I0727794

MONARCH RISING

BOOK FOUR

REMEMBER

THE GREATEST OF THESE IS LOVE

SYLVANA CANDELA

This is a work of fiction.

Copyright © 2022 by Sylvana Candela

All rights reserved. No part of this book may be reproduced or used in any manner without written permission of the copyright owner except for the use of quotations in a book review. For more information, contact sylvanaccandela@gmail.com

ISBN (softcover): 978-1-7376706-6-7
ISBN (ebook): 978-1-7376706-7-4

Cover art by Michelle Popkes
Cover design by Glenda Nowakowski
Interior design by Wendy C. Garfinkle
Edited by Wendy C. Garfinkle
Proofreading by Leanne Sype

www.sylvanacandela.com
www.peacefulworldpublishing.com

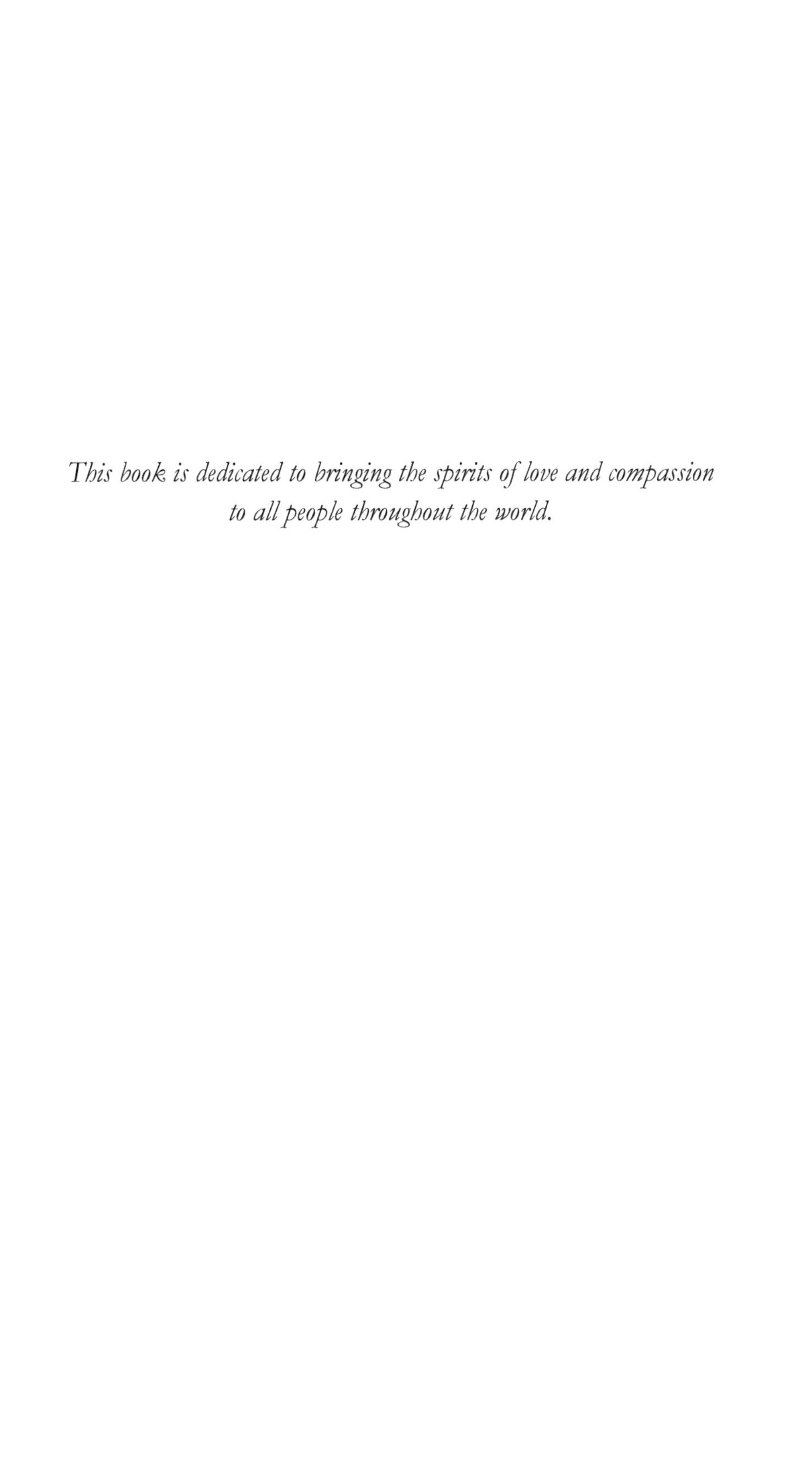

This book is dedicated to bringing the spirits of love and compassion to all people throughout the world.

Table of Contents

Preface

IT HAS BEEN 18 YEARS since the downfall of the Council and Upper Crust of One World. A new world called One Garden has grown and is thriving everywhere. It is a world where people are free to become who they were meant to be. But who exactly are they? During the dark times of slavery, mind-control, and the forbidden education of their past, the people had all but forgotten who they were, including their individual cultures of generations past.

With the help of Lord Emeka and his restoration of libraries, people are catching up just as quickly as they can. They have also put a great effort into learning all three official languages of the world: English, Russian, and Chinese. So, for the most part, universal translators are not necessary anymore. But the people must also learn about the cultures of their own continental territories, as well as the suffering of their people in the past.

In REMEMBER, book 4 of the Monarch Rising Series, our heroes of One Garden realize that in order for the people of the planet to move forward into a higher form of universal, or divine love, they must first remember their past. In that way they can understand the transgressions that were perpetrated against them, and learn to forgive the evildoers of the former ruling class.

Lucifer, of course, will honor no such thing, as he is bent on revenge toward the ones who took his victory away from him: the heroes of One Garden—Kookie, Yakov, Liling, The Major, and all the rest.

As we return to the world of Monarch Rising, Lucifer is determined to interfere with the progress of the people and not let them return to the Garden of Eden. In fact, he is determined to gain absolute power over the people of the world, and this time, make *all* of them his slaves.

PART 1
THE STRUGGLE

Chapter 1 – Brethren

PA, ES, AND SPA are staring out of the portal window, looking up at the sun. They have been trapped in their polar palace under ice for the past 18 years. The horrors they experienced during their captivity brought them to a place of emotional depravity and a living hell. They certainly did not think that they would ever see the light of day again. And now that they are looking at the sun, they can barely catch their breath. The hearts of the three elderly brothers are overflowing with fear and awe as they stare out of the prison bars that now melt before their very eyes.

The greed and corruption that PA, ES, and SPA perpetrated against their fellow humans, in league with the devil, brought them to this hell; to a grotesque 18 years of ghoulish existence in isolation. And now, as the ice imprisonment of their horror chamber melts, a voice from above speaks to their hearts:

By the Grace of the Creator, you are set free. May you use your freedom to choose a new way. But first, you must learn what that way is, and I will show you. Come, follow me.

"Did you hear that, my brethren?" asks PA, full of awe and wonder.

"Why yes brother, I did indeed hear it," replies ES.

"And I heard it as well. But not with my ears, brethren. Oh no, not with my ears," says SPA.

PA continues in utter amazement, "No, not with my ears either, not at all. Whatever could that be, then?"

ES agrees, "Very strange, yes indeed, truly very strange."

SPA scratches his head as he says to his brothers, "And what did the voice mean about learning a different way?"

"And *to 'follow me'*?" says PA. "Who is this *voice*, my brothers?"

PA, ES, and SPA look at each other in curious wonder, not knowing what to think or say. Then, PA speaks:

"Perhaps we should do what the voice says."

ES replies, "Yes, yes indeed. We must find out what has happened to One World, while we have been . . . (he pauses) . . . down below."

SPA continues, cautiously, "And whether or not we have any family or friends left."

PA responds to his brothers sadly, "What family? What friends?"

The three of them hang their heads in shame.

* * *

The brothers of the former Council of One World have packed a few meager belongings. Now that the ice is clearing over the portal area and entryway to the subterranean palace, they will be able to leave in any one of the Cloudtransporters that were buried with them. They board the aircraft and cruise to the portal. Just as they are about to leave, they see a figure in a red, hooded cape standing in the entryway. The face of the figure is in shadow, so PA, ES, and SPA cannot tell if it is a man or a woman.

"Now who might that be, brethren?" asks SPA, suspiciously.

"Dear me," ES replies. "I wonder if it is the one who just spoke to us."

"Ah!" PA responds. "Now that does make sense. Perhaps that is what the voice meant when it said, *Come, follow me.*"

"Yes, truly it must be!" exclaims SPA.

All at once, the person in the red, hooded cape speaks to the brothers. "Where are you going, men of the Council of One World?"

It is the voice of a woman, pleasant and soothing to PA, ES, and SPA, who have not heard a woman's voice in a very long time. They are instantly mesmerized by the sweetness of her soft, gentle tones. She approaches their craft, pushing back her hood so the brothers can see her face.

They recognize her features at once, although she does not appear to be altogether human. Flames of fire seem to be shooting out of her eyes as she says to them, "Yes, yes, oh Highest Ones. Do come. Come, follow me!"

They look at each other in amazement as the woman they now recognize does not appear to have aged a day, though 18 years have passed. And she is quite as beautiful as ever. . . except for the strange, unearthly flame in her eyes. ES speaks up and addresses her:

"Have you come to show us where to go? Are our people still alive and well? Yes, we shall indeed follow you," the three of them nod in agreement, "most beautiful Lady Bella!"

In the bowels of hell another voice smirks, *Ah, yes! My woman . . . my queen . . . my beautiful Bella!*

* * *

Deep in the rainforest of the Yucatan, there is a small garden community called the Village of Chiconahui, named after the Pyramid of Chiconahui, nearby. The ancient stone structure adds a mystical beauty and feeling of serenity to the area.

The highly evolved loving, super humans known as the Chrysalenes, and the rest of the villagers are rising to the morning sun. The sweet smell of forest earth and the sound of birds singing fill the hearts of all who inhabit this lush, tropical paradise. There are two guests in the Village of Chiconahui learning all about the flowers, herbs, and trees of the area. Phil, an elderly gentleman of Sioux descent feels a strong kinship to the people of the village, and even considers the local flora and fauna to be his brothers and sisters. His wife, Doc, is fulfilling her childhood dream. From the time she was a little girl on a farm in California, young Penny communicated with the natural world. She got her nickname, Doc, by helping others to know what herbs to take for different ailments. And now Doc is living her dream with her husband, traveling from one garden community to another all over the world, learning and sharing new local healing herbs with everyone.

Phil, Doc, the Chrysalenes, and the other villagers are out tending the gardens when Doc is the first one to see it. Looking up at the sky she gets all excited and cries out:

"Look! They're here! They're here!"

Everyone stops what they are doing and look up to see a Cloudtransporter just overhead making its descent onto a nearby clearing. On the side of the craft is a portrait of two pigeons with #3 and #4 written next to them. And next to that are the words "BIG KAHUNA" painted in bright blue.

"It's Kookie and Angie!" Doc howls with joy.

All hearts are filled with great anticipation to meet the legendary Big Kahuna himself. For the past 18 years, Phil and Doc shared with everyone throughout One Garden about the brave and heroic actions of all their friends, especially Kookie and Angie. The one and only High Lord Kenneth, also known as Kookie, was willing to sacrifice his own life to save the people of One World from genocide. And of course, there is his heroic wife Angie, who courageously stood up to Lucifer himself in their battle to free the people. They arrive with their 15-year-old son David and a new generation of homing pigeons . . . the offspring of #3 and #4.

"Come on, everybody!" Doc cries out to one and all. "Come meet Kookie and Angie!"

The Chrysalenes and the other villagers all follow quickly behind Doc and Phil as they run to the clearing where the Cloudtransporter has just landed.

"Oh my, but surely we are blessed with such an honor!" exclaims Chrysalene Eve Sophia.

"Heavens, yes!" Sergio shouts with joy.

The villagers and Chrysalenes are all excited as they reach the aircraft just in time for the portal to open. Out steps David, followed by his Mama Angie and Papa Kookie. Angie is carrying the two little pigeons #3 and #4 on her shoulders snuggled closely against her neck, just like their parents, the original #3 and #4 used to do. Then, to everyone's surprise and absolute thrill, three other people emerge from the craft: Lord Emeka, and his wife Eve Elli who is holding their baby, little Lady Bi.[1]

---

[1] *Chinese girl's name pronounced Bee*

Kookie and Angie wave to Doc and Phil as they all rush to greet each other with open arms.

"Hello, hello my friends!" Angie exclaims joyously, dancing her way down to Doc and the others. The pigeons flap their wings to steady themselves on her shoulders. When she reaches Doc, the two old friends embrace in a warm hug, with #3 and #4 excitedly hopping back and forth between them.

"It's so great to see you, Angie! How's David? How's Phil? How are #3 and #4? How's Suzie of the Seashells, and Rudolpho?!" The two women jabber back and forth, laughing with delight.

"My goodness David, you get bigger each time I see you! Pretty soon you'll be as big as your dad here!" Doc says, patting David on the back. David looks down, smiling and blushing while Kookie taps the tips of his fingers together, beaming with pride.

Then Doc remembers. "Oh, my goodness! I got so excited that I forgot to introduce you all to the Chrysalenes and the villagers!" They smile and nod as Doc says, "Everyone, this is Sergio." Looking at Kookie, she continues, "Sergio is the Big Kahuna here in Chiconahui!" They all have a chuckle while Sergio smiles, blushes, and bows his head. Doc continues, "And these are two of the Chrysalenes of our village, Adam Mateo and Eve Sophia." They smile and bow their heads as well, while Doc continues introducing everyone from Kookie and Angie's group to the rest of the Chrysalenes and villagers.

Kookie says, "We are honored to meet you all. Thank you for receiving us so warmly."

"The honor and pleasure are all ours," says Sergio.

Eve Sophia bows her head saying, "May we serve you well, as you bless us with your presence."

After the introductions are made, Kookie turns to everyone and says, "Angie and I were in Johannesburg visiting Lord Emeka and Eve Elli. We told them that we were coming here and what we are about to do."

Emeka looks at Kookie and exclaims, "And we got so excited about the project that my wife and I absolutely *had* to join you guys!"

Everyone chuckles, and Eve Elli pipes in, "We are so honored to be here and serve in whatever way we can for this great project." Little Lady Bi starts to wave her arms around, smiling and clapping in agreement with her mama.

"The honor is all ours, Eve Elli, my sister Chrysalene," Eve Sophia says tenderly. Eve Elli bows her head graciously, revealing to one and all the creatures nestled snuggly in her hair. "My goodness!" exclaims Eve Sophia. "There are three Monarch Butterflies in your hair, my sister! And they appear to be most comfortable!"

"They sure are," says Lord Emeka. "The Monarchs and Eve Elli are quite inseparable." Little Lady Bi leans forward to kiss the butterflies in her mama's hair.

"Ooo, aww!" folks twitter, as little Lady Bi giggles with delight.

Phil steps forward and says to Kookie and company, "It is so good to see you all again, my brothers and sisters. Won't you come join us as we break bread together? We are having a most wonderful harvest!"

"Truly," says Chrysalene Adam Mateo. "The Creator has blessed us with such an abundance of fruits and vegetables. It is our privilege to share His fruit with you. Do come and join us." Putting his hands out to everyone in a gesture of friendship, Adam Mateo leads the way to their garden of paradise.

* * *

In a nearby village in the Yucatan, another Cloudtransporter lands. The portal opens and out step three men looking bedraggled and confused.

"Where are we?" asks SPA.

"Didn't Lady Bella say that she would meet us here?" ES inquires.

"Yes, indeed she did," PA replies. "And after she programmed the coordinates of our Cloudtransporter to bring us here, Lady Bella just seemed to vanish into thin air!"

"Indeed, brother! We turned around for a second and she was gone!" exclaims SPA.

"Well, I suppose she will show up soon and tell us what to do next," ES says, as he notices a small house off in the distance. "Perhaps we should go over to that cottage and see if anyone is there."

"Sounds like a good idea, brother." PA replies. "Let's go."

The men of the former Council of One World make their way toward the cottage. As far as they can see, there are no other signs of human life around them.

Deep in the bowels of hell a voice says to his bride, *Go to them, my Bella. Go to the cottage where their destiny awaits.*

Bella replies, *Yes, I will show them the way . . . YOUR way.*

Lucifer smiles and says, *Ah yes, my queen. And for that you will be well rewarded. I have yet another whip for your exquisite collection waiting for you upon your return!*

With lustful anticipation and excitement, Bella's spirit is on its way to the Yucatan.

* * *

PA, ES, and SPA arrive at the cottage tired and hungry. As they open the door and walk in, a fire burns in the hearth and a sumptuous spread of food is arranged on a long, wooden table. The fare consists of all the food they were accustomed to before their captivity. There are platters of turkey, beef, and lamb, as well as an assortment of pasta salads, quiche, pastries of every description, and warm, creamy soup. With wide eyes, the brothers sit down and feast on food they have not tasted in years. About halfway through their frozen imprisonment, the food had pretty much run out. Except for an underground spring that ran through the palace and the few vegetables they were able to grow, there was really nothing else to eat, except the unmentionable. And that was how they survived.

Closing their eyes and savoring every morsel, PA, ES, and SPA eat until they are completely stuffed. They are so over-filled that they become sleepy.

PA says to the other two, "Look, my brethren, there are three large, soft chairs right by the hearth."

"Indeed!" says ES. "In fact, there is a pillow with a blanket folded up on each cozy chair."

SPA remarks, "Yes, and it all seems as though someone was expecting us."

The three of them chuckle. "Well," says PA, as he goes over to one of the chairs and gets all snuggled-in with the pillow and blanket. "I shall not disappoint our host." ES and SPA are in total agreement about this, and they too nestle into the soft chairs. Within minutes the three brothers are fast asleep . . . and their dream begins:

They are in a forest, and it is late afternoon. The sun is beginning to set with the colors of yellow, orange, red, and gold filling the sky. PA, ES, and SPA feel very much at peace when they look up and see a ray of bright White Light breaking through the soft, puffy clouds. From within the White Light a celestial Being begins to materialize before them, with magnificent wings the colors of the sunset. They hear a voice from the celestial Being, speaking to their hearts:

"Human creatures, I Am the Monarch Angel. I have come to give you a message from the Creator. He has set you free from captivity, that you might follow Him if you decide to do so. There is much healing and love that you can bring to the people of the world, as well as much damage and destruction. The choice is yours, former Council Creatures. Always know that you are free to choose." As she begins to fade, Angel says to the brothers, "Call on me if ever you need my help."

The Monarch dissolves into the colors of the sunset leaving behind peace and serenity in the hearts of PA, ES, and SPA.

Then the sky begins to darken, snuffing out the stars. The brothers are aware of a chill in the air and they are unable to get warm. Presently they become aware of a red glow coming from beneath their feet. Booming thuds sound off in the distance as a familiar fear begins to fill their hearts.

The red glow becomes brighter and more intense as the booming becomes louder and faster. PA, ES, and SPA are now filled with terror as the throbbing pierces their very souls.

Then they see her, rising from the chasm of red, glowing thunder. With fire shooting from her eyes Bella speaks to the hearts of the three brothers:

"Dearest brothers," the sweet voice begins, "Highest of the Council of One World, PA, ES, and SPA, the world has gone to chaos while you were gone. The people whom you once called slaves, have taken over. They are growing into a mighty force of vermin who would gladly send you back into captivity, or worse. Do not forget the misery and starvation you experienced these past 18 years, and those who are responsible for your suffering. The Upper Crust has been all but crushed by the slaves. And those of you who are left are wandering around like lost sheep. It is your task, brothers of the former Council, to bring back the glory of the Lords and Masters and avenge the wrongdoing of the slaves!"

PA, ES, and SPA are filled with confusion, anger, and fear as Bella points to the three of them and says, "Our Lord of the underworld, Lucifer, has chosen YOU for this task. I am queen Bella, wedded to Lucifer. And I am here to help you carry out the will of the fallen angel."

The brothers are suddenly shaken out of their sleep. They wake to find themselves back in the cottage, in their soft chairs, with Bella standing before them. With a fire in her eyes and a grimace across her face, Bella says to PA, ES, and SPA: "Okay. Let's get to work."

* * *

Gathered around a campfire at the center of the Village of Chiconahui, Kookie and his companions are about to break bread with the villagers and the Chrysalenes. They have all heard rumors about Kookie and Angie's plans and are anxiously waiting to hear the details. Sergio passes around a loaf of bread, and everyone breaks off a piece. When each person is holding a chunk of bread, Kookie raises his glass of pure spring water and says:

"To the high love of philia,[2] the love between friends. As we sit here together around this warm fire, may we all experience the warm love among us, which is now growing throughout our new world of One Garden."

"Amen, brother!" they all exclaim as they share their bread and water.

"I would also like to mention to all of you," continues Kookie, "that tomorrow the rest of our group will be arriving. We have been sharing our progress with them and they are going to be an integral part in helping us get our plans underway."

"Really?" says Doc, excited. She can hardly wait to hear who else among their friends will be arriving.

"Yes!" Angie chimes in. "Yakov and Liling have been helping us as well as Rudolpho and Suzie of the Seashells. We really have put our best brains together for this one! And of course, they are bringing their families. We will have Yakov and Neely with their daughter Beth, as well as Liling and Dumaka and their daughter Meiling."

Eve Sophia says, "How blessed we are to have such cherished folks joining us here."

---

[2] *Greek word for the pure love of friendship. It was considered to be the highest love of all in ancient Greece.*

Phil and Doc can hardly contain their joy at the thought of seeing their dearest friends again, not to mention their excitement over reconnecting with their daughter, Suzie of the Seashells. Yakov, Liling, and Rudolpho all did their heroic part, together with Kookie, Angie, Phil, Doc, and the rest of the Alliance, in saving the former One World from destruction at the corrupt hands of the Council. The bond of love that grew between them remains strong to this day and has now been passed on to their offspring.

The community shares a delicious meal of soup and salad, with more bread and pastries, giving thanks for the friends they will connect with tomorrow. The villagers have heard about Kookie's passion for chocolate chip cookies so they have whipped up their own, unique cookie recipe, presenting it to their beloved guest for dessert.

"Oh my goodness!" Kookie exclaims with sheer delight. "These are absolutely divine! Please do share your recipe with David. He is the master chef of our house and is particularly fond of baking."

David nods and looks down, smiling and blushing. He is a shy young man who looks up to his dad – the Big Kahuna – with awe and respect. Kookie sits back with a beaming smile, tapping the tips of his fingers together.

"Well," says Angie, "I guess we shouldn't keep everyone waiting any longer. Shall we roll out the new program the three of us put together?"

"Oh my!" exclaims Doc. "David, did you help your folks on this project?"

"Well . . . I . . . um . . . yeah!"

"Wow!" everyone chuckles, and those sitting next to him give David a pat on the back.

"Oh yes," says Angie, with much mama pride. "David is brilliant in logic *and* creativity. And this project has required both from all three of us." Looking at Kookie, Angie continues, "May I explain it to everyone now?"

"Go right ahead, my darling," says Kookie, beaming from ear to ear.

Angie takes out her Metatron device, the little black box that contains all their advanced programs including the 369-programs that foiled PA, ES, and SPA years ago. She begins:

"We are now in a time of healing the pain, sorrow, and fear of the past, in our new world of love and freedom. We of the Alliance who fought against the Council back then, knew that we had to wake people up from the mind-control programming that PA, ES, and SPA, aided by the corrupt people of the Upper Crust, perpetrated on all of us, turning us into their slaves. In the process of doing that, Kookie and I discovered many amazing uses for this little black box, and we knew even then that its uses were probably limitless."

Looking at Kookie, Angie wants him to explain things further at this point. So Kookie takes it from here:

"All my life I knew that the worst thing we were dealing with among my people, that is, the Lords and Upper Crust of One World, was the way in which the Council took complete control of people's minds. The Creator gave all people free will and we of the UC," Kookie momentarily hangs his head staring at the ground in shame, "took that free will away from the people. We had no right to do that. And that is why many of us in the UC rebelled and risked our lives to give everyone back that which PA, ES, and SPA had no right to take away."

Kookie looks down at the floor again and Angie tenderly touches his arm. Everyone knows the struggle that Kookie has been through his whole life with this, so they quietly allow him the space that he needs to process the sadness he still feels. When he is ready Kookie continues:

"The program we have created with Metatron which will manifest its energy through the pyramids of the world, should ensure that the minds of the people cannot be tampered with in such a manner anymore. Once the 369-program of Metatron has been connected to the pyramids, it should help to activate them and emit a higher frequency. This in turn will raise the loving vibration of people, bringing us all into a higher state of awareness, with greater intuitive skills and memories of the past. It is also the intention of this pyramid activation with the 369-program of Metatron, to help us heal our bodies, minds, and spirits. Finally, it should also help to diminish the power of fear and evil over us, and over our lives. This will bring in a higher divine love, somewhat like the hearts of our beloved Chrysalenes."

Everyone is left speechless. Sergio, Doc, Phil, the Chrysalenes, and the other villagers who have come to join them are all stunned. Lord Emeka and Eve Elli have been aware of the plan for a while, but this is the first time they are hearing it from Kookie and Angie as an expression of their compassion for people.

Eve Elli breaks the silence: "Bless you, Kookie, Angie, and David, for bringing this sacred gift to us. And thank you, Father in Heaven, for inspiring and guiding our courageous and creative friends in their work for the people of One Garden."

Everyone nods and says, "Amen."

* * *

In the bowels of hell, Lucifer fills with hatred and anger as he hears Kookie's plans.

Oh no! Lucifer hisses and growls in his bestial voice, *No, No, No! My Lord Kenneth! You have done quite enough harm . . . my sssson! QUITE ENOUGH! You will NOT stop me from striking fear and hatred in the hearts of all you pitiful, weak, and foolish dolts! YOU WILL HAVE ME **AND** MY BELLA TO DEAL WITH!*

And high up in the heavenly realm another voice is heard speaking to Lucifer saying, *"We shall just see about that, beastie creature. We shall see!"*

Chapter 2 – Stones

HIGH LORD YAKOV, AND his sister High Lady Liling are just finishing up at a global conference on gardening. Liling and her husband Dumaka are experts on herbal gardening, while Yakov and his wife Lady Neely both have a natural green thumb. Everything Yakov and Neely touch seems to just grow and thrive, including their sweet and charming 17-year-old daughter, Beth. Liling and Dumaka's daughter Meiling is 16 years old, and the two young women have enjoyed themselves immensely at the conference, making friends and learning new recipes.

When Yakov and Liling heard what their High Lord brother Kookie was up to at the ancient pyramid of Chiconahui, they knew they would have to fly there just as soon as possible. So when the conference is over, they round up the girls, say goodbye to everyone at the conference, board their Cloudtransporter, and head straight for the Yucatan.

Speaking in Chinese, Meiling exclaims: "Oh, mom! Will we actually get to see a real-life ancient pyramid?"

"Yes, honey, we sure will. And I just know that your Uncle Kookie will allow us all to help in whatever way we can for their project," says Liling.

"*YAY!*" Meiling and Beth exclaim in unison.

The children of the super-intelligent Kookie, Yakov, and Liling, have all been raised to be tri-lingual, and freely converse back and forth in the language of their parents: English, Chinese, and Russian.

Dumaka turns to his wife Liling and says, "It is still such an honor and pleasure for me to be with your brothers and their families, my angel. Whatever we do together is always filled with love, which I can feel extending outward to all of One Garden."

Liling smiles and snuggles close to her husband.

"We will be there in just a few hours, everyone!" Yakov announces, "so get ready for a day of adventure!"

"Yes dad, I know!" Beth says as she rolls her eyes, and the two cousins shoot a knowing glanced at each other with a chuckle. "Every time we get together with Kookie, Angie, and David, you always say the same thing!"

Neely interjects, "That's because every time we get together with them, sweetie, it truly *is* an adventure!" They are all filled with anticipation, preparing themselves for whatever awaits them at the Pyramid.

* * *

At the Village of Chiconahui, the Chrysalenes are out in the gardens, loving on the blossoming fruits and vegetables, and the villagers are preparing for more visitors. Although the Cloudtransporters are well equipped for sleeping and living in, the lords and ladies who visit the small villages are always respectful of the dignity of the local people. They recognize the villagers' need to be treated as the good hosts that they are to the members of the former Upper Crust. So Kookie and his fellow lords and ladies always graciously accept the accommodations and offerings of the people in the small villages and garden communities.

Sergio and his family, as well as the other folks of Chiconahui, are happily scurrying around preparing tents and sleeping areas for all the guests who are expected.

"Papa!" shouts young Tomas. "Are the great warriors coming from across the ocean to see our pyramid?"

Laughing at his intuitive eight-year-old son's "great warrior" reference, Sergio explains, "Yes, Tomas, they are coming to see the pyramid and to see us as well. However, though we may see them all as great warriors, especially Kookie, I don't think they really see themselves that way."

Tomas looks rather perplexed as he says to his papa, "Why not? *Especially* Kookie! He is the greatest warrior who has ever lived!"

Still chuckling Sergio says to his son, "You may be right about that, but oftentimes a hero's journey requires that the hero be blind to who he truly is."

Now Tomas is more confused than ever. "That makes no sense at all, papa! It just makes no sense at all!"

Lord Emeka has been listening nearby to the conversation between father and son. He is overcome with emotion as he understands exactly what Sergio is saying to young Tomas, thinking of and missing his own father Lord Ekene, in Heaven. Lord Emeka feels the need to go over and share his thoughts and feelings with Sergio and Tomas. Touching the boy gently on his shoulder, Emeka says to him:

"My good young man. You may think of us as warriors and in some ways we may be. But I can tell you this." Looking at Sergio, Emeka says to him with a quiet sadness in his eyes, "A father who gives so much love to his son as you do kind sir, is the greatest hero of all."

With that, Emeka's gaze drops to the ground, and young Tomas, who has heard all about the story of little Lord Emeka and his late father, begins to understand. Eve Elli comes over to her husband and puts her arms around his waist. She says to him with much love in her heart:

"My dearest Emeka, you always think with your heart for the people of the world, giving so much love to one and all. And for that, you are, and always will be, a truly great hero and righteous man. I love you so very much, my husband."

Eve Elli leans over, kisses him tenderly on his neck and snuggles up close to him. In her heart she hears the voices of the Monarchs in her hair going, *Aww!*

* * *

In a nearby cottage in the Yucatan, PA, ES, and SPA are sitting in the soft chairs, dumbfounded by what they are hearing from Bella.

"You mean the slaves have taken over One World?!" shouts ES, unable to digest what Bella has just told them.

"Yes. Yes, indeed they have," she replies.

"But how, My Lady? How is that possible?" asks ES with incredulity.

"We had a great plan. *You* had a great plan, dear Lady. What happened?" exclaims ES.

The three brothers look at each other with shock and dismay knowing now, after all this time that their worst nightmares have come true.

Suddenly, Bella opens her mouth to speak and the voice coming out of her changes. It is a deep growl, bellowing at PA, ES, and SPA:

"It was the three of you that happened! Dolts! Idiots! Fools! You allowed yourselves to trust Master Howard, and to be deceived by Lord Kenneth, Lord Yakov, and Lady Liling!"

PA, ES, and SPA look at each other in terror as they hear the voice of their former master coming back to haunt them, years after he sealed them in their tomb of ice. It is becoming all too clear to them now, knowing who they are dealing with once again.

"So you see, Your Highest of the Council," Bella continues in her own spirit and voice, "We all have work to do now. Kookie and the others are well hidden by the same technology that fooled us the last time, but we know that they are not very far from here.

"Brothers, the lord and master Lucifer has sent me to tell you that it is time, once again, for the three of you to follow him and do his bidding."

* * *

Yakov, Liling, and company are flying low over the lush green rainforest. There appear to be trees everywhere as far as the eye can see. Here and there they come across a clearing or a waterway winding through the jungle. They see all sorts of strange creatures wading through the shallow waters. Neither the waters nor the creatures are in any particular hurry to go anywhere. The pace of life they witness below is much slower than anything they have ever seen before, and everyone on board the Cloudtransporter is mesmerized by the vast and tranquil beauty of the tropical rainforest.

Presently they come to a clearing where they see two Cloudtransporters below. One has a seashell mural and the other has two doves and the words "Big Kahuna" painted on the side.

"We're here!" Yakov announces enthusiastically to the group.

Just a little way off in the distance, Meiling and Beth see it . . . and their eyes become the size of saucers as their jaws drop.

"THE PYRAMID OF CHICONAHUI!" the girls shout with great excitement. "Yippee! Yeeha! Woof!" they exclaim, as Liling, Dumaka, Yakov, and Neely share a chuckle over their daughters' enthusiasm.

"We'll be down there soon, ladies!" says Dumaka, "And then you will get to visit the ancient sacred site."

The Cloudtransporter lands gently in the clearing next to the other two. Looking at the aircraft with the painting of the seashells Liling exclaims, "Oh my! I didn't know that Suzie and Rudolpho would also be joining us! What a wonderful surprise!"

As the portal opens and the group steps out, they are greeted by the villagers and their guests. Suzie of the Seashells rushes towards Meiling and Beth with huge hugs and lots of giggles.

"What a wonderful surprise!" says Liling to Suzie. "When did you and Rudolpho arrive?"

"Just before you guys did," replies Rudolpho, coming to join the hug-fest. "Phil was telling Suzie and me all about it, and we wouldn't miss Kookie and Angie's launch of their new program for anything!"

"Well, we are certainly most happy to see the two of you," says Dumaka.

Everyone gathers around, hugging, laughing, and filling each other in on the latest goings-on in their lives. They especially enjoy passing little Lady Bi from one to the other.

Phil remarks, "It kinda reminds me of when you were my little one, Suzie, and everyone delighted in you so much. And now look at you! Why, you will be 20 years old soon!"

Doc chimes in affectionately, "And to all of us you are still our Little One."

"You betcha! Absolutely! Aww! Still such a sweetie pie!" several friends chime in. Suzie just smiles sweetly and Rudolpho gives her a big squeeze.

Kookie puts his index finger in the air and says: "Well folks, why don't we all break bread together and then head on over to the pyramid. There is a lot for us to do today!"

"Amen brother!" the crowd enthusiastically agrees as they all start heading towards the village.

∗ ∗ ∗

Everyone is about finished with their meal when David gets up and excuses himself. "I'll get everything ready now dad," he says to Kookie.

"Ok, son. We are all just about ready to go." Kookie smiles and taps the tips of his fingers together.

He is so proud of David and the fine young man he is turning out to be. For a moment Kookie thinks of his own father, as he lowers his head and stares at the floor. He does not want to think of such painful memories on this wonderful day. So he puts his arm around Angie and kisses her gently on the cheek, brushing aside the thought of his last encounter with the evil one; the day he found out his father's true identity.

Kookie suddenly looks up at the group, points his index finger in the air and says, "Ah! Here comes my son with the equipment. Are you all about ready to go to the pyramid?"

"Oh yes! Yes! *YES!*" says Beth, as she and Meiling are on their feet in two seconds flat.

Everyone laughs and Liling says to the girls, "Well, I think we have kept you two waiting long enough."

"Okay folks, just follow me." Kookie says as they all get up and make their way to the Pyramid of Chiconahui.

The crowd arrives at the site of the ancient stone structure. Kookie says, "Before we begin, I would like to explain why we have chosen a pyramid to work with."

The group gathers around staring at the remarkable structure before them. The stones are worn, covered in grass and other assorted forest flora. But the powerful energy radiating from the majestic pyramid is palpable to everyone standing before it.

Kookie begins to explain: "Many years ago there were visitors to the great pyramids of the world, including several located in the Yucatan. Their origins, purpose, and powers were talked and written about by many, with wild speculations about what the pyramids truly were. However, once the Council took over such knowledge that hinted at empowerment of the people was forbidden. Books were destroyed and almost all the ancient knowledge was lost."

Kookie pauses, remembering how he rescued and hid many books for safe keeping. The thought saddens him for a moment but then he continues, "PA, ES, and SPA kept some of the books on ancient wisdom for themselves. My guess is that they figured the books might be useful to them one day. As one of the three High Lords of the Council, I was privy to the existence of these books and was unhappy with the Council for withholding the information from the people. Of course, Yakov, Liling, and I knew that PA, ES, and SPA had another agenda with the populace, and part of that included keeping them numbed and dumbed-down, or numbed and dumbed as we would say.

"So when I saw the opportunity to rescue the books, I did so without PA, ES, and SPA ever knowing that they went missing. Unbeknown to anyone, including my brother Yakov and sister Liling, (both smile, shake their heads and roll their eyes) I hid them all in the basement of the secluded cabin on the grounds of my estate. The books remained there until the downfall and disappearance of the three brothers. Back then when I discovered the books on the ancient wisdom of the pyramids, I got to work creating the Metatron device, based in part on pyramid energy. And now, Angie and I, and our son David, are going to attempt to bridge the modern technology of the Metatron device with the ancient pyramid wisdom, right here at this sacred site."

The group of Chrysalenes, villagers, and old friends are awestruck. Rudolpho speaks up: "So, what do you expect to happen once you connect Metatron to the Pyramid of Chiconahui?"

"Well," Angie begins, "Metatron can do many things, especially regarding intuition and other higher forms of energy."

David continues, "And what we are interested in is healing the collective human consciousness, which includes raising our intuitive skills, opening up our memories of the past, and moving into a higher love frequency. That, of course, will involve activating other pyramids around the world as well. But this is our test run before we hook up and activate the whole shebang!"

"Wow!" says Doc. "So, what's any of this got to do with our intuition and memory?"

Kookie looks at all of them and with sadness in his voice says, "With the numbing and dumbing process that the Council perpetrated on all of you, your memory was severely affected. Once we get other pyramids activated too, as Angie just said, we hope to reawaken human awareness. Then we can *all remember who we truly are, why we are here, and what our purpose is.*"

"Wow! Oh my goodness! That's incredible!" the collective voices exclaim.

"Can you really do that?" asks Rudolpho in amazement.

Yakov and Liling chuckle as Liling says to him, "If our big brother says he can do something it is as good as done, no matter how outlandish, crazy, or just plain impossible it may sound."

Rudolpho shakes his head and says, "Yes, I guess I should know that by now."

"Okay," says Kookie. "Let's get started! I would like us all to climb onto the pyramid, spread out, sit down and get comfortable. Those of you with your own Metatron devices please take them out and turn them on."

Eve Elli puts her hand up and addresses the group. "Before we begin, I would like to say a blessing." They all reach out and join hands as she begins: "Heavenly Father, we humble ourselves before you at this, your ancient site of wisdom. We thank you for the beautiful hearts of all who are gathered here today, and know that through us, the people of the world can begin to heal from the past and raise their vibration to the divine frequency of Your Love. Lord, I understand that this will be a challenging process, as there are many painful feelings that may come to the surface. I ask that You help the people feel protected, comforted, and healed, by Your Loving Grace."

Up above in the celestial realm, another voice is heard speaking to the hearts of all present saying: *Human creatures remember, you are not alone. The Creator loves you and sends us to watch over and protect you. May we guide you through the times ahead, offering comfort and love. Remember how much we love you, human creatures. I Am the Monarch Angel, and I shall always be with you.*

The Monarch Butterflies in Eve Elli's hair hear the voice of Angel. Suddenly they rise, circle around the group of people and dance in rapturous joy. The "human creatures" feel the love of the dancing butterflies and their collective soul swells with ecstasy.

Everyone is eagerly awaiting with great anticipation what will happen next.

* * *

Deep in the bowels of hell, Lucifer snickers and sneers as he looks up to the heavenly host saying, *Aha! So that is where they are hiding! At the Pyramid of Chiconahui! I have a host of my own and we are on our way! And I shall take for myself the power that you wish to unleash!*

And the Monarch Angel says to Lucifer, *I don't think so! beastie creature!*

* * *

Everyone is seated on the pyramid and those with Metatron devices have turned them on.

"Whoa!" David exclaims.

Ordinarily, when turning on the device the golden pyramid appears and begins to rotate slowly. However, this time it is spinning furiously as Metatron is getting hot in his hands. The others are having the same experience, and they all have to put the device down on the stone next to them.

Kookie points his index finger in the air. "This is looking very promising, folks!" The ones without Metatron look at the devices of those who do, as Kookie says to the group, "Okay! Here we go!"

He enters the program code not knowing for sure what will happen next.

* * *

At the nearby cottage in the Yucatan, Bella left PA, ES, and SPA to mull over their predicament while searching for other masters of the UC who were always loyal to the Council. She knows that this is going to take more than *"three incompetent buffoons,"* as Lucifer continuously refers to them, to reinstate a reign of terror across the world. It will have to be done slowly with much subtlety and tact. However, Bella also understands something that Lucifer does not, regarding PA, ES, and SPA. As incompetent as they may seem, they do have the respect of the remaining members of the UC who were loyal to them before their disappearance. And in life, Bella proved herself to be a very effective and heavy-handed leader. Now that she is a disembodied spirit, and the number one henchwoman of the devil, her powers have the potential to be exponentially greater than they ever were.

Bella knows of such a group of mercenaries as she heads for a small town in Euroslavica. She will tell them that PA, ES, and SPA have returned and are ready to give them their lives back. Bella figures that rounding up enough of these former Master Commandants, and a few other remaining members of the UC who were loyal to the Council, will give Lucifer the power that he needs to stop Kookie and the others from carrying out their plans.

* * *

Kookie and company are watching their Metatron devices with great excitement and some trepidation. The golden pyramids on Metatron are spinning so fast that they are glowing like hot embers. Meiling sees what is happening to the Pyramid of Chiconahui right before their eyes.

"Whoa!" Meiling exclaims as she jumps up from her seat. "Look you guys, look!" She is pointing to the weathered, eroded stones covered in grass and flora when everyone else suddenly notices it too.

"Yeeow! Eek! Oh my goodness! What the . . .?" they all cry out in turn. The stones that have eroded over time are smoothing out right before their eyes! And the grass and flora are . . . disappearing!

"WHOA!" shouts Kookie. "Can you all see what's happening?"

"Is it going back in time?" David mutters somewhat fearfully.

"I don't think so," exclaims Phil. "It is . . . sharpening, or something, and losing its debris!"

"Getting cleaned up. Detoxifying!" Dumaka says excitedly.

The Chrysalenes smile with delight as they have a full understanding of what is happening.

Adam Mateo explains, "The pyramid has been in a deep slumber just like we were before we became Chrysalenes, and just like you all were until you stopped listening to My Buddy and the other mind-control techniques of the Council."

Adam Mateo has the group's complete attention as this is all somehow making sense to them. He continues, "And now that the pyramid is hearing its own earth frequency that Kookie's Metatron program is singing to it, the pyramid is coming alive again."

"*WHOA!*" everyone cries out.

Suddenly, Kookie becomes excited and says, "So now the pyramid should be able to communicate with us, helping us to communicate better with each other and improve our intuitive skills."

Angie interjects, "And help us to remember whatever it is that we need to know."

Looking at the Chrysalenes, villagers, and their friends, Angie reminds them of the words that will bring them to a whole other level of freedom: "The Truth will set you free."[3]

Eve Elli and the Monarchs in her hair have been listening to the heart of the pyramid. She now stands and announces to the group, "The stones are talking to me. Close your eyes, put your hands across your chest, and you will hear them too."

---

[3] *John 8:32 (KJV)*

As they all do so, a gentle pulsation and tranquil feeling comes over everyone. And a voice from deep within the stones speaks to their collective heart:

Beings of Light, know that you are most precious and adored by the Creator. He loves you with a love that is beyond your comprehension. And for this, He will uphold you and never let you truly fail. The dark lord of the underworld is preparing to do battle for your souls by instilling you with fear and challenging your love and faith. And we of the great stone structures of the world have been told that you need our guidance and assistance. We are asked to remind you of who you truly are; that you are spirits filled with Divine Light and Love. Your purpose here on earth is to share your Light and Love with each other, healing the darkness within the hearts of your fellow beings. The dark forces have pulled you apart so much that you have forgotten the most important thing. You are all ONE, COLLECTIVE Being of Light, and your separateness from each other is only an illusion created by the underworld. It has been their way of disempowering and controlling you. As you raise your vibration to a higher divine love, that separateness will begin to heal.

Remember, precious beings of the Creator that the dark forces are gathering. But do not fear them. Remember that love is the most powerful force of the universe. And that your true self, IS PURE LOVE."

The voice of the stones goes quiet, and the Metatron devices turn themselves off.

"Holy shmoly!" exclaims Kookie.

The Chrysalenes, villagers, Kookie, Angie, David, Yakov, Neely, Beth, Liling, Dumaka, Meiling, Rudolpho, Suzie of the Seashells, Phil, Doc, Lord Emeka, Little Lady Bi, Eve Elli, and the

Monarch Butterflies in Eve Elli's hair, all breath out in unison: *"WHEW!"*

Yakov reflects upon what they are all feeling when he looks at their faces and says, "The dark forces are . . . *gathering?*"

Those words fill the air with a stillness and sense of foreboding, felt in the hearts of everyone present.

Chapter 3 – Witness

LATER THAT EVENING, the friends decide to spend their time in quiet reflection. Eve Sophia, Eve Elli, Lord Emeka, and Adam Mateo commune in nature with the other Chrysalenes, while Sergio, Tomas, and the other villagers are engaged in light activities or just keeping to themselves in their huts. They all seem to have a sense of foreboding as Kookie and his companions settle down in the visitor's hut.

Angie looks around and says, "Hey everybody, I wonder if we could all talk about what happened today, and, you know, how we are all feeling right now."

"Sounds good to me," Liling sighs.

They gather around Angie and she begins: "That was quite an experience at the pyramid and I'm so glad we are all here together."

"Amen! You said it, sister. Totally weird!"

"What is bothering me, as Yakov pointed out," Liling says, "is what the stones meant by, *the dark forces are gathering.*"

"I hear you, mom," says Meiling. "That has me totally spooked."

"Me too," Beth groans.

The others nod in agreement, muttering amongst themselves.

With much understanding and compassion in her heart Angie says, "No matter where our memories lead us, be it a place of light and love or down a dark corridor, always remember my dear friends that *The Truth Will Set You Free.*"

"Yes, my love," says Kookie tenderly, placing his arm around Angie and giving her a squeeze. "And how grateful I am that we all have each other."

At that moment, Lord Emeka, Eve Elli, and Lady Bi return to the hut. They are just in time to hear what Angie said.

"Remember what the Monarch Angel told us," Eve Elli says, "that the Heavenly Host is always with us, and we can call on them anytime we need their help."

Hearing those reassuring words everyone manages a smile and a sigh of relief.

"Well," continues Kookie who is also feeling relieved, "why don't we all turn in for the night.

* * *

During the dark hours before dawn, all is peaceful and quiet in the hut. Outside, the nocturnal sounds of the rainforest are slowing down as a stillness settles in. The sleeping folks in the hut are lost in their dreamworlds, including Suzie of the Seashells who is in a world of colors, feeling and images.

There are soft lights coming and going with soothing sounds of a woman's voice. Suzie is aware of a warm, cozy feeling in her soul with arms wrapped around her, holding her in a loving embrace. She hears a soft, rhythmic thumping sound against her ear. The woman's voice is singing to her as she feels herself swaying to and fro.

Suzie hears words coming from the woman: . . . "Sweet . . . baby . . . angel . . . mine . . . Martina . . . sweet . . . little . . . Martina" as the swaying continues.

Suddenly, the sunlight grows stronger as she feels the movement quicken. The soft rhythmic thumping sound turns into hard rapid pounding. There are other voices now, lots of them; loud men's voices. The embrace around her body turns into a tight grip as the pounding sound becomes frantic.

Suzie is fearful as she begins to wiggle and squirm. All at once there is a loud BANG! The embrace holding her releases and little Suzie begins to fall . . . and Susie of the Seashells wakes up screaming.

The silence in the hut is shattered and awakens everyone. Rudolpho is right by Suzie's side.

"It's okay, it's okay, honey. I'm right here."

Suzie shakes so badly she can hardly catch her breath. Doc and Phil are at her side in seconds as the rest look on with concern.

"Oh, sweetheart," Doc whispers to her little one.

"We're all here, my Wakanjeja,"[4] Phil says tenderly.

Suzie whimpers softly. She has heard the story from her "Papa Phil" of how he rescued her at the Shelter when she was only about nine months old, but Mimi, Angie and Doc never told her about her mother's cold-blooded murder, which they witnessed, while little Suzie was in her mother's arms.

Rudolpho holds her close rocking her in his arms, triggering the memory of Suzie's dream. She has stopped crying, and with a sad little smile says to everyone, "My name was once Martina."

Kookie's eyes widen. "That just came to you in a dream?!"

"Yes."

____

[4] *Lakota word for sacred child*

"Wow!" Kookie exclaims, furiously tapping the tips of his fingers together.

"My Little One, little Suzie," Phil says tenderly. "I called you that because I did not know your name." Bowing his head with humility, Phil adds, "And now I do, Miss Martina."

Suzie takes Phil by the hand and looks warmly into his eyes as she says, "Papa, my name is Suzie of the Seashells and I honor *you*, the one who rescued me and gave me that name."

A collective, tearful "Aww!" resounds in the hut.

Phil looks at his grown-up Little One and says, "Bless you, Wakanjeja." Taking Doc by the hand he says to both of them, "And bless the Creator for bringing us all together as a family."

The Monarch Angel looks down from the heavens and says, *Bless you all, sacred human creatures. May the love that you have for each other spread like the Heavenly Light, throughout One Garden.*

And the fallen angel looks up from the bowels of hell and snickers, *We shall see, Monarch Creature! We shall see!*

* * *

Master Howard has just arrived at the main plant of Howard Pharmaceuticals in California. His old office suite is now occupied by his son Master John, who folks still like to refer to as the Major. Since his retirement, Master Howard and his wife, Mistress Henrietta, have been spending a lot of time with their friend Judy, at Judy's Garden Community. His favorite pastime is cultivating Henrietta's Rose Garden, which he started years ago right after the downfall of the Council. Today he decides to drop by and see how the Major is doing.

Entering his old office, Master Howard says: "Well, hello there, son! How are you today? And what's new here at the plant?"

"Oh hello, father," the Major says without looking up. His face is buried in inventory reports. "I'm doing fine and so are our herbal products. In fact," he looks up at Master Howard, "we are just about to get some new herbs in from Phil and Doc."

"Oh? Where are those two, these days?"

"They are in a tropical rainforest in the Yucatan. Phil said something about a sacred site . . . a pyramid!"

"Wow!"

"In fact," the Major continues, "the whole gang is down there right now. I haven't gotten all the details yet, but it is something to do with Kookie, Metatron, and a new program that he, Angie, and David have come up with."

"Whoa!" exclaims Master Howard. "Whenever Kookie comes up with a brilliant idea you can bet it will have those *other guys* shaking!"

Both men chuckle as Master Howard continues, "Well son, it's good to see that you have everything under control here. Would it be okay if your mother and I take the kids to Judy's Garden for a coupla days?"

"Sure thing, dad. Vi is in the lab. Just go on down there and make arrangements with her."

Master Howard finds his daughter-in-law Violet, working in the lab with the senior shop manager Reggie. When he sees them, he blurts out at Reggie, "Hello my good man! So good to see you today!"

Reggie looks up from his herb grinder machine. Happy to see his old boss, he says to Master Howard, "And a good day to you, sir! I trust that you and the Mistress are well?"

"Yes we are, very well, indeed."

Vi looks at him and says, "Hi there, dad! I suppose you want to take the boys with you and mother to Judy's Garden."

Master Howard chuckles, "Well my goodness! I am always amazed at your intuitive skills and how you hit the nail on the head!"

Vi laughs. "I was hoping that they would have some time with Judy and the Chrysalenes, working on the herb gardens there. Go up to the house and take them. I'm sure you'll all have a blast."

"Thank you my dear. We shall have them back safe and sound in a couple of days," says Master Howard.

"You betcha, dad. Have fun! And say *hi* to Judy, Adam Tate, #9 and #10 for me, won't you?"

"Absolutely!"

Master Howard goes off to collect his wife and their grandkids, and head on out to Judy's. He is unaware that two others have been listening to him making plans.

From the bowels of hell, Lucifer says to Bella regarding his former henchman Master Howard: *So! The bad boy thinks he can just turn his back on us! Turn over a new leaf, does he?!*

Yes husband. Bella moans at the painful memory of how Master Howard was instrumental in her own demise. *He seriously tricked us didn't he,* Bella winces, *joining forces with Kookie and the Alliance, and working to bring the Council down! Even after I threatened him!* she wails.

Lucifer sneers, *Thinks he can trick the REAL trickster here and get away with it, does he? Humph! We shall see about that! Go to him, my bride. We shall see what that miserable rat is willing to walk away from now!*

Yes husband, I will go to him. And do you remember your promise of the new whip we talked about? You know, the "living whip." The boa with protruding fangs . . . Andre! You won't forget to have Andre ready for me when I get back, now will you my DEAR? Bella sneers at him with a sarcastic tone.

My queen, Lucifer protests, *have I ever disappointed you?*

Bella is off to Judy's Garden, anxious to get even with one of the main characters who was responsible for her downfall . . . and her death. Of course, she is also looking forward to rekindling her relationship with her favorite pet and soon-to-be new whip, Andre.

* * *

Master Howard and Mistress Henrietta arrive at the Garden of Judy, just a little way up the California coast from Howard Pharmaceuticals. They have brought their three grandsons; Jason, age 15, Michael, age 13, and Charles, age 10.

Judy sees the Cloudtransporter landing in the field and gets all excited. Jabbering away at her pigeon buddies #9 and #10 who are pattering around on the kitchen table eating all the leftover crumbs, Judy exclaims, "They're here! Yay! Come on, you two! Let's go out and greet Master Howard and his family!"

The pigeons stop munching on the table treats and hop onto Judy's shoulders. She gives her little buddies a quick snuggle and bounds out of the cottage toward the field. Master Howard, Mistress Henrietta, and the boys see Judy and wave to her.

Jay, Mike, and Charlie are thrilled to see #9 and #10 as they run to greet them, and the birds are just as excited to see the boys. Charlie gets there first and #9 and #10 hop onto his shoulders. He giggles with delight, scratching their little heads while the pigeons snuggle against his neck.

"Grandpa!" Charlie shouts out to Master Howard who is trailing behind. "I want pigeons of my own, Grandpa!"

"Me, too!" exclaims Mike who is now petting the birds on his brother's shoulders.

Master Howard and Mistress Henrietta catch up with the boys, the birds, and Judy, and they all hug each other. Judy exclaims with much enthusiasm, "It is so good to see you all again, my sweet friends!"

"You too, my dear," says Master Howard. He holds Judy's hands and bows his head graciously to her.

Mistress Henrietta is all smiles as she turns to her husband and says, "Well Howard, what do you have to say about getting the boys some homing pigeons of their own?"

"Oh yes! Yes, yes, Grandpa! Yes, *please!*" the boys cry out to Master Howard with Charlie jumping up and down.

The three grown-ups laugh and Judy says, "Well, I'm sure Kenny and Lisa can accommodate you with that request. If you like I can send #9 to them right away with a pigeon order."

"Yay! Woof! Yes!" the boys respond enthusiastically and Master Howard just smiles and shakes his head.

"All right then," he chuckles at his family. "Judy, let's place that order with Kenny and Lisa!"

"You're the best, Grandpa!" Jason says, as he and his two younger brothers throw their arms around Master Howard, giving him a big, juicy grandson squeeze.

"I'll take care of that for you right away," Judy says. "But first let's get you all settled in the guest cottage and then we can break bread together at my place."

Mistress Henrietta looks forward to sharing new baking recipes with Judy while Master Howard thinks about something else that he must do with his grandsons.

* * *

Meanwhile, at the Village of Chiconahui, Sergio comes running to the visitor's hut frantically looking for Kookie and the others.

"Lord Kookie! Lord Kookie!" Sergio calls out as he reaches the entrance to the hut.

"They are not here right now." Yakov says. He and Neely are the only two there at the moment, preparing food. "They have all gone out exploring. Phil and Doc have taken a group to check out some jungle flora, and I believe that Kookie said something about going back to the pyramid."

Neely detects something urgent in Sergio's voice as she says, "Is there something we can help you with?"

"Oh, My Lady!" Sergio says, quite beside himself with concern. "It is Tomas, my son."

Neely and Yakov both drop what they are doing and come over to Sergio, putting their hands on his shoulders.

"What is it?" asks Yakov.

"Is Tomas alright?" Neely says to him, gently.

"I don't know. I just don't know. I went out to the garden this morning and when I came back a little while ago, I found Tomas sitting in the hut staring up at the ceiling. I called out to him, but he would not answer." Sergio starts wringing his hands in despair. "My son! What is happening to him?"

"We'll be right there, Sergio. But first I must get Kookie and the others. Go back to Tomas and we shall be there just as soon as we can."

Sergio goes back to his son to find him sitting in the same spot, still staring at the ceiling. This time, Tomas slowly rocks back and forth. He lowers his eyes for a moment and then closes them as if he is thinking deeply about something.

"Tomas," Sergio whispers softly. "What is happening to you? My son, please speak to me. What is happening?"

As he continues to rock, with his eyes still closed, Tomas begins to speak. His voice sounds far away as if he is in another world:

"I am running . . . there are others . . . we are all running . . . some have fallen . . . laying still on the ground . . . shouting . . . yelling . . . gunshots . . . babies crying . . . mothers screaming . . .

"We get to a clearing . . . there is a beach up ahead . . . boats are in the water . . . I look back and see many people laying on the ground . . . more gunshots in the distance now . . . we run to the boats . . .

"Men in the boats are yelling . . . I do not know the language . . . the word is VAMONOS![5] . . . I hear it again . . . VAMONOS! . . . We climb into the boats as fast as we can . . . gunshots ringing out behind us . . . some people are shot down in the boats . . . they are tossed overboard . . .

---

[5] *Spanish for "Let's go."*

We are drifting now in the boat . . . water everywhere . . . where are we? . . . it has been a while . . . much fear . . .

Suddenly we see it . . . way off in the distance . . . a shoreline appears . . . everyone begins to cry . . . but they are not tears of sadness . . . they are tears of hope."

Tomas opens his eyes and looks at his papa. "I was hearing the voice from the stones, Papa, the stones of the pyramid of Chiconahui. She calls herself the Soul of the Stones and she's been talking to me all morning, telling me many, many stories."

Sergio is on his knees hugging his son. "Bless you, my boy." Looking up to the heavens with tears in his eyes, he says, "Thank you, Creator, for returning my boy to me.

By now a crowd has gathered outside the hut. Kookie and his friends, as well as the Chrysalenes and villagers have gotten word and slowly congregated outside Sergio's hut. They have been listening to Tomas sharing his vision, imagining that this was something that happened in the past. The Chrysalenes all nod at everyone and confirm this to be true. And that the language Tomas spoke, the word "vamonos," is from a language that was spoken at that time in this part of the world.

Eve Sophia explains to everyone, "The language is called Spanish. Some of you may even remember a few words, or songs from that time, especially now that the Chiconahui Pyramid has been activated."

The villagers are lost in thought as each one has a sudden memory come into his or her consciousness. They all look up to see Tomas appear before them in the doorway of the hut. He looks around at everyone, smiles, and begins to sing softly, in Spanish.

The song is a love poem by a man to a woman, who comes from a place called Guantanamo.

As Tomas sings, all the villagers suddenly remember the song in their collective *alma,* and they begin to sing along with Tomas. Then a miracle happens. The song continues to flow in Spanish from everyone else present as well, including the Chrysalenes, Kookie, Angie, Yakov, Neely, Liling, Dumaka, Phil, Doc, and all the rest of their friends. Even little Lady Bi is "singing" the tune going, "ahhh," with everyone.

Nearby, the Soul of the Stones listens and is elated at what she hears. This ancient soul goes all the way back to the birth of Mother Earth herself who is connected to rocks and crystals, and all life on the planet. And just as a mother loves her children, so does Mother Earth love all her inhabitants. She has heard the cry of her children ever since they left the First Garden, and now she is overjoyed that they are on a journey back to their earthly paradise.

The Mother is also filled with gratitude that her children are reaching out to each other in unity and love. Mother Earth has come to the Soul of the Stones, of the Pyramid of Chiconahui and speaks to her:

My precious daughter, Soul of the Stones: The time has come for you to awaken your sisters: the other pyramids, everywhere. You must all help the people of earth on their journey of love, healing, and remembering. The dark forces are going to do all they can to stop them and take the good people of the earth away from the Creator and each other. When you see that they are in imminent danger, you are to step in and help. Thank you my child, sweet Soul of the Stones. Thank you.

* * *

At Judy's Garden, Master Howard has taken Jay, Mike, and Charlie to a sacred spot out in the field. It is Henrietta's Rose Garden which he planted 18 years ago, right after One World won its freedom and became One Garden. The boys have been there before, but their grandpa has never told them the story of why it is his outdoor sanctuary, apart from the fact that he named it after their grandma.

The roses are in full bloom in a variety of colors, with little stone benches planted among the bushes. Master Howard likes to come to his little rose sanctuary, sit on one of the stone benches, close his eyes and let the roses speak to his heart. Today however, he has the boys sit directly upon the soft earth.

"Have a seat, guys," he says to his grandsons, sitting down on the earth and patting it.

Jay, Mike, and Charlie, follow their grandpa and sit down next to him.

"Now run your hands through the dirt and tell me what you feel."

As Master Howard instructs his grandsons to do this, he looks at the stone bench nearby. Somehow, he feels a voice calling to his heart. The voice says, *You are a righteous man, my brother. Do not ever forget that.* The voice is warm and comforting to him, but it also carries a sense of foreboding that Master Howard cannot understand.

He tries to block it out as he continues with the story he brought his grandsons there to hear. Feeling the soft earth beneath them the boys smile at each other, waiting for the tale that their "wonderfully weird grandpa," as they like to call him, is about to tell them. . . for the umpteenth time. Master Howard begins:

"A long time ago I was not the nice, loveable grandpa that you see sitting here before you today."

The boys smile and chuckle with delight.

"No, I was actually a selfish, greedy, money grubber, and I did not care much about what I did to get ahead in the business world. So when it all came crashing down on me, I felt completely worthless and unworthy of anything good and decent."

The boys are now looking at their grandpa seriously. There is a more somber tone to his story which they have not heard before. Jay, Mike and Charlie are feeling somewhat sorry for him as he continues:

"I came out here to this very spot and the Chrysalene Adam Tate taught me a lesson that helped me to forgive myself for being a really bad boy. As I sat here and ran my fingers through the earth, I pulled up a worm. And it occurred to me that I felt about as low as the little guy that I was holding in my hand. Then Adam Tate told me of all the wonderful things that worms do to give us healthy dirt that can produce healthy fruits and vegetables. And I realized that our Creator uses all of us, the high and mighty, which I thought I was, as well as the small and lowly, which I knew I had become, to do his bidding here on earth."

Jay, Mike, and Charlie are now beaming at their grandpa as he finishes his story.

"It helped me release my guilt of the past, that I might move forward in life and be a much better person to all whom I love, and everyone else whom I can serve."

"Wow, Grandpa. That's just beautiful," says Jayson, and the other two nod in agreement.

"Thank you, my boys. Thank you. And now I would like the three of you to close your eyes, put your hands in the dirt, and see what the rose garden has to say to each one of you. We can talk it over later at Judy's cottage, over cookies and juice."

"You got it, grandpa!" they all agree smiling.

And the four of them sink their hands into the dirt and close their eyes."

As they sit there, Master Howard notices a breeze beginning to blow. It is a gentle breeze at first but within a few minutes it picks up. He looks at the boys who are lost in meditation with peaceful smiles on their faces. And then out of nowhere, he is sure he can hear a voice speaking to him. He forgets about his meditation and begins to listen to the voice in the breeze, and an eerie sense of foreboding grows within him. It is the sound of a woman's voice. And though he has not heard this voice in a long time, it sounds strangely familiar. The dread in his guts becomes worse as the voice grows louder and clearer.

Now he can make out the words that the female voice is saying to him:

Master Howard, Master Howard, I am SO sorry, Master Howard! Can you ever forgive me?

Master Howard freezes with fear when he looks up to see where the voice is coming from, and down at the far end of the field he sees her; a woman wearing a red, hooded cape.

Chapter 4 – Succubus

AS MASTER HOWARD SITS in Henrietta's Rose Garden trying to meditate, the Soul of the Stones is crying out from the Yucatan all the way to Howard's heart in California. She is trying desperately to warn him of the impending danger. But he hears nothing except the pleading of the woman in the red, hooded cape, causing him great anxiety. Frozen from the loud fear in his mind, he cannot hear the soft voice of love calling to his heart. And while the boys are in quiet meditation, Master Howard is driven from his place of love and devotion, headed towards the she-demon from hell.

* * *

A long time ago, when the Council took control of One World, they told the Upper Crust that the people would be easier to control if their languages were limited to only three: English, Russian, and Chinese. The people were told that it was for their own good, especially if they wanted to be of service to a master and have a roof over their heads. They would have to learn the language of the lords and masters of whatever Continental Territory they lived in, or they would have no place to serve or to live. School children were only taught in the official language of their Territory, and the masters had language instructors brought into their places of service for the rest of the populace.

Anything spoken other than English, Russian, or Chinese became forbidden, with the threat of serious consequences to anyone who broke the rules. So, within one generation the native languages of all the other peoples of One World were all but forgotten.

There were, however, a few courageous elderly folks who sang songs to the young ones in their mother tongue, with the stern warning to their beloved offspring that they must always remember who their people are; their language, customs, and ways. But most of all they must *"NEVER FORGET"* the suffering of their people. For surely, should they ever forget, it will happen again. And indeed it did, to all the people of One World, with the ultimate enforcement of global slavery and genocide.

* * *

In the village of Chiconahui, Sergio and Tomas are gathered around the firepit with Kookie, Angie, David and several villagers. Suddenly they all hear a flurry of words entering their hearts in the beautiful language of their ancestors . . . the language of Spanish. They are also experiencing feelings and visions of things which they have never known before.

Young Tomas has a 10-year-old friend, Daniela, who has been his bestie from early childhood. And she is having a vision too. Daniela gets down on her knees and with her eyes closed, shares with everyone what she is seeing:

"I see a house filled with people. They are happy . . . talking and laughing together. A woman comes in from the garden . . . carrying lots of vegetables in her arms. She just picked them from their garden. The woman goes over to a big table to put the vegetables down . . . lovingly . . . giving them to her family."

Daniela is quiet for a moment as something else comes into her vision . . . something she has never seen before and has a hard time explaining. With her eyes still closed and furrowing her brow she describes what she sees:

"There is an object on the wall above the table. It is made of wood . . . about the size of the woman's hand. It has been held by many hands . . . many times. It is shaped something like the letter 't'. The woman looks at the "t" when she puts the vegetables down on the table . . . she feels joy in her heart . . . I hear a voice . . . it is saying a word . . . but I do not know what it means . . . as I look at the "t" it keeps saying this word over and over . . . LA CRUZ . . . With this word, I can feel the woman's love in her heart."

Daniela opens her eyes. A feeling of peace and joy is with her. It transmits to all the other villagers as well as the Chrysalenes and the visiting friends.

Eve Sophia explains to Daniela and everyone else, "It is another Spanish word which means THE CROSS. In days gone by when people used to have such things it made them very happy."

"It looks like it is still making people happy," says Kookie with a smile, as he sees peace radiating from Daniela and everyone else. "Thank you for the gift of your visions, dear children. We will be leaving soon, and I am so grateful for the time we have spent here with you."

The others agree as warm hugs and expressions of gratitude are exchanged all around.

"Come on," Kookie says to Angie and David. "Let's see the pyramid one more time before we leave. We've got to be at

Howard Pharmaceuticals later this afternoon and we mustn't keep the Major waiting!"

"Yes Dad!" says David pointing his index finger in the air just like his father. "Mustn't keep the Major waiting!"

"Oh! You two!" quips Angie as the three of them take off for the pyramid.

When they arrive, most of the others are already there. They are all seated on the ancient stone structure in various states of meditation or reflection.

Yakov comes over to Kookie looking a bit apprehensive as he says to his big brother: "I don't know, bratan.[6] It seems that we have all been called here but we do not know why. Liling has gotten the message in her heart that we are to wait until everyone arrives."

"Hmm," says Kookie. "I guess that explains why *I* had the sudden urge to drop everything and come here too. Are we all here now?"

"Not yet," says Liling, "But I'm sure Phil, Doc, Suzie, and Rudolpho will show up soon. Whatever it is that has brought us all here right now, must be calling them as well."

"Look!" says David, turning around. "There they are!"

Sure enough, Doc and family are right behind and rather surprised to see everyone else there too. "Hey there!" Doc calls out. "So what brings us all back here again?"

Kookie shrugs his shoulders as they reach him and says, "We're not sure. But I think we had all better get ourselves to the stones and have a seat along with everyone else. Since it seems we are all expected to be here I guess we'll find out soon enough."

---

[6] *Russian slang for bro'*

"You got that right, brother!" Phil exclaims.

* * *

Master Howard has left Henrietta's Rose Garden and is walking across the open field toward the woman with the red, hooded cape. There is no one else around since the Chrysalenes and farm hands are all at Judy's Cottage preparing for the celebration of Master Howard's visit with his family.

The woman is still calling to him, pleading, with words of remorse. Her voice is awakening an excitement in him that the 87-year-old man has not felt for a very long time. His step quickens, and as it does, the woman ducks into the nearby trees. Master Howard has now forgotten his fear. He is only aware of the burning passion deep within which is filling his heart with overwhelming lust. He begins moving quickly to the place where the woman disappeared behind the trees, and he enters the wooded area.

Suddenly the air goes still, cold, and dark, and Master Howard feels light-headed as if in a dream. Then he hears the woman's voice again:

"Howard . . . Dearest Howard . . . Do you remember me? Do you remember all the things you once did to me? . . . Mmm, Yessss! I remember! . . . I remember well!"

The woman suddenly appears before him, her hood down. And he recognizes her at once as a woman that he had an affair with many years ago, right after his son was born.

"And didn't you just looove all those things I did to YOU, my Dearessst Howard! Ooo, yesss! Yes indeed, you did, my darling!"

Howard cannot speak. He is inextricably drawn to her. She puts her arms around him and pulls him in close. Whatever free will he had is all but gone as he gives his will over to hers. At that moment she reveals herself to him, as Bella's true face appears.

Howard is shocked but he still cannot speak or move. He knows now that he is lost . . . lost to a succubus . . . lost to the beast. With no control left inside of him, he reaches out and grabs her. And Bella opens her red cape to reveal her seductive, irresistible naked curves.

"I am here for you," she whispers in his ear, "all of me. You can take me now."

With his will surrendered to hers, Howard begins to run his hands up and down her back and all over her body, his mouth firmly planted on hers. Then she pulls back a little and gives him the final command:

"For that which you are about to receive, the lord Lucifer asks only one thing of you."

Master Howard is lost in lust as the final words from Bella reach his ears: "Lucifer wants your help in taking the souls of your grandsons: Jayson, Michael, and Charles."

* * *

In the Yucatan at the Pyramid of Chiconahui, a group of people hit the proverbial roof and scream their collective brains out: *"AAAAAAAAAHHHHHHHH!!"*

They have been listening with their hearts through the Soul of the Stones, to Master Howard's entire ordeal. Yakov is the first one to jump up and yowl: *"MERCIFUL CREATOR IN HEAVEN! HELP HIM! PLEASE! HELP MASTER HOWARD!"*

Dumaka is next: *"Oh, Heavenly Kind One! Please be with our dear friend Master Howard."*

Then comes Phil: *"Great Spirit, Holy One, Creator of all life, Loving Father in Heaven. Please help our brother, Your son Master Howard. Please let him feel Your most loving presence as he is faced with this evil."*

Meanwhile, the Soul of the Stones has been trying to get the attention of all present. But like Master Howard, the sacred stone notices that humans are not able to hear the quiet voice that is speaking to their hearts when they are in the throes of fear.

Hmm. They are not responding to subtlety, she ponders.

So, the Soul of the Stones decides to get their attention another way. She tosses a rather large rock from a point just above where they are all sitting, bowling right down their center, barely missing everyone. Suddenly they all stop dead in their tracks. Eve Elli of course, has been sitting there cool as a Chrysalene and feels much compassion for Master Howard.

That's better, says the sacred stone to herself. Then she continues to the people gathered on her stones, speaking to their hearts:

Good people, you have nothing to fear. Your friend Master Howard is in the hands of the Lord now. His time here on earth is almost at an end, and the Creator has sent an angel to watch over him and guide him home. The ones who need you most now are his family. You must go, good people . . . go to Master Howard's family. And whenever you need me, I Am here.

The Soul of the Stones goes quiet and Kookie jumps up and yells: *"Let's go! To the Cloudtransporters! NOW! VAMONOS, AMIGOS!*

* * *

Bella's words slam Howard in the gut. Something inside his soul kicks him hard as he suddenly wrenches himself completely free of Bella's evil grip. His head reels and he feels like he is about to topple over. Howard's vision becomes blurry as he looks into Bella's eyes and sees the red fires of hell burning in them.

With his last ounce of free will that he didn't even realize was still in him, Howard looks into the eyes of the succubus and says, "No! The devil will NOT have my grandsons!"

"Well Howard, if that is what you wish. But I shall still have my way with you!" Then Bella screams: "ANDREEEEEE!!"

In an instant, a 13-foot-long boa constrictor, endowed by Lucifer with 6-inch fangs, appears in Bella's hands. Holding the snake high above her head, stretched out stiff with his fangs protruding, Bella screeches a maniacal laugh and screams to the bowels of hell below: "THANK YOU, HONEY!"

With one quick lash Bella brings down the wrath of hell on Howard. Andre's fangs tear into Howard's flesh and rip open his torso from the neck down to his thigh. He goes down instantly and lays on the ground unconscious. And although he feels no more pain, Bella cannot control her raging lust. She screams with pleasure, tearing him to shreds, with lash upon lash to his fallen body.

Howard is now in the tunnel of Light and sees the beautiful, golden Angel of the Lord before him. "I have been here watching over you, Howard creature," Angel says to him, "that you would be released from your body quickly, and not suffer." For this he is truly grateful.

"Thank you, most beautiful angel," Howard says, and with a heart full of hope he asks her, "Am I going home now?"

"Yes, human creature, and I Am honored to show you the Way."

Taking Howard by the hand, the Angel of the Lord guides him up the Tunnel of Light. His eyes go wide with wonder, as feelings of peace and love fill his heart. Howard reaches the Gate and sees his mother and father on the other side, joyously waiting to see their son again. And Angel turns to Howard one more time saying, "Welcome, righteous, human creature. Welcome home."

* * *

Jay, Mike, and Charlie have been meditating in the rose garden. When they open their eyes and see that their grandpa is not there, they figure he must be wandering around the roses nearby.

"Hey, Grandpa! Where are you?" Mike calls out, expecting him to pop out from behind one of the rose bushes. But there is no answer.

Jay remarks, "I'll bet Grandpa found a Chrysalene to talk to. You know how side-tracked he gets with those folks!"

The three brothers chuckle and Charlie says, "Hey! I've got a great idea! While we're waiting for Grandpa I would love to see if I can dig up a worm. Then I can bring it back and tell everyone at the cottage a story about the great miracles of a little worm!"

Jay and Mike laugh as they each throw a handful of dirt at their little brother.

Charlie starts to dig and Jay says, "I've got another idea. Why don't we pick some roses for grandma and our celebration meal this evening?"

"Now *that* sounds like a plan," says Mike, and the two of them start checking out the rose bushes.

"Well," says Charlie, "You guys can get the roses, and I'll get the worm," as he keeps on digging.

Jay and Mike roll their eyes, smile at each other, and begin their rose selections.

After a while they have a nice bunch of roses gathered, and Charlie announces that he has found a special new friend. He holds up the worm and inspects the little guy, who also seems to be inspecting Charlie. But as he does so Charlie sees something quite unexpected out in the field. "Hey you guys, look what's coming in for a landing!"

They all look up and see four Cloudtransporters landing in the field. Jay is puzzled. "We didn't hear anything about other guests, did we?"

As they watch the portals open, they recognize each and every one of their parents' dearest friends step out of the aircraft. And then, lo and behold, Vi and the Major step out of Kookie's craft as well.

Jayson notices that they are all holding each other; Kookie's arm around the Major, and Angie holding Vi close to her. But instead of heading towards Judy's cottage they stay where they are, talking to each other. The boys are too far away to hear what they are saying, but the look on everyone's faces and the scene unfolding before them begin to alarm Jay and Mike.

They can hear Kookie's voice although they cannot make out the words. He appears to be directing a few of the men to the wooded area nearby while motioning everyone else to stay where they are. Kookie, Yakov, Dumaka, and Phil go into the wooded area.

"That does it!" says Jay defiantly! "Let's go check it out!"

Mike and Charlie agree without hesitation and the three of them start heading in the direction of their mom, dad, and everyone else at the Cloudtransporters.

The Major is the first one to see his sons coming towards them, and he suddenly bolts across the field before the boys can get any closer. Reaching them, the Major is all out of breath and obviously shaken.

Kookie, Yakov, Dumaka, and Phil do not have very far to go before they see Master Howard's body just ahead. He is covered in blood and has been badly mutilated and dismembered.

Suddenly, Kookie stops. He thinks about this man whom he has known all his life. A man who praised him and held him in high esteem when he was a child through all his growing years, and who treated him like his own son. Kookie watched Master Howard go through his darker days and eventually come out of it, shining, in his beautiful real soul. He was the closest thing that Kookie ever had to a real father. And now he sees him lying on the ground in bloody pieces at the end of a battle with a succubus, who took this man's life. But the she-demon from hell could not capture Lucifer's real prize . . . Howard's soul.

Kookie can go no further. He drops down to his knees, puts his head in his hands, starts rocking back and forth, and has a complete breakdown.

* * *

The Major tries to compose himself as he looks at Jayson, and then glances at the other two.

"What is it, dad? What's going on?" Jay says to his father with trepidation.

"It's your grandpa."

"Is he okay?" Jayson asks.

The two younger brothers look imploringly at their dad and all three of them now know that something is very wrong.

In a soft voice the Major replies, "I don't think so. Kookie and the others have gone to find him."

The boys try to comprehend what their father has just told them, and the Major continues, "Kookie and the others came to pick up your mother and me when they sensed what was going on. And now they have gone to check it out."

He puts his arms out to his sons and they all stand there holding each other. Then they hear Yakov's voice as the men come out of the woods.

The Major looks at them for a moment and catches a glimpse of Kookie who is walking slowly, head down, trailing behind Yakov, Phil, and Dumaka. Yakov looks around and sees the Major standing there holding onto his boys. The two men lock sorrowful eyes as Yakov slowly shakes his head . . . *no*.

The Major tightens his grip on his sons' shoulders and lowers his head in grief. With tears falling he whispers softly, "Your grandpa has gone home."

Jayson, Michael, and Charles all begin to cry as they snuggle up against their dad. Within moments they feel another pair of arms around them all when Vi takes her husband and her sons into her embrace.

The rest of the group walks slowly over to the Major and his family, their eyes expressing the sadness that their hearts are feeling. But when the Major sees the deep look of sorrow on his soul-brother Kookie's face, the two men throw their arms around each other and release the immense sadness they both feel for the loss of their "dad."

* * *

At the cottage, Judy is startled when she sees everyone coming. Instinctively, she goes to Adam Tate who is out in the front garden with the other Chrysalenes and residents. She asks him quietly what is going on.

"My dearest Judy," Adam Tate says with heart-felt sympathy and compassion. "The other Chrysalenes have taken Mistress Henrietta back to the guest cottage. They wanted to give her the news, surrounding her with their love and some good herbal tea. We have already made a few pots for the others who we knew would also be coming."

He puts his arms around Judy with much tenderness. "Master Howard has gone home to be with the Creator."

"*WHAT?!*" Judy shrieks. "*What are you talking about?! What happened?!*"

At that moment Judy hears everyone coming in at the back of the cottage.

Adam Tate simply says to her, "His son will explain it all."

Everyone is gathered in the cottage with a few Chrysalenes who have come in to care for them. They find a place to sit down while the Chrysalenes begin serving the soothing herbal tea. The Major looks at everyone as he says:

"My mother is at the guest cottage being cared for by the Chrysalenes. She has been told that my father has passed but does not know exactly what happened yet. So, I will ask one of the Chrysalenes to please bring her here."

Adam Tate goes to bring Mistress Henrietta to Judy's cottage, and moments later they return with her. When she sees the Major, she falls into her son's arms.

As mother and son cry together, the Major says to her through his tears, "It's okay, Mother. The Monarch Angel was with him when he passed. And she told us that he did not suffer much."

Vi approaches and says, "Come, Mother, sit with me and let John tell you what happened."

The two women sit together on one of Judy's sofas. And the Major bows his head and begins to speak in a soft, sorrowful tone: "This afternoon my father Master Howard, passed from this world and is now with the Creator. When Kookie and all the rest of you came to Vi and me and told us what happened at the Pyramid of Chiconahui, at first I didn't believe it."

He pauses for a moment, thinks about the *entire* story and how Kookie and the others said they were leaving it up to him to tell it in his own way.

Looking at his mother the Major tells her, "The evil spirit of Lady Bella came and called dad into the woods. And when Bella told him that Lucifer wanted his help in taking the souls of his grandsons, he refused."

He stops to look at Jay, Mike, and Charlie. "And that was when Bella took your grandpa's life." Looking down once more, the Major says, "She killed him with a blow from a sharp weapon."

Henrietta, Vi, and the boys all look down and weep. And the loved ones sitting next to the family reach out and hold them tight.

Eve Elli stands and says, "Dearest sweet friends; Mistress Henrietta, Major, Vi, Jayson, Michael, and Charles. All of us here love you so much and our hearts are with you in this very sad moment. I am here to reassure you that the Monarch Angel was with Howard when he passed, and she made sure that his passing was quick. I am also asked to tell you that the Creator and all the angels of Heaven also love you very much, and today they are welcoming their beloved son Howard home."

Mistress Henrietta stands up and goes to Eve Elli. Putting her arms around the sacred Chrysalene she says, "Thank you, Eve Elli. And bless you . . . bless you . . . bless you."

Mistress Henrietta and Eve Elli hold each other in a warm embrace. Then Eve Elli continues: "The evil one may have taken a life today, but the beast lost the battle for Howard's soul. And for that we are truly victorious."

Everyone nods in agreement and then Charlie stands up and says, "I have something to say about my grandpa."

The room hushes as all eyes and ears are on young Charles.

"Today, my grandpa told us the story of the worm, again, and how the little critter inspired him to plant Henrietta's Rose Garden for my grandma."

Everyone smiles at Charlie, remembering their own fond memories of Master Howard's favorite story about his life.

"But today when he took us to the rose garden and told us the story, it felt different. As I was sitting there on the soft dirt with Grandpa, Jay, and Mike, it just gave me a whole new feeling about it. So I decided to try to find one of those little guys myself."

Pulling something out of his pocket Charlie holds up a worm for all to see. "I found this little critter. I'm going to keep him and take good care of him." Pausing for a moment, fighting back tears, he continues," And I will call him Grandpa Howard."

There is a soft and loving murmur around the room, as Charlie says proudly, "And this little guy will always remind me of the love and courage my grandpa had when he stood up for my brothers and me, and said *No,* to the bully."

Vi hugs and kisses her son.

And the rest of the day and evening is spent sharing memories of Master Howard, by his loving family and friends.

* * *

In a small cottage somewhere in the Yucatan, PA, ES, and SPA are mulling over their fate. They have now had some time to consider the forces they are dealing with and what they are going to do about it.

SPA says to ES and PA, "My brothers, we all know too well the power the beast wields and what he did to us the last time we, how shall I say, *disappointed* him.

"Yes brother," says ES with hesitation, "We . . . uh . . . certainly do know what the beast can do."

PA adds, "And we also know that he can do a lot worse. That is, we are still here and still alive, where we could easily have been with him in the underworld by now."

SPA says, "Yes indeed, brother PA, along with Lady Bella and all the other lost souls who inhabit that dreadful place."

"It was not the beast who set us free you know," PA says.

"Hm," ES ponders, "We never did figure out who that voice belonged to, did we?"

"You mean the voice that said, *Come, Follow Me?*" SPA considers.

"Yes brother, that one exactly," PA continues. "I believe it was *that* voice and not the voice of Lady Bella that we heard after the ice melted from our prison."

As the three brothers reflect upon this they hear another voice right outside the cottage. It is the voice of Bella the succubus, calling to the brethren: *"I have returned to you, most high, PA, ES, and SPA. Open the door and let me come in."*

Chapter 5 – Masters

PA, ES, AND SPA look at each other. There is a knowing glance and subtle nod that passes between them which says, *Yes, we have been here before and we know what to do.* Words are not necessary for each one to know what the other two are thinking.

PA goes to the door and lets Bella in.

A pale glow emanates from her face. Bella's eyes look deep into the eyes of the three men, piercing through the very bottom of their souls.

The she-demon smiles and speaks to them: "Well, your Highest, brothers of the former Council of One World. What have you three to say for yourselves? You may have all your wealth and power returned to you should you decide to do the master's bidding."

PA, ES, and SPA regard Bella in silence as she continues. "Of course, if you haven't quite decided what to do I have a friend who can help you make up your minds." An evil grin crosses her face. "His name is Andre!"

Bella holds her hands up over her head ready to receive her boa buddy when PA raises his own hand and says to her, "My Lady, that won't be necessary. My brothers and I have decided," he gives them an almost imperceptible sideways glance, "that we are indeed at your service."

Bella puts her hands down.

PA puts his hand down too.

They smile at each other and Bella says, "Very well then. Let's get to work, shall we?"

And the three brothers say, "Indeed!"

* * *

It is late afternoon in the village of Chiconahui, and Tomas, Daniela, and the other children have just finished picking the fruits and vegetables for the day. They bring them around to all the huts of the village and leave the food, along with their sweet smiles. The delicious fragrance of bread baking and soup cooking permeates the entire village making everyone's mouth water.

But Tomas and Daniela have discovered another hunger coming from a deeper place within. It is the hunger for knowledge and wisdom, especially of their true heritage and identity. Being born and raised in the Continental Territory of Panamerica all they have ever known is that culture, including the English language. So as soon as their chores for the day are done they cannot wait to go talk to their new, ancient friend, the Soul of the Stones.

"Hurry, Tomas!" Daniela calls to her buddy.

She is way ahead of him down the well-worn familiar jungle path leading to the pyramid.

Tomas also feels the hunger for other nourishment, munching on a piece of fruit which is slowing down his steps. But he manages to finish his food and catch up with Daniela just as she enters the clearing.

The pyramid stands majestically before them.

"Can you feel it, Daniela?"

"Yes, I can." she replies.

They both feel strangely confused by the heaviness that has suddenly come over their hearts.

"It feels like the Soul of the Stones is speaking loudly to us today," Tomas remarks.

"Yes, yes it does!" Daniela agrees.

The two of them approach the pyramid with a bit of caution unsure about what message the Soul of the Stones is about to reveal to them.

They each climb to their favorite spots, close their eyes, and wait for the voice to speak to them.

The children do not have to wait long:

Blessings to you, young ones of the earth. There are many other earth beings, especially those of the air, who have asked me to send their love and blessings to you today.

Daniela and Tomas are smiling deeply from the heart.

We are all filled with gratitude that you are listening to our voices. There is so much we need to tell the other earth beings of your kind, but they cannot hear us as well as you do. We have much hope now that you two young ones will carry our words to others.

The children are filled with awe as they nod.

There is a dark lord of the underworld who has caused much suffering and destruction on the earth. He has hurt the earth beings very much in the past by turning you against each other.

The Soul of the Stones brings up an image for Tomas and Daniela to see:

It is the image of a young girl about the same age as Daniela. She is in a room with other children, with small tables and chairs. A woman stands in front of them talking and smiling at the children. Daniela and Tomas feel her kindness and the love that the young girl has for her.

The woman stops talking and peers out the window as if she hears something. There are loud noises outside and the young girl becomes fearful. She gets down on the floor, crawls under her little table, bends over and covers her head.

To Daniela and Tomas, it sounds like thunderous bangs going off suddenly, one after another.

The young girl opens her eyes and sees that the woman and the other children have all gone and she is the only one left in the room. She leaves quickly and tries to run away from the sudden, loud bangs. Tomas and Daniela can feel her fear and they both become sad.

Daniela opens her eyes and wants to leave. But Tomas is still listening, so she closes her eyes again and hears the rest of the message:

"There are many things that the dark lord has done in the past which have hurt the young earth beings very much. We will show you some of these things so that with your love you may learn to help other earth beings defeat the dark lord. We wish for you all to be happy, joyous, and free in your new world of One Garden. Remember always, young ones that The Truth will set you free."[7]

"Is there something we can do?" Tomas asks the Soul of the Stones.

---

[7] *John 8:32 KJV*

"You are both being called to take a journey up to California, to a place called the Garden of Judy. On your journey you will be guided by your hearts and the visions that you will both receive. Be brave and true, precious young beings. And remember how much the Creator loves you."

The voice goes quiet, leaving Daniela and Tomas staring at each other with confusion. They know intuitively that their hearts are about to be opened to the suffering of other people, *their* people, of the past. They also feel a foreshadowing of what is about to happen in One Garden.

But most of all the two children know that they must follow the voice that guides them from the Soul of the Stones.

* * *

At the Garden of Judy later that evening, Mistress Henrietta is with her grandsons and Eve Jennie. Vi looks in on them periodically. Kookie and the rest are in Judy's cottage involved in a serious discussion about where they all need to go from here.

Vi comes back from looking in on her family and everyone asks how Mistress Henrietta is doing.

"As well as can be expected," Vi says with a sigh. "Eve Jennie is looking after all of them and she is especially mindful and attentive to mother's needs. I am so grateful to be blessed with the Chrysalenes in our lives."

"Here, here!" Everyone strongly agrees with this.

Liling speaks up about what is on her heart. "What is most disconcerting to me," she says, "as we started to discuss on the way over here, is the reemergence of the evil spirit of Lady Bella. When we were fighting with a disease, or human greed, or a corrupt Council and UC, we knew who the bad guys were and what we were fighting against. But now it is a much deeper enemy. It is well-hidden in the hearts of people and too easy for the dark side to have its way with us."

Angie chimes in, "Yes. That is *oh* so very true, Liling. When I was with the beast in his underworld of lost souls, I could see how and where his power came from. It all came from our fears of each other, and it is so easy for him to crawl under our skin and exploit that."

"And until we learn how to really deal with our fears," Doc exclaims, "the dark side will continue to be a threat to all of humanity."

Phil adds his own thoughts. "Great Spirit has given us free will and allowed trickster to tempt us and make us fearful and divided for a reason."

Phil has everyone's attention now and they have all gone quiet.

"The Creator has given us the choice to allow His loving spirit to enter and open our hearts, or for trickster to close our hearts. But for those whom trickster has shut down the Creator is especially compassionate, loving and patient. We have only to see His compassion and love expressed through the Chrysalenes."

Everyone smiles and nods in agreement as they look with mutual gratitude and affection at the Chrysalenes in the room.

Phil continues, "It is through trickster's challenges that the Creator allows us to learn and grow, becoming more like the Chrysalenes. And as long as we continue to keep our hearts open to the Creator's loving spirit we will always win in the end.

"And I do believe that Master Howard did just that. As young Charlie said, his grandpa died defending his grandsons against a bully. That, to me, is the true value of trickster. And once we learn that lesson, as many of us here already have, then we do not have to fear him anymore."

Dumaka adds, "In fact we can even thank trickster for how he truly helps heal the divide between us, by bringing us *all* closer to the Kind One in the end."

Kookie has been listening closely to what everyone has been saying, and how this all translates into the imminent threat of Bella.

"It seems to me," Kookie says, "that in the long run the best protection we can have in every stratum of society is to never forget the harm done by the evil doers. Also, we must always remember where the true power, the ultimate power, the *absolute power* comes from. And that, is LOVE."

Kookie ponders what he has just said for a moment, and smiles. "There is no force in the universe that is greater than Love. Therefore, when we plug into that sacred power we truly can do anything."

"As for the matter at hand," Kookie continues, "the first thing we need to do is open our hearts to the truth and be prepared for whatever Bella is up to."

Rudolpho is the next one to speak up and says, "And I am looking at a whole room full of people right here who have already had plenty of experience in outsmarting her ladyship, AND trickster!"

The friends all break out into a much-needed chuckle.

"I completely agree," says the Major, "and I want to go to Kenny and Lisa's as soon as possible. I really feel that we need to connect with the crowd at Bear River Garden. And besides, I want to get a pair of pigeons for the boys . . ." He pauses, lowering his head with sadness, "especially now."

"Sounds like a plan," says Yakov looking at Neely. "I say we leave for Bear River, Oregon, first thing in the morning."

"Yes! Let's do that, bratan!" says Kookie, and the others agree.

That evening before they all turn in, Kookie asks Judy to send a message with #9 to Lisa and Kenny.

It reads:

Will be arriving tomorrow, 21 total. – Big Kahuna

* * *

The next morning, Judy decides to offer Mistress Henrietta and her family a burial place for Master Howard in his beloved rose garden. The Major and his family are overwhelmed with gratitude by Judy's kindness.

"My good woman," the Major says," you honor us all. I can think of no other place in the world where my father would want to be buried."

"The honor is all mine," says Judy.

The garden residents and Chrysalenes clear a spot in the rose garden and lovingly attend to the burial. Adam Tate and the others plan to find just the right stone and set it there with a small bench for meditation.

Judy has a feeling that Henrietta needs to spend a little time in the rose garden with the Chrysalenes, so she invites the Mistress to stay there for as long as she needs. Eve Jennie offers to stay with her giving comfort and support to Henrietta.

As the group prepares to leave, everyone gathers around to give lots of love and hugs to Judy, the good people of her garden community, the Chrysalenes, and Mistress Henrietta. And as everyone walks back to the Cloudtransporters, they all stop at the rose garden to say farewell to their beloved friend Master Howard, one last time.

* * *

At the small cottage in the Yucatan not far from Chiconahui, Bella barks at PA, ES, and SPA.

"You will prepare to leave at once!"

The brothers look at each other warily as PA says to her, "Where are we going, My Lady?"

"It is not very far from here, Brother PA. Oh . . . may I call you that? *Brother* PA?"

Again, the brothers exchange uneasy glances as PA says, "Yes, indeed ma'am, you may call me Brother PA."

"Well then Brother PA, the three of you are to get back in the Cloudtransporter and I will program it to bring you to your next destination. It will only take about five minutes for you to get there." With an eerie smile Bella continues, "I do believe you will recognize the place once we arrive."

She disappears and the brothers board the craft.

They are flying low over the tropical terrain of the Yucatan. Except for the occasional clearing there is not much to see, or for the brothers to recognize. But, then they do see it, just a little way up ahead. And the memories of PA, ES, and SPA become crystal clear.

It is the former residence of the late Lord Josef who died 18 years ago in the same blast that took the life of Lady Bella and many other lords and ladies.

Bella's band of mercenaries, former Master Commandants of One World have arrived. They look up and see the Cloudtransporter coming in for a landing.

Bella found most of these men in Euroslavica and the rest in the other two continental territories of Sinopacifica and Panamerica.

After the fall of the Council they were broken, dispirited and quite lost. Bella found them and rounded them all up saying that the Highest of the Council had returned and would once again unite the Upper Crust. She promised these men that PA, ES, and SPA would regain control and leadership of One World with their help. Then Bella told them to come to the estate of the late Lord Josef and await the arrival of their leaders. And with that, the former Master Commandants of One World have renewed hope and a sense of purpose again, united in their love for power and their hatred and fear of the former slaves.

The men are all wearing Universal Translators. And when they see the approaching craft, several of them cry out in their own languages, Chinese, Russian, or English:

"Kan! Smotret![8] Look! It is Our Lords! The Highest have returned!"

---

[8] *Chinese and Russian for "look!"*

As they hear the cries of their fellow Master Commandants, other men come running excitedly out of the big house. They were all told stories of their heroes PA, ES, and SPA, how they did their best to eliminate the slaves and keep One World for the UC. The Highest of the Council allegedly died bravely in battle against the enemy . . . the people of One World. And now, not only have they learned that their heroes are still alive, but they have returned to unite and lead them once more.

As the Cloudtransporter lands and the portal opens, the Master Commandants are gathered waiting with bated breath. And then PA, ES, and SPA walk out of the portal in full view of the crowd of men who once worshipped and followed them. An awestruck hush comes over them. No one has ever actually seen the faces of the Highest of the Council since they were always heavily guarded and their identities well protected. However, the men know in an instant who they are and many of them begin to break down and cry.

Their leaders have come back to them and they shall all rise once more.

* * *

At Bear River Garden, in Bear River Oregon, Lisa and Kenny scurry around preparing for the arrival of their 21 guests. The garden residents and Chrysalenes also joyfully prepare for the return of their friends.

Two other heroes of the former Alliance of One World, Mimi and Ryan, come dancing into Lisa's cottage excited about the arrival of Kookie and company, and especially Eve Elli, Emeka, and little baby Bi.

They have been part-time residents at Bear River Garden for the past 18 years, spending the rest of their time in Johannesburg at the estate of Lord Emeka. They share a uniquely special relationship with him. Mimi and Ryan are the grandparents of Eve Elli and great-grandparents of little Lady Bi, who are their most precious jewels.

"Hurry everyone! They are almost here!" Lisa exclaims as she is putting the finishing touches on her cookies, fruit pies, and assorted quiche pastries.

The residents prep the little guest huts for the visitors, and the Chrysalenes pick fruits and vegetables from the gardens and hothouse. Kenny, of course, has the honor of selecting the pair of birds from his coop who will become the beloved friends of Jayson, Michael, and Charles. He is truly having a hard time deciding which ones to choose though and finally gives up.

"I think I had better just let the boys pick their own little buddies," Kenny says to the pigeons, chuckling, and scratching their little heads.

Lisa finishes up in the kitchen with the most tantalizing aromas imaginable coming from her cottage and wafting through the back gardens.

Mimi says to Lisa, "Do let me help you with those exquisite pastries of yours!"

"Absolutely!" exclaims Lisa. "Nothing tastes quite as good as a cookie baked by a grandma!"

The two women have a chuckle and Ryan says, "How about cookies baked by a grandpa?"

"Now those are truly the best of all!" Mimi lovingly says to her husband, giving him an affectionate squeeze and a smile.

The Chrysalenes and residents are also just about ready.

Kenny looks up from the coop and sees four Cloudtransporters making their descent out in the field.

He rushes into the cottage to tell Lisa: "Honey! They're here!"

"Oh my!" Lisa exclaims as she drops what she is doing.

She and Kenny head for the Cloudtransporters which have just landed, as Lisa calls out, "Come on everyone!"

The garden residents and Chrysalenes, who are beaming with delight, trail after Lisa and Kenny. They all arrive just as the portals open.

* * *

From the bowels of hell, the beast watches with disgust as the loving energy emanating from the folks at Bear River Garden is more than he can handle.

"Sickening!" he says to Bella. "Just sickening. We cannot allow such treachery to divert our plans, my queen, now can we?"

Bella replies, "Do not worry, husband, we have the finest team assembled. Their hatred of the slaves and fear of you makes them perfect soldiers for this war."

Lucifer ponders Bella's words for a moment.

"And remember" she continues, "they are quite devoted to PA, ES, and SPA."

Lucifer lets out a long screaming howl of hideous laughter: "EEEYYYAAAHAHAHA! Those idiots! If they were fruit flies they could not find their way to the nearest piece of fruit!"

Bella thinks about it and agrees, "This is true. However, do not forget that they now have ME to deal with as well as my buddy here, Andre!"

With an evil grin and maniacal laugh, Bella holds her hands high up over her head, and in an instant her 13-foot-long boa buddy with six-inch fangs appears in her grip. Andre looks down and winks at her.

Bella says to Lucifer, "We are both here, my husband, to deal with those treacherous slaves."

"Do you really know what this war is all about, my charming Bella?"

"Why of course, my fallen angel. It is for the souls of humankind."

"It is more than that, my delicious succubus. It is to show that other One up above which one of us is boss! It is to show Him that I, NOT He, reigns supreme!"

Then Lucifer looks up and shakes his fist in a fit of rage, screaming: **"I** *HAVE THE TRUE POWER!* **I** *HAVE* **ABSOLUTE POWER! NOT YOU!!"**

The beast snorts and says to Bella and Andre, "Well, the two of you had better get up there and take care of business!"

* * *

At the estate of the late Lord Josef, PA, ES, and SPA stand in front of the open portal of the Cloudtransporter looking out over a field of Master Commandants. Some are in tears, some are calling out their names, and some have fallen to their knees. The brethren walk slowly down the ramp and the rest of the mercenaries drop to their knees. As the brothers continue their procession towards the entryway of the Big House, suddenly an old familiar feeling becomes aroused in all three of them.

Lucifer takes it all in. He closes his eyes to feel the power-lust that PA, ES, and SPA are beginning to feel once more.

They get to the entryway and Bella comes out to greet them.

"Welcome, PA, ES, and SPA, your most high. Welcome to your new home!"

Addressing the group of commandants on their knees, she cries out:

"YOU WILL ALL RISE!"

They do.

"YOU WILL NOW PLEDGE YOUR LIVES, HEARTS, AND SOULS TO THE BRETHREN OF THE COUNCIL, BY REPEATING THE WORDS THAT I HAVE TAUGHT YOU!"

They begin:

"We, the Master Commandants of One World, do hereby give our Will over to the Brethren of the Council, PA, ES, and SPA. We shall follow their command, under torture or unto death, without question or hesitation. Our hearts and souls are now as one, belonging only to the Council of the Brethren. And so it is. And so it shall be.

Lucifer smiles with his eyes still closed. *"Now you are all mine!"* he says.

* * *

At Bear River Garden, in Bear River, Oregon, the group of friends disembark from their Cloudtransporters and see the people and Chrysalenes coming toward them. They are all so happy and excited to see one another, but none are quite as thrilled as Mimi to see her great-grandbaby, little Lady Bi!

Eve Elli and Lord Emeka see Mimi moving as fast as she can as they both rush to her.

"Gramma! Gramma!" squeals Eve Elli with great excitement sounding just like she did when she was three years old.

Mimi cries out, "My sweet darlings!" as she reaches her precious family and squeezes everyone with her big gramma hugs. "Oh my! I have missed you all SOOO much!"

Little Lady Bi giggles with pure delight as Mimi cannot stop hugging her and dancing around with her baby.

Her Chrysalene daughter Eve Lydia laughs at her 70 plus-year-old mama. "Take it easy, mom. Remember your knees and lower back."

"Oh nonsense!" Mimi says to her daughter with indignation. "Why I am just a young girl. Don't you know?" she says, nuzzling little Bi still swinging her around. And then she gets a twinge in her knee that says, *I don't think so, woman!* Mimi stops with a yelp, "OY!"

Her loving hubby Ryan puts his arms around Mimi and says, "You will always be my girl, twinges and all." He gives her a peck on the cheek and another peck on little Bi's cheek.

Lisa waves her arms around at everyone and says, "Well, hello! It's so wonderful to see you all again! Look at all the young ones! My! How you've all grown!"

Meiling, Beth, David, Jay, Mike, and Charlie all come over to give Lisa big hugs. They smell the most fabulous aromas coming from the kitchen of Lisa and Kenny's cottage. Their mouths begin to water imagining the tantalizing meal that Lisa has prepared for them, to which she says: "Let's all go break bread together, shall we?"

The youngsters can't get there fast enough.

* * *

At Lord Josef's estate, Bella nods at two Master Commandants who are standing in front of the group. They come over and introduce themselves to PA, ES, and SPA.

"I am Master Commandant Pasha," the first man says to the brothers.

"And I am Master Commandant Haitao," says the second man. "We are here to take you, highest ones, to your living quarters."

SPA says to the men, "Yes, do take us."

The two men lead PA, ES, and SPA through a maze of corridors in this very old, large mansion, passing a great gathering hall along the way. The Brethren of the Council know that this will be a most adequate room for gatherings with the men. They finally get to their suites which are very comfortably furnished and well-equipped with a full, high-tech surveillance system.

PA looks pleased as he says to Pasha and Haitao, "Thank you. You will tell all the men that we shall be meeting in the great gathering hall within the hour."

"Yes, your highest!" they say as they click their heels together and salute.

Pasha and Haitao leave the three brothers alone. They look around for the familiar cameras and other assorted surveillance equipment, although they know that the one who is watching them does not need a camera.

One thing PA, ES, and SPA got very adept at during their 18 years in captivity was a silent form of communication between the three of them. When they knew that it was particularly unsafe to communicate, they learned how to say it all with their eyes and body language.

For the moment they are saying nothing of any consequence other than the usual that has always been expected of them by their lord Lucifer.

PA begins with, "Well, my dear brothers. This is a rather charming and comfortable place, is it not?

"Oh my, yes! Yes, indeed it is!" chirps ES.

"Do tell!" exclaims SPA. "It is most comfortable, indeed!"

"I should like very much to get settled in before we go out and address the Master Commandants," says PA, matter-of-factly.

"Yes brother, that does sound like a very good idea," says SPA.

"Indeed!" says ES.

The three of them give each other one of their special looks as they go off to their private rooms.

Master Commandant Pasha and Master Commandant Haitao are busy rounding up all the men. They tell everyone that the Brethren of the Council expect them to be in the great gathering hall ready to receive their first set of instructions, shortly. There is much excitement in the air and great anticipation as to what plan of action there will be. Most of these men are in their late 40s by now and figure this will not be the same sort of combat that they were trained for and engaged in, in the past.

Pasha says to the men, "It seems that the last time we had our confrontations with the people of One World, it was technology and mind games that took down the UC." They all nod at the painful memories of their defeat. "So maybe that is what we will be doing this time."

"You mean outsmarting them?" asks one of the commandants. "Considering the brains they have on their side that won't be easy."

"No," says Haitao, "it won't be easy. But we were the warriors of One World and the top ones at that."

"That's right," Pasha agrees, "and they have been busy planting gardens and learning how to kiss seedlings to make them grow big and strong!"

The men all laugh out loud at the thought of the great High Lord Kenneth, High Lord Commandant Yakov, and all the others, on their knees in the gardens around the world kissing plants.

Pasha, Haitao, and the other Master Commandants begin to gather in the great hallway. They are discussing possible ways they could mentally outwit such geniuses as Kookie, Yakov, Liling, and Rudolpho.

Master Commandant George suddenly has an idea and says to the men, "My brothers, I do not give a hang how brilliant a man is. *No one is perfect!* Kenneth, Yakov, Liling, and Rudolpho are subject to the same temptations and weaknesses as the rest of us. I believe that we must first discover what their weaknesses are," he pauses for a moment, "and then exploit them!"

PA, ES, and SPA have been listening to the men for a little while, standing outside the great hallway. Once again they nod at each other in a language that only they can understand.

A trace of a smile crosses the lips of PA. He motions to the entrance of the great hallway and says to ES and SPA: "Ready?"

They both nod, returning the trace of a smile.

PA says, "Good. Let's go in."

Chapter 6 – Decisions

AT THE FARM COTTAGE of Bear River Gardens, Lisa serves up cookies and pastries to round off a truly exquisite meal. After bringing several platters from the kitchen, she goes back to get one more; a full plate of chocolate chip cookies that she sets down right in front of Kookie. Everyone around the table laughs.

"Hey bro, is that enough for ya'?" the Major asks.

Kookie looks at the Major with a smile as he takes his tuba mouthpiece out of his pocket and blows raspberries at him. More gales of laughter follow including little Lady Bi, who lets out a big, baby-belly-laugh from Mimi's lap.

Kookie looks at her and says, "Well, just for that, young lady, I will have to give you something." He holds his plate of chocolate chip cookies out in front of her. "Here you go, little one. Help yourself!"

A collective "Aww" echoes around the table and little Lady Bi manages to find the biggest cookie.

After polishing off his plate, Kookie sits back and taps the tips of his fingers together. He is truly stuffed.

Kenny looks at Jay, Mike, and Charlie and asks them, "What would you guys say about coming to the coop with me and picking out a pair of pigeons?"

"*WHOOOA!*" the three of them cry out and quickly glance at their mom and dad.

The Major rolls his eyes, nods, and grins, and Vi smiles with an approving nod.

"Okay," Kenny says to three very excited young gentlemen. "Let's go!"

Jay, Mike, and Charlie race each other to the pigeon coop with David, Meiling, Beth, and a very happy Kenny trailing behind. When the young folks reach the pigeons, they immediately pick up the little critters, scratch their heads and do the pigeon handshake with them. It is a very endearing maneuver which Kenny teaches all the baby birds how to do.

Charlie puts his hand out to one little guy and offers to shake hands as he says, "Hello!" And he is completely enchanted and blown away when the baby pigeon offers Charlie his foot in return. He picks up the little bird, puts him on his shoulder and the pigeon walks up to Charlie's neck. The two of them snuggle each other as Boy and bird are instantly bonded.

Upon entering the coop, Kenny observes the same bonding experience happening with the pigeons and all three brothers, as well as David and the young ladies. Kenny is overjoyed as he just knows that he will be giving away lots of pigeons today.

Back at the cottage the table is cleared, and everyone knows that they are about to have a serious discussion. Lisa brings out a few flasks of fresh coffee. Bi has settled into a cozy nap on Great-Gramma Mimi's lap, and everyone lets out a sigh. The room goes quiet as Kookie begins:

"The loss of Master Howard and the way in which he died, is a wakeup call. The beast is most assuredly angry at us for robbing him of his victory. But I have been asking myself, what does he really want from us?" Kookie pauses for a moment as he glances around the table. "I believe that what he ultimately wants is something that he cannot have."

"What is that bro?" the Major asks, thinking of his dad with sadness.

"Simply put, he wants *MORE.*"

Kookie pauses again observing the expressions on the faces around the table. There is a mixture of confusion, pensiveness, and assorted looks that say, *huh?* The only one who is sitting with her eyes closed smiling blissfully is Eve Elli. In fact, Eve Elli is doing her Chrysalene glow, giving Light to the others in her presence.

As always Mimi is the first one to notice her all-knowing, all-glowing granddaughter, and as usual she cannot contain her curiosity for very long. "Okay, kid! So what does this all mean?" Mimi asks.

Everyone chuckles in agreement with Mimi, and they all turn to Eve Elli.

With her eyes still closed, expression unchanged and glowing with more intensity, Eve Elli speaks softly to her beloved family and friends:

"Once, when Lucifer lived in Heaven, he was a beautiful, brilliant angel. He had everything including the love of the Creator. He had so much going for him that he thought himself to be just like the Creator. And eventually he thought himself to *BE* Him. At that point Lucifer decided that he had Absolute Power and that his word was *The* Word . . . the Word of the Lord Himself.

"When the Lord realized what had happened to Lucifer, he expelled him from His House and sent him to where he is now, where his corrupted soul turned him into a beast."

Eve Elli opens her eyes and looks at everyone. "It is a lesson and warning to us all that ABSOLUTE POWER CORRUPTS

ABSOLUTELY.[9] The only one who has, and can wield Absolute Power, with love, is our Creator.

"And the reason Lucifer always wants *more* is because whatever he has, whatever he does, and whatever he gets will never be enough. Right now, he probably wants our souls, all of us. But if he were to get that it would not be enough for him either. Anyone with such a lust for power, whether it is control over people or a passion for more and more things, is truly to be pitied. Because that lust can *never* be satisfied."

Mimi looks at her precious granddaughter with love and gratitude in her eyes. "And do you pity Lucifer, sweetheart?" Mimi asks.

Suddenly, Eve Elli breaks out into an ear-to-ear grin. "Oh yes gramma, I certainly do! And it drives him crazy!"

"*HAHAHAHA!*" The entire room erupts into fits of laughter.

But there is one who is not laughing.

In the bowels of hell, the beast, the prince of darkness, Lucifer, screams with a hateful rage that resounds throughout the universe.

And way up above in the heavenly realm a chipper voice speaks to the heart of her beloved human creature Eve Elli. "*You go, girlfriend!*"

* * *

In the Yucatan, the Master Commandants in the Great Hallway of the late Lord Josef's estate are fully captivated at what their comrade George has just told them. The idea of outsmarting the

---

[9] *Lord Acton of England, 1834*

smartest of the smart; Kookie, Yakov, Liling, and Rudolpho, is *not* about trying to be cleverer than they are, which is probably impossible, but to uncover and exploit their weaknesses. PA, ES, and SPA have been listening to this from behind the door. And now they walk into the room and join their minions.

When the men see their high lords walk in, they jump to their feet and stand at attention. PA smiles at them and motions for his men to sit down.

"Hello Master Commandants. Thank you for joining us here so quickly," PA says.

The men all respond in one voice, "AT YOUR SERVICE, HIGH ONE, *SIR!*"

PA continues, "My brethren and I have heard a few of your comments just as we walked in. And I must say that we are very impressed with what we are hearing."

"Yes, we are, indeed," says SPA.

"Indeed," says ES.

"We do understand that life has been difficult for you these past 18 years. When the slaves took over, they also took away your power and your riches."

The men begin to mutter and grumble as PA continues.

"However, my fine warriors and heroes of One World, now that we have reunited, we shall take all of that back!"

The men cheer as PA's passion swells.

"And all of you here will have even more than you ever dreamed of as we shall bequeath to you the titles and honors you all deserve!"

The cheering gets louder, and PA finally arouses the men into a state of ecstasy as he proclaims, "And you shall all become lords of your own estates!"

The men jump to their feet and the Great Hallway explodes into a thunderous uproar.

After a while, PA motions for them to calm down and return to their seats. He looks around the room and says, "Would the man who just spoke about exploitation of weaknesses stand up."

Master Commandant George rises to his feet and PA looks him square in the eye. "What is your name, Commandant?"

"My name is George, High One."

"Well then George, you are right. We have tried most unsuccessfully in the past to outwit those of whom you have spoken and to no avail. In fact, it has always seemed to backfire on us. We even tried what you suggested once and it almost worked. But it too backfired in the end."

At this point SPA interjects, "Yes, indeed we did, George. We tried it once with Master Howard and it almost worked. I daresay that with a little bit of effort and, how shall I say, ingenuity, we might be more successful at it this time.'

ES stands up and shouts, *"AND THIS TIME WE SHALL NOT FAIL!"*

The minions jump to their feet once again, pounding their fists in the air shouting:

"SHALL NOT FAIL!

SHALL NOT FAIL!

SHALL NOT FAIL!"

PA raises his hand to get their attention and motions for everyone to sit back down.

He elaborates, "Their weakness is that they seem to have lost all fear of the dark side of human nature. And for that they have been thrown off their guard. In other words, men, they are not looking where they are going and do not recognize danger when it is right before them."

The crowd mutters and snickers in agreement with more sarcastic references to kissing plants.

"So, I firmly believe," exclaims PA, "that if we throw such a danger at them on a much larger scale than we did with Master Howard, this time men, yes . . . this time *WE SHALL NOT FAIL!*"

The minions fly out of their seats, pounding and shouting:

"SHALL NOT FAIL!
SHALL NOT FAIL!
SHALL NOT FAIL!"

At that moment, PA, ES, and SPA notice servants standing in the entryway with trollies of food. They look at each other with a knowing grin.

PA motions for the Master Commandants to calm down as he says, "Before we break for dinner, my brethren and I are leaving you all with the task of coming up with a most excellent strategy."

SPA concurs. "And by this time tomorrow we expect to have our plan of attack underway."

"Indeed!" ES exclaims. "Now *do* enjoy your most excellent meal!"

The Master Commandants applaud while the food trollies come in. And the brethren of the former Council of One World quietly slip out.

In the bowels of hell Lucifer grins, Bella pets her boa, and Andre gives a knowing wink at the two of them.

* * *

Kookie continues his discussion at Bear River Garden. "Bella can strike at any moment and in a devious manner. We defeated Lucifer once," says Kookie, "but it is an ongoing struggle.

"What can we do then?" asks the Major with concern. "How do we come up with a plan that can protect everyone from an enemy that will never die?"

Lord Emeka has been listening quietly but intently to all that has been said. Looking at his wife Eve Elli and his sweet baby girl fast asleep on her great-gramma Mimi's lap, he knows in his heart what it is that the dark lord from the underworld can never defeat.

He turns to the Major and says, "I have been reading the books that PA, ES, and SPA kept hidden from all of us until Kookie rescued them years ago. And those books talk about many good things."

"Like what?" asks Doc who has also been reading the books from the new libraries that Emeka has helped to establish throughout One Garden.

"Like history for one thing, and how we must study the past if we are ever going to learn anything from it."

"And also about love," says Angie. Looking at Kookie she says, "I have been reading those books too my darling. And I *do* know from my own experience with the beast that LOVE is one thing he cannot tolerate . . . and cannot defeat."

Phil interjects, "The Creator has given us everything we need to live a good life, which we have all been a part of these past 18 years. I believe that He has also given us the tools we need to protect and defend our world from all forces that would have us return to slavery."

All eyes are glued on Phil as he continues, "He has given us the incredible love and genius of Kookie, Yakov, Liling, Rudolpho, and all the rest of the great souls who are sitting right here around this table. And I do believe from what we have all seen that there are more, *many* more souls in the world such as all of you, who live in the Light, than those who are in league with Lucifer."

"Here, here!" everyone joins in.

"The Creator has also given us some wonderful tools of technology, and books that can help us learn more of what we need to know as Lord Emeka has just reminded us," Phil says with great confidence smiling at everyone around the table.

Kookie has been listening to Phil while holding his Metatron device in his hands, and a thought occurs to him as he points his index finger in the air.

"I've been thinking. You know, the activation we did at the Pyramid of Chiconahui was a great beginning. It really brought out some significant memories of our past. And the more we remember, the more we heal and raise our collective, human awareness. And as we move closer to the highest form of love, humanity will hopefully never forget the evils of the past and learn the lessons that will keep us truly happy, joyous, and free.

"It is also important to realize though, that once we achieve full activation of pyramids around the world all kinds of memories, dreams and visions will be revealed and some of them will not be pleasant or easy to deal with. But as the Monarch Angel says, when that happens, she, and all the benevolent forces of the heavens and the natural world will be here to help us. All we have to do is call upon them."

"Yes," says Angie, "the Truth is not always easy to handle. When I confronted the beast, I learned that lesson very well. But I also saw that the beast has a much harder time dealing with the Truth than we do, because basically the Truth and Love are inseparable."

Kookie feels very grateful knowing that Truth and Love are the very essence of Angie. He taps the tips of his fingers together, smiling away and happy as a clam.

Just then a joyous sound from outside comes bursting into Lisa and Kenny's cottage. Four young men and two young women come laughing and bouncing back from the pigeon coop with a very happy Kenny following right behind. Each one of the youths has a pair of birds snuggled up to either side of his or her neck, and the whole party of young people and pigeons are cooing away together with sheer delight.

"Ooo, Mama! Papa!" says Meiling to Liling and Dumaka. "Can I keep them? Please? Can I keep them?"

Beth goes skipping over to her folks with the same exuberance, "Aren't they simply adorable?" she says to them, as the pigeons on her neck each hold a foot out to Neely and Yakov.

David takes the two pigeons off his neck and perches them on Angie's shoulders. They immediately snuggle up against her neck as if they are in pigeon heaven. And of course, Angie is right there in pigeon heaven with them.

Last but not least, Jayson, Michael, and Charles, stand in front of the Major and Vi, kissing, cuddling, and scratching the little heads of their new companions. Charlie speaks for all three of them when he gives mom and dad a doe-eyed stare and says, *"Puleeease?"*

The parents of the six young people all look at each other and then at Kenny. In one seemingly simultaneous maneuver, the four dads take out their official One Garden Barter and Trade card and hand it to Kenny.

"This should help you at the next Barter and Trade Market, Kenny," Dumaka says.

"Here, bro, they are well worth it," says the Major handing Kenny his card.

"Thank you, bratan!" says Yakov.

"It is always a great pleasure, my good man," says Kookie.

"Thank *you!* Thank you all!" exclaims Kenny. "The pleasure is all mine."

Glancing at Lisa for a moment he turns back to the group and says, "And having you folks as our friends is the greatest pleasure and honor of all."

Lisa looks at her husband with a loving nod and the others all smile and say, "You too."

The new little feathered friends are passed around the table, taking turns "shaking hands" with everyone and just being their charming little pigeon selves.

Finally, Kookie speaks up. "Well folks, what do you all think? Anyone interested in a little journey to activate pyramids?"

"Just tell us what we have to do and where we have to go, my brother," exclaims Liling. She and Dumaka look at each other and at Meiling and the two pigeons. The birds have already become a permanent fixture on their daughter's neck. "It looks like we will be taking a couple of new little companions along with us," Liling says, smiling and shaking her head.

Everyone has a chuckle and one by one hands go up in the air, beginning with Phil and Doc, followed by Rudolpho and Suzie, and Yakov and Neely.

Mimi looks at Ryan. "Honey, what do you think?" she asks.

"We're in!" Ryan says and his hand goes flying up in the air.

Everyone smiles and Lord Emeka says, "Of course we are in too," as he raises his hand.

The Major says, "I would love more than anything to go with all of you, but" and he looks at Vi, "I've got a really strong feeling that someone has got to stay and keep a watchful eye at Howard Pharmaceuticals. Not that I'm expecting anything to happen, but we never know where or how the other guys might strike. I just don't want to leave the plant unprotected."

Vi nods at him and says, "It's okay, honey. I've got the same feeling in my gut."

The others understand. And Lisa and Kenny look at each other and express the same thoughts as the Major and Vi, feeling that they too need to stand guard at their central guesthouse at Bear River Garden.

"Totally understood," says Kookie to the Major, Vi, Kenny, and Lisa. "We *do* need our people at their home bases, for all that you folks do."

Phil adds, "I think we should go right back to the Village of Chiconahui and see what is happening there since the activation and if everyone is okay. Especially if we are going to be activating other pyramids around the world."

"That sounds like an excellent idea," Kookie says to Phil. "I say we figure out our assignments tomorrow and then get going. But for now, why don't we all take some time to enjoy a good healing visit with the Chrysalenes and do some loving on the seedlings."

"Sounds like a plan! You got that right! Lovin' on the seedlings – it's been a while!" they exclaim in turn.

The group of friends enjoy the rest of their day with each other, their beloved Chrysalenes, and the beautiful natural surroundings of Southern Oregon at Bear River Garden.

* * *

In the village of Chiconahui, Daniela and Tomas talk to the villagers about their sudden memories of the past, and much to their surprise they discover that almost everyone has been having dreams and visions.

Eve Sophia tells them, "Yes, it is strange how most of the villagers have been experiencing these things. As Chrysalenes we are familiar with the voices and messages of the heavenly realm, and we are so very happy now that others are experiencing them too."

Daniela asks Eve Sophia, "Have others also been called to go to California to the Garden of Judy, as we have, ma'am?"

Eve Sophia chuckles. "Not exactly. But we all seem to receive our own special calling." Then she adds, "And I have been called to help you two on your journey to the Garden of Judy."

Tomas and Daniela's eyes grow wide with excitement. Tomas says to her, "Really?! Are you going to go with us, then?"

"I am here to serve you my child," Eve Sophia says with a warm smile.

Standing right behind her is Adam Mateo. "And so am I," he says. "I have heard the same voice in my heart which has told me that I am to go with the two of you, guide you on your journey and serve you both as best as I can."

Daniela and Tomas look at each other with expressions of great joy. "We've just GOT to go ask our parents!" Tomas says to her.

"You bet!" exclaims Daniela as they both scurry off to find their folks.

Tomas reaches his hut and finds his dad outside tending to the vegetable garden. "Papa!" he cries. "I have been to the pyramid with Daniela and we both had another vision!"

Sergio looks up from his work, wipes his hands and says to his son in a playfully mocking tone, "Hmm . . . now let me see. The Stones told you that you and Daniela are to go to California, to the Garden of Judy."

"*YES!*" Tomas squeals at Sergio, who puts his hands out to Tomas, laughing.

"We have all been having dreams and visions, my son. And while I was here tending to the seedlings, the Soul of the Stones came to me and spoke to my heart. She said that I was to go with you on your journey of seeking Truth and knowledge. So, I went inside and spoke to your mother, and it is all settled."

Tomas can hardly believe his ears! "Daniela is also asking her mama and papa, so I hope they will also—" but he does not have a chance to finish his sentence because he sees Daniela and her mama Elena coming down the path toward them. Elena is all smiles and Daniela is skipping with delight.

"Hello, Sergio and Tomas!" Elena says. Clapping her hands, she says to father and son, "The voice in my heart told me that there is no time to lose, and we should get going as soon as possible. Daniela tells me that Eve Sophia and Adam Mateo will also be joining us. How exciting to be going on a vision quest with Chrysalenes!"

"What is a vision quest, Elena?" Tomas inquires.

"I was told that a vision quest is what our ancestors used to do. There were different reasons for them, but for our purpose it is to journey into the unknown seeking knowledge and wisdom and being guided by the Creator and all those He sends to help. These can be people or elements of nature such as the Soul of the Stones."

Daniela interjects, "And the Monarch Angel!"

"Who?" the other three say as they look at her quizzically.

"The Monarch Angel," Daniela says. Then she explains to the others, "There is an Angel of the Lord who decided a while back to have an earthly experience. She knew that her help would be needed by people down here, so she lived among us for a while as a Monarch Butterfly. The first one who got to know her was Vi, of Howard Pharmaceuticals. Well, Angel has been talking to my heart and she has told me many things. But mostly, I feel just how much she loves *Human Creatures,* as Angel calls us. And I just love her too."

Everyone chuckles, and Daniela continues, "In fact she is talking to my heart right now. The Monarch Angel is saying, *There's no time to waste young human creature! Hop to it!*"

Everyone laughs and Sergio says, "Ma'am, yes, ma'am!"

***

Deep in the bowels of hell the beast is becoming agitated. Upon hearing the reference to the Monarch Angel he remembers the last encounter he had with her when she "dropped in on him" unexpectedly with Angie. Lucifer knows that he has no time to waste.

He turns to Bella and sees her still petting Andre who is licking her with his long, forked tongue.

"My queen!" he says to her abruptly. "Quit playing with that thing! There is work to be done up above! Go and tend to those idiots of the former Council before they ruin everything once more!"

"Yes, husband." Bella replies. And turning to Andre she says, "Come on, sweetie pie. Let's go upstairs and have some fun!"

Andre winks at her and off they go to the former Lord Josef's Estate in the Yucatan.

***

After leaving the meeting at the Great Hallway of the estate of Lord Josef, PA, ES, and SPA return to their quarters. They do not speak to each other except for a few brief words here and there.

PA says, "I thought it best to have our meal here without the others around."

"Yes indeed, brother," says SPA.

"Indeed," says ES.

Their tone is somber and trepidatious. Knowing that anyone could be listening to them, on earth or in the underworld, makes them quite fearful indeed. What they do not realize however is that there are others who are also listening to them, others from the heavenly realm.

The Monarch Angel has been listening to their hearts. She listened to them during their captivity and knows what they had to do to survive, trapped in their palace under the polar ice for 18 years. Like the Creator, Angel has much love and compassion for all human creatures on earth, even those who have fallen from grace. She decides to make an appearance in the quarters of PA, ES, and SPA.

The brothers are quietly finishing their meal. They are ready to go to their rooms and be alone with their thoughts for the rest of the day when suddenly, they are aware of a soft, glowing Light. It fills the room with its presence although they do not see where it is coming from. PA, ES and SPA look around, confused and somewhat apprehensive.

"What is that?" asks ES.

"It seems to be other-worldly, does it not, my brothers?" asks SPA.

"Yes, it does," says PA, "only . . ." and he pauses for a moment, "only it does not feel like Lady Bella, does it?"

"No, no indeed," the other two agree.

Suddenly Angel materializes before them in all her sparkling golden glory. Their eyes go wide, their hearts race, and their jaws drop to the ground.

"Uh . . . uh . . . who are you?" asks SPA.

The brothers are abruptly frozen in their seats and cannot move. Speaking to their hearts the Angel says:

"I Am the Monarch Angel. You have nothing to fear for I come with wonderful news for all of you, but especially for you, Brother SPA."

SPA looks at Angel with confusion, somewhat leery of what she is about to say. Angel continues:

"You may recall a woman who bore you a child once; the Lord Ekene."

Now PA and ES look at SPA in utter disbelief.

"You may also recall how your son Lord Ekene left this earth, accidently going over a cliff."

SPA nods. He did not know that anyone else knew about this and he chokes back tears. Angel continues:

"What you may not know is that after his death your son found himself in the underworld, condemned to the desolation and despair of hell. But what you also do not know is that his son, your grandson Lord Emeka, who was only five years old at the time, went down to the depths of hell to rescue him. He brought with him, among others, the Chrysalene Eve Elli who was only three years old at the time."

The three brothers are in absolute shock by this news and the Monarch Angel continues to tell SPA the rest of the story.

"Well, thanks to your grandson Lord Emeka and the Chrysalene Eve Elli, Lord Ekene is now in Heaven. And one more thing Brother SPA . . ."

Brother SPA is in so much shock that he does not know if he can handle one more thing.

"Lord Emeka and Eve Elli are now young adults. They have married and now have a baby girl. Her name is Lady Bi. She was named after the Lady Bi who was Lady Bella's younger sister. The one whom Lady Bella murdered.

Therefore, SPA creature, you now have a great-granddaughter who is herself a Chrysalene.

"I love all human creatures, men of the former Council, but Eve Elli holds a special place in my heart. And nothing will make me happier than if one day all three of you decide to follow me instead of the one whom you are now following."

The Monarch Angel begins to fade until she disappears altogether. But her Light and her Love continue to fill the room and the hearts of the three broken men left behind.

Meanwhile, Bella has been standing outside the door of PA, ES, and SPA's quarters. She heard everything, including the part of Lord Ekene and Eve Elli's baby being named after her sister Lady Bi; the one who deceived her, the one she tortured and killed.

Bella's grip on Andre tightens as she thinks back to that time and feels the rage and hatred she felt for her sister. Not only did she hate Bi then but throughout her childhood as well, for Bella's sister Bi was their mother's favorite. She now has a new enemy, Eve Elli. And her hatred feeds her bloodlust, giving Lucifer's queen an even stronger desire to do her husband's bidding.

Bella knocks on the door of the brother's quarters. They are expecting her. Already familiar with her knock, they look at each other with a knowing silence as they hear her say:

"It is I, Bella. Let me come in."

PART 2

THE JOURNEY

Chapter 7 – Visions

EARLY IN THE MORNING, in the tomato hothouse at Bear River Garden, Eve Elli sets her daughter down next to a seedling. "Okay sweetie, give the baby tomato plant some lovin'."

Little Lady Bi has watched her mama and papa love on the seedlings many times. It makes baby Bi happy since she can feel the thrill it gives the seedlings to receive human love and light.

Bi gets all excited, giggling and flapping her arms. And Great-Gramma Mimi who is watching her little darling cannot contain her enthusiasm either. She comes over to her little one and starts giggling and flapping along with little Lady Bi.

Then Ryan comes over to his wife and their little angel. "Can I join in, too?" he asks, flapping his arms with delight.

Jay, Mike, Charlie, David, Meiling, and Beth are watching all this from the other end of the hothouse. They roll their eyes at each other and do their best to stifle huge guffaws. And then they all go quiet as little Lady Bi begins.

She closes her eyes and starts to glow, smiling and feeling love enter her heart. Then she leans over and kisses the baby tomato plant, *Mwah,* patting her chest and saying, "Wuv baby! Wuv baby!"

All are witness to the purity of Chrysalene-baby-love as they heave great sighs together.

When everyone has done their rounds for the morning of seedling loving and enjoying their time in nature, they slowly regroup at Lisa and Kenny's cottage. The friends now must choose their pyramid assignments and begin their journey.

Yakov is the first to speak up. "There are so many pyramids scattered throughout the world, bratan. How many do you suppose we actually need to activate?"

"Oh, it's really quite simple," says Kookie tapping the tips of his fingers together. "Thanks to Metatron I have figured out that we only need to activate a total of three in the right locations. That includes Chiconahui which means we only need to activate two more. Combined with Metatron we should be able to get a good positive chain reaction going with the rest of them around the world."

"Wow! No kidding! That's awesome!" the others exclaim.

Yakov continues, "So where are the other two pyramids located?"

"I have chosen a kind of triangulation of pyramids," Kookie explains, "which should set up a matrix of global activation. So, to triangulate with the Pyramid of Chiconahui the two other locations that I think will work well for us include one only about 11 miles from Johannesburg. It is an area that was uninhabited for a very long time and has recently been repopulated as a garden community."

"Oh, my goodness!" exclaims Lord Emeka. "I know that place! Eve Elli and I helped the people there get that garden community going. I guess that's where we will go."

Eve Elli glances lovingly at her little Bi. "Yes. And they also chose to name their garden after our sister Bi in Heaven, as we did with our daughter. It is called The Garden of Bi," says Eve Elli.

Everyone pauses for a moment and remembers the gruesome death of Lady Bi who sacrificed her life for the Alliance. And she is now cherished as one of the greatest heroines of freedom for the people of One Garden.

Mimi looks at Ryan and pipes in, "Well, I guess we know which assignment *we* will choose, honey!"

Kookie continues, "The other location is in your neck of the woods, Yakov. It is not far from the town of Moscow, also in a nearby area that was deserted until recently.

"Well, bratan," Yakov says, "In that case, I guess we should go there."

Looking at Neely he adds. "Is that okay with you, sweetie?"

She smiles and nods in agreement.

Kookie goes on to explain, "The villagers of the garden community there have named it after little Suzie, to honor her and all the other children who died as she did. . ." Kookie pauses for a moment looks down at the floor and then continues, "from the Ebola bioweapon."

All eyes turn affectionately to Suzie of the Seashells. She was the first child named after the original Suzie, by Phil.

But no one is more taken by this than Vi. Sitting there frozen in time to her own memory of the original Suzie and Vi's unwitting part in the little girl's death, tears begin to well up in her eyes.

The Major also remembers that terrible time when he first met his wife. Seeing her emotional reaction now reminds him of how he had to grab a knife away from Vi before she did harm to herself after learning that she was the one who unknowingly administered the Ebola bioweapon to a two-year-old child.

Taking his wife's hand the Major says to her, "Honey, do you want to go with them?"

Vi closes her eyes and begins to weep, and everyone feels sorrow and compassion for her. "Thank you, my darling. Yes, I would like to go."

Looking at Yakov and Neely, Vi asks them, "Okay if I join your group?"

Neely puts her arms around Vi and says, "We would be delighted to have you."

The Major looks at his wife and says, "I guess it's all set then."

Vi and her husband have a tender, quiet moment together. Then the Major looks at his sons and smiles. Nodding at the three of them he says, "Looks like we'll be holding down the fort with Reggie back at Howard Pharmaceuticals. You guys up for that?"

Jayson exclaims, "Actually, dad, my brothers and I have been talking about it. We really feel like we want to be with grandma at Judy's and even spend some time at Henrietta's Rose Garden."

Michael and Charles nod in agreement.

Vi says, "That would be very sweet of you boys and I'm sure Grandma Henrietta would really appreciate that."

The Major smiles at his sons and is in full agreement.

Phil and Doc know that they must return to the Village of Chiconahui. They turn to Suzie and Rudolpho as Doc says, "Would the two of you like to join us at Chiconahui?"

They all notice that Suzie is holding her seashell necklace and her eyes are closed. A vision begins to unfold before her:

Suzie is traveling along a dirt road in the tropical rainforest. The aromatic fragrances of the earth are sweet and soothing, and the sounds of the birds and other animals lift her spirits. She is enjoying the beauty of the colorful rainforest flowers as the warm breeze blows freely through her hair.

After a while the sights and sounds of the jungle fade away and the dirt road turns into an old abandoned paved road. Small buildings appear that have also long since been deserted, with obvious signs of corrosion and decay.

Suzie now sees something up ahead that she cannot make out. It looks like a gateway of some kind stretched across the road. As she approaches the gateway, she is suddenly surrounded by vehicles from a very long time ago. The road becomes packed with the old-time vehicles, and in her vision, she rises and floats over them. As she floats over the gateway, Suzie notices that there are only a few vehicles on the other side.

Suddenly the sky goes dark as if a storm is brewing, and a cold, grey building appears before her. Suzie is gripped by a sense of foreboding that something is very wrong in the cold, grey building. She wants to keep going down the road, but something is forcing her to hold back.

And then a ray of Light appears in the sky breaking through the darkness above. She hears a voice calling to her from the Light saying, "Bear witness and remember . . . Never again!"

Suzie opens her eyes and realizes that she has been crying.

Rudolpho puts his arms around her and whispers softly, "What is it, honey? What did you see?"

She gives Phil and Doc a quick glance and then looks at Rudolpho saying, "Yes, we must go to Chiconahui."

Rudolpho kisses her on the forehead, smiles and says, "Okay."

Dumaka looks at Liling and says, "I guess you will want to go to the Garden of Bi, my darling."

Liling nods and replies. "It will be nice to return to Johannesburg where we first met and fell in love."

They look at each other with tenderness remembering the love they found together during those dark times.

"We must honor the path that the Kind One is calling you to follow," Dumaka says to her.

Liling smiles sweetly at her husband. "Thank you, my love."

Meiling says to her mama Liling and papa Dumaka, "Beth and I have been talking it over and, like Jayson, Michael, and Charlie, we too feel called to spend some time at the Garden of Judy. We want to get to know the Chrysalenes better and spend some time with Henrietta and her rose garden. Is that okay with you guys?"

"Of course it is, honey." Liling says to her daughter, proud of the compassion she sees in both young ladies. "You go and we'll stay in touch through our Metatron devices."

Then she says to Yakov and Neely, "Is that okay with you two, that is, if Beth joins them?"

Neely looks at her daughter and then at her husband who are both smiling and nodding. "I guess that takes care of that!" Neely says with a chuckle.

"Thanks, mom!" both girls exclaim joyously.

Dumaka smiles and looks around at everyone. "I wonder if perhaps before we all leave, we could take a little fun break and visit the local Coffeehouse here in Bear River?"

Immediately, a collective sigh permeates the room, and everyone expresses agreement at such a wonderful idea.

The Centers and their Coffeehouses were always a hub of activity and social gatherings before the demise of the Council. Since then, they have become people-owned cooperatives, providing a trader's market where everyone comes to barter for supplies and services. The Coffeehouses are filled with even more love, laughter, and great fellowship now that the people of One Garden are free. Some of the Centers have even been turned into garden communities.

Kookie points his index finger in the air and exclaims, "To the Coffeehouse!"

And everyone else points their index fingers in the air as they cry out, "The Coffeehouse!"

* * *

In the Yucatan at the estate of Lord Josef, Bella stands outside the door of PA, ES, and SPA's quarters. She has knocked a few times already and is awaiting their response.

"It is I, Bella," she says one more time. "Let me come in."

A few more moments go by. Then, slowly, the door begins to open.

"Come in, My Lady," says SPA.

Bella walks in and looks at the three brothers. She is smoldering inside after eavesdropping on their conversation with the Monarch Angel, hearing that Eve Elli named her child after Bella's traitorous sister Bi. What really infuriates Bella though is knowing that this is Eve Elli's way of honoring Bi. And her hatred of Eve Elli is now growing. However, she knows that she must keep this to herself for now and just deliver the message to PA, ES, and SPA that Bella was sent by Lucifer to convey.

"Your master has been watching you and listening to your plans with the Master Commandants. I have come to tell you that Lucifer is pleased with the three of you."

"Indeed," says SPA.

The others look at her and bow slightly. It is more of a deferential nod. They are staring at Bella flatly with no emotions, waiting for her to give them their instructions from the fallen one.

Glaring at the brothers, Bella states: "Lucifer says that Kookie and the others are about to break up into three groups, traveling to high-energy zones where they will attempt to hook up with powerful earth forces.

"You are to send a mole to each one of their groups. The mole must gain their trust and never let them suspect that he is working for the lord of the underworld. When the time comes that Kookie and his cohorts have formed a matrix and are ready to activate the energy source around the world, Lucifer will step in. Through the three of you he will take that energy source for himself, giving him Absolute Power over the people of One World."

PA, ES, and SPA remain unmoved. Through their years in captivity, for their own survival, they have learned how to bury their feelings deep down inside.

"And for your part in this," Bella concludes, "You shall all be *very* well rewarded. The fear and division Lucifer will create when he gains control over this power source will bring the people, *all* the people of One World to their knees. You will have absolute control over them as they return to slavery and the three of you will reign together as supreme rulers. No one will ever be able to challenge you again."

She pauses for a moment, giving PA, ES, and SPA an evil grin and finally cries out, *"NO ONE!"*

The brothers never take their eyes off her as PA finally says, "Yes, My Lady Bella."

"Yes, indeed," ES says.

"We are ready to move into action," SPA concurs.

"Excellent! Most excellent!" Bella exclaims.

Andre has been wrapped around Bella's neck this whole time. She takes his head, nuzzles him against her cheek, kisses one of his protruding fangs and says, "Come darling. We have another group to eaves-drop-in on."

Andre winks at her and they disappear.

$* * *$

Kookie and company walk into the Bear River Coffeehouse. It is a lively place, bustling with energy and activity. Kenny and Lisa take their trader card to the Trader's Market. With the points Kenny just received from the sale of 12 pigeons to the youngsters, he and Lisa are looking forward to getting supplies for the constant flow of visitors that come to Bear River Garden.

Lisa turns to the others and says, "Why don't you all find a couple of tables in the Coffeehouse, and we'll catch up with you in just a bit."

"Sure thing, Lisa!"

Kookie already has his eye on the display shelf filled with Lisa's very own chocolate chip cookies. After they all choose their purchases, they scan their trader cards through a card reader. This records the purchase amount in points, as well as the identities of the buyer and seller. In this way, "Barter and Trade" functions as one simple monetary system throughout the world of One Garden.

"Over here people!" the Major calls. He has secured a cozy spot for their group.

The youngsters chatter and laugh as they carry their drinks and pastries to the café tables while Kookie tries to balance a few plates of cookies in his hands.

Angie shakes her head and chuckles, "Here honey! let me help you with that."

Making their way towards the tables, the other patrons recognize and greet them.

"Hey, Major! How's my man?"

"Great to see you guys again!"

"Aww! Look how big Lady Bi is getting!"

There is much admiration expressed throughout the Coffeehouse. Kookie and friends are the heroes of One Garden, known and loved across the globe.

Lisa and Kenny have finished trading and have now come in to join the others. The mood is lighthearted, and spirits are high. Laughter fills the Coffeehouse and love is felt among all those present.

No one notices when the door opens, and another person enters.

She carries a wooden staff with the head of a serpent. She sits down quietly at a corner table and keeps her face concealed. . . with the hood of her red cape.

* * *

It is evening in the Yucatan. PA, ES, and SPA have each gone off to their private bedrooms in the estate of Lord Josef, ready to retire. They lie down in bed and begin to drift off, fading into a synchronized dream.

They are in a brightly lit room with lots of people seated around small tables. The light is so bright it appears to be glowing. They see people engaged in lively conversation, joking, and laughing with each other. Then they notice a Golden Light shining above everyone. It begins to take the form of wings, radiating in the colors of orange, yellow, white, and gold. A voice begins to speak saying, "SPA creature, behold your grandson Emeka, and your great-granddaughter Bi." The colorful wings shine down upon Emeka and Bi giving them a heavenly glow. And the Angel of the Lord continues, "There is still time for you brother creatures, if you choose to come to the Light."

Then the light dims and the people in the room stop moving as if they are suddenly frozen in time. A darkness looms over everyone. The walls begin to drip with dark red blood and a maniacal laugh resounds, "HA HA! PA, ES, and SPA! You have no place else to go! You MUST come to me! Do you really think that the One above will welcome you into his home after what you have done?! That unspeakable thing you all did in your captivity under the polar ice when the food ran out. When you slaughtered and butchered your Overlords and techies, one by one. Were they TASTY MORSELS?! HAHAHAHA!" The voice shrieks at them.

The voice fades and so does the dream. The three brothers awaken slowly with absolute terror in their hearts.

The next morning PA, ES, and SPA call three Master Commandants into their quarters: George, Haitao, and Pasha. SPA greets them at the door. "Do come in Master Commandants."

They look at SPA with much eagerness ready and willing to serve their highest ones. The men follow him into the main living room of the brother's quarters. There is a spread of food laid out where PA and ES are ready and waiting.

"Do sit down," says PA.

"Yes," says ES, "And do make yourselves comfortable."

"Oh, and do help yourselves to a little repast," SPA says.

George, Haitao, and Pasha sit down and dig in to the food.

After a few moments SPA says to them, "We have an assignment for the three of you."

The men stop munching and look up from their food.

"Good," SPA notes, "We are glad that you are all so eager to be of service."

"Sir, yes, *sir!*" The three of them mumble, mouths full of food.

SPA explains the assignment to them. "You are each to go to a garden community posing as one of the people. We shall give you each a story that the villagers should find believable, in how you came to be among them. You will pretend to be their friend but always remember who you are *really* working for."

Pasha looks at the other two and then at SPA. Somewhat confused he suggests, "You mean that we are working for the three of *you*, our Highest Ones."

PA, ES, and SPA look at each other with a knowing glance. Then SPA responds to Pasha, "Yes. Remember that you are working for the three of us."

George, Haitao, and Pasha simply nod in agreement.

"Then," says SPA, "you are to find the pyramid which is right near the garden community. You are to go there and await further instructions."

Leaning forward and staring straight into their eyes, SPA gives them a cold-blooded stare and says, "Is that clear . . . men?"

"Yes, sir! It is very clear, *sir!*" the three of them say together.

"Good," says SPA. "Now finish your meal go back to your quarters and be prepared to leave shortly. A Cloudtransporter will be ready and waiting to drop each one of you off at your destination."

"Sir, yes, *sir!*"

* * *

Kookie and friends are up early at Bear River Garden, ready to embark on their pyramid assignments. One thing Kookie and Angie did not decide the night before was where *they* are going to go. Like the others they too have been waiting for a sign. This morning while Angie is still in bed slowly opening her eyes, she gets a wake-up call from Angel.

Speaking to her heart, Angel says to Angie: *Good morning, sister human creature! Time to wake up! There is much to do today!*

Angie closes her eyes and smiles, speaking out loud to Angel. "Good morning, Angel, my sister! So where do you want us to go? I am at your command!"

But instead of answering her in words Angel shows her a place.

Angie sees a cornfield. There are commandos wandering around in a daze and farmers lost in grief. She sees a younger Kookie, a three-year-old

Eve Elli, a five-year-old Emeka, and others offering comfort and support to all the emotionally distraught people.

Then the scene changes and Angel shows Angie a cave near the former Wyoming battlefield of the dark times. Spreading her large golden wings and wrapping her arms around Angie, Angel lifts her up in the air and carries her through the cave. Slowly they pass the most exquisite crystals, glittering in the heavenly Light radiating from the Monarch Angel. Gradually they come upon a large underground chamber, sparkling and shimmering with magnificent colors. Angel sets Angie down upon a large flat piece of clear quartz crystal which begins to shimmer with a warm, soft glow from within.

Peace comes over Angie with a deep love that fills her heart.

The vision fades and Angie opens her eyes. She hears the voice of Angel saying to her heart, *That is where you must go, Angie creature. You and Kookie creature must activate the pyramids of the world from the Great Quartz Crystal of the Hidden Cavern at Cavern Village, Wyoming.*

Angie sits bolt upright in bed calling out to Angel, "But how will we find the cavern? And how will we know what to do with the crystal?"

You will know, sister Angie creature. When the time comes you and Kookie creature will know . . . Angel's voice fades and disappears.

Kookie has just come in from tending to the new seedlings with David, Eve Elli, and Lord Emeka. Seeing that Angie is awake he says to her, "Good morning my love. David and I were just talking about our assignments and thought that perhaps we should go with Yakov and Neely to the Garden of Suzie. It sounds like a fine idea to me, but I am not so sure that is where we are supposed to be."

"It isn't." says Angie.

"Uh . . . what's that, my angel?"

"Exactly!"

"Huh?"

"Angel."

"Angel?" Kookie is scratching his head. He has no idea what his wife is trying to tell him.

Angie chuckles and says to her husband, "You silly! Angel came to me this morning and told me that we are to go to Wyoming."

"What? Wyoming? Why Wyoming?" Kookie asks, totally confused.

She tells Kookie about Angel's visit, her vision of the battlefield in Cavern Village, Wyoming, and the Great Quartz Crystal of the Hidden Cavern.

"Wow!" exclaims Kookie trying to make sense of it all. "Well," he says, shrugging his shoulders and shaking his head, "if there's one thing I know, it is never to question Angel. Like she always says, *"Time is a wasting! Hop to it, human creatures!"*

Angie nods in agreement and they prepare to leave Bear River Garden, Oregon, for Cavern Village, Wyoming.

All the friends have one last meal together with Lisa and Kenny. They take turns thanking their hosts profusely for their hospitality, generosity, friendship, and love. Kookie explains to everyone that he and Angie have been instructed by the spirit of the Monarch Angel to go on another assignment and will not be joining them at the pyramids.

He says, "Angel has told Angie that we are to go to Wyoming."

"Wyoming? Why Wyoming?!"

They both laugh as Angie explains, "There is a place called the Hidden Cavern of the Great Quartz Crystal. The energy there is powerful, and it will boost the energy transmission through Metatron and the crystal to the pyramids. This will give us maximum effectiveness for activation."

Kookie goes over the instructions for activation with everyone and says, "We must all launch the Metatron matrix at the same time from our four designated points around the globe. This will cause total, worldwide activation of the *other* pyramids on earth, as well. Are you guys with me?!"

"We got this, bratan! It's all good! No problem! We're ready!"

"Oh . . . just one more thing," Kookie says pointing his index finger in the air. "After you have completed the activations let's all meet back at Judy's Garden."

"Okay! We're ready! Rock and roll!"

"Bless you Angie and my brother Kookie," Liling says. "May we all complete our missions quickly and without incident. Then we will join you all at Judy's."

With hearts full of hope, the groups head out to their Cloudtransporters.

* * *

Tomas and Daniela have left Chiconahui and the rainforests of the Yucatan behind. They are now traveling down small dirt roads.

It has been a pleasant trip for them so far with Sergio, Elena, Adam Mateo, and Eve Sophia, as well as the sights, sounds, and sweet, woody fragrances of nature. The nighttime is especially warm and peaceful when they drift off to sleep on the soft earth, with nocturnal creatures singing lullabies to them. They have had no dreams or visions on their journey so far, and they are simply enjoying good conversation and each other's company.

Daniela is the first one to wake up and is all smiles and sunshine. "Good morning! How did you all sleep last night?" she asks as the others awaken.

"Very well, my child," replies Eve Sophia. "And you?"

"Mm!" Daniela says, stretching and holding her arms out to the heavens. "Just wonderful!"

From the looks of it everyone else had a very good night's sleep too. Sergio says, "Well, let's have something to eat and then get going. From my calculations, we are less than a day's ride now from the California border. Once we get there it will not be that much further to Howard Pharmaceuticals. I am really looking forward to meeting the Major, Reggie, and a bunch of other folks once we get there."

"Yes indeed!" Elena chimes in. "And I am looking forward to spending time with Judy and Adam Tate as well, once we get to the Garden of Judy."

They are all excited and looking forward to visiting their favorite people and places in California.

The traveling companions finish their morning meal, pack up their gear and are on the road. A little while later they reach the coast approaching the Southern California border. The sounds of the waves crashing against the shore and the smell of the ocean breeze uplift their spirits.

"Look!" says Tomas, pointing to a Trader's Market and Coffeehouse up ahead. "Can we stop there for a little while, dad?" he asks Sergio.

"Sounds like a good idea, son. We can load up on supplies and say 'hello' to the locals."

The others nod in agreement, and they head that way.

After a light meal at the Coffeehouse, speaking to a few people and getting a few needed supplies at the Trader's Market, Sergio and company are back on the road.

The group is sullen, riding along in silence before Elena speaks up. "Something was wrong in there, very wrong. I don't know what it was. But it was just plain creepy."

Sergio, Tomas, and Daniela have the same uneasy feeling and they do not know what to say.

The Chrysalenes feel much compassion for their friends because they know what lies ahead. It is the reason Adam Mateo and Eve Sophia knew that they had to accompany the four villagers on their journey.

The Southern California border is looming up ahead. They can see the gateway stretching across the road from one end to the other. The group's sullen mood since leaving the Trader's Market and Coffeehouse has suddenly grown worse and no one can understand why. Sergio rides a bit ahead of everyone and he starts to slow down. The others do the same.

The border is now right before them, and Daniela and Tomas come to a stop.

"What is it, honey?" Elena says to her daughter.

"I don't know mama," Daniela replies softly and somewhat fearful.

"This is ridiculous!" exclaims Tomas. Putting on his game face, he turns to Daniela and says, "Come on! Let's go!"

* * *

Phil, Doc, Rudolpho, and Suzie come in for a landing at the village of Chiconahui. Since her dream, Suzie has had a feeling of foreboding about that place especially regarding Tomas and Daniela. She has a gnawing feeling that the two youngsters could be in some kind of trouble, and she is anxious to see them again.

The Cloudtransporter lands in the open field next to the village. As the portal opens, the four people step outside. The villagers always see the Cloudtransporter coming in for a landing and many of them go to the nearby field to greet the visitors. But not this time. Instead, Phil, Doc, Rudolpho, and Suzie are greeted by an eerie stillness in the air. They see one man in the distance coming toward them.

They have never seen him before and know that he is not one of the villagers.

"Hello there!" Phil calls out to the man. "My name is Phil, and this is my wife Doc. The others here are my daughter Suzie and her friend Rudolpho."

Phil extends his hand to the stranger who simply looks at him and nods. The man then says, "I hope you have come here to help everyone."

Now they all become uneasy, and Suzie of the Seashells remembers her dream. She anxiously asks the man, "Why? What's wrong?"

"They are not doing so well," the man says. "It is hard to explain. You will have to come and see for yourselves."

Phil, Doc, Rudolpho, and Suzie are now worried.

As the man turns around to lead them to the village Doc says to him, "Excuse me, sir, we did not catch your name!"

"Oh, yes. I'm sorry. Please forgive me. My name is George."

Deep in the bowels of hell Lucifer smiles, and Bella pets Andre who winks at his mistress.

Hmph! snorts Lucifer with a sarcastic grin, *I wonder if those three idiots, PA, ES, and SPA actually got it right this time. Master Commandant George is definitely one of my boys!*

Chapter 8 – Serpent

GEORGE WALKS WITH PHIL and his family into the village of Chiconahui. No one is around and the place appears to be deserted, which greatly increases their uneasiness and anxiety.

"Where *is* everybody?" Doc asks with trepidation.

"Come, I will show you," says George. He brings them over to one of the huts and announces himself to the people within. "Good morning. It is I, George. How are you all doing today?"

There is no answer. Phil and Doc look at each other and begin to feel something else inside their guts; an inexplicable, rising sense of dread.

George calls out to them again saying, "I have brought some friends with me." He looks at Phil, Doc, Rudolpho, and Suzie, and nods.

Phil says, "It is your friend Phil. Doc is here too. Are you folks okay?"

After a moment of silence, a soft, meek voice is heard from inside the hut. "Phil?"

"Yes, it is I. May I come in?"

A young man appears at the door. He looks pale and drawn, as if he has not eaten or slept much or seen the sun for a while. He stands there for a moment staring off into space unable to look at anyone.

Suzie is filled with dread when she sees him. She asks, "What is it, sir? Can you tell us?"

The man looks up at her and with much fear he says, "Bad dreams. Very bad dreams. Bad people in bad dreams. Bad people make us work very hard. Hit us with a snake, big snake, to scare us."

Doc and Phil look at each other. They are hearing echoes of their past . . . but *is* it the past?

"Being hit with big snakes?" Doc questions, looking at her husband. "Is that the past or an omen of something worse to come?"

Those and similar thoughts are going through Phil and Doc's minds.

They look at George, and Phil says to him, "By the way, who are you my good man? That is, where are you from and how did you come to be here?"

"I come from a nearby village," George replies. "For some reason everyone in my village started having nightmares just like the folks here. Began happening only recently. No one knows why or what started it all. Then the other night I had a vision that said something about Chiconahui and a pyramid. So, I had to come here. And this is what I found; an entire village affected just like this young man here. Everyone's nightmares seem to vary, but they paint the same grizzly picture of a world that's gone backwards to how things were 18 years ago, only worse. Much worse."

The others are now filled with confusion and fear, but Rudolpho has an idea. He says to them, "It seems that we have all been drawn to the pyramid. Perhaps it would be a good idea if we were to check it out and see if the Soul of the Stones has anything to say to us."

"Yes! Excellent!" Suzie, Doc, and Phil agree. George simply nods.

The young man looks at them imploringly. "Can you make the bad dreams go away, then?"

Suzie touches his shoulders tenderly and whispers softly, "We are going to try my friend. We shall do our best and try."

"Thank you," the young man says and quietly goes back inside his hut.

Rudolpho looks at his sweetie and says, "I guess this is why you were called here, honey, instead of the other two pyramids."

Upon hearing that George jumps in. "The other two pyramids?"

"Yes," says Rudolpho, "but we can discuss all that later. Meanwhile let's see what we can do here."

As they all walk toward the pyramid, Phil asks George, "By the way my good man. Is everyone in Chiconahui experiencing the same thing?"

"Yes, pretty much," he says, "and in my village as well."

As an afterthought Phil says to him, "Oh, and how are Sergio and Tomas doing?"

"I couldn't tell you sir. They were just leaving as I arrived."

Suddenly they all stop short, and Suzie of the Seashells is about to have a fit. "They did *what?*" she wails.

"Oh, my goodness!" howls Doc. "Did they say where they were going?"

"Something about visiting friends in California," George replies.

"Good heavens!" exclaims Suzie, who now hears voices screaming in her gut. "I'm absolutely certain that we are supposed to be with them. That even now they seriously need our protection!"

"Yes honey, I agree with you," Rudolpho says, "And I think we will find out what we need to know at the pyramid."

They get to the clearing where the Pyramid of Chiconahui stands fearlessly before them. The Soul of the Stones is ready to tell Rudolpho and Suzie about Tomas and Daniela, and what awaits them at the Southern California border.

No one except George sees the 13-foot-long boa constrictor stretched out on the first level of stones of the pyramid. And no one except George sees the serpent wink at him while speaking to George's heart, "With you, Lucifer is pleased."

* * *

Tomas and Daniela speed toward the gateway of the Southern California border. They move with such determination and courage that they ignore every voice inside of them that is crying out to the brave young souls, *SLOW DOWN!*

Sergio, Elena, Adam Mateo, and Eve Sophia have a hard time keeping up with the young daredevils, and their sense of foreboding increases the closer they get to the gateway.

The youngsters slow down as they arrive at the border. There is a Trader's Market and Coffeehouse just before the border crossing with a few people milling about. Tomas and Daniela are not interested in stopping there, especially considering the last Coffeehouse they stopped at and how grim the mood was there. They all have a gut feeling that the same is going on in this one.

But a worn-out Sergio says to Tomas, "I'm afraid the adults need a break, son."

"Aww gee, dad!" Something inexplicable is drawing Tomas and Daniela across the border and the last thing they want to do now is stop.

Sergio laughs and says, "Okay. I know there's another rest stop not too much farther ahead. Besides," he continues, while looking at Elena and the Chrysalenes, "I feel rather anxious to get to Howard Pharmaceuticals now and see the Major."

What Sergio does not tell anyone is that he has a horrible feeling about the energy in the area and wouldn't mind just moving on. Everyone agrees and Tomas, Daniela, Sergio, Elena, Adam Mateo, and Eve Sophia pass through the gateway and cross the border.

As they enter California, the sky darkens. Sergio and Elena look at each other.

Sergio says, "Hmm, must be a storm coming. Perhaps we should move a bit quicker to the next rest area."

But he looks at the children and sees them stopped dead in their tracks. They are fixated on an old, abandoned building nearby. Before Sergio can say anything, Tomas and Daniela move in that direction. The sky grows darker, and a cold wind starts blowing.

Sergio and the others are behind the children when suddenly a 13-foot-long boa constrictor slithers in front of the adults, coming between them and the children. The serpent is staring at Sergio and suddenly winks at him. And he is helplessly frozen in fear.

Tomas and Daniela enter the old, abandoned building.

* * *

Rudolpho and Suzie of the Seashells are in the Cloudtransporter heading full speed to the Southern California border. When they heard what was happening from the Soul of the Stones, they knew there was not a moment to lose.

Phil and Doc have stayed behind. They must help the villagers of Chiconahui with herbal preparations and emotional support before they start going into shock.

Suzie looks down anxiously watching the jungle whiz by and seeing the ocean loom up ahead in the distance. She is frightfully worried that they might be too late.

* * *

Inside the old, abandoned building at the California border crossing, Tomas and Daniela find themselves in a large empty room. It is dark and gloomy, filling them with an unnatural cold feeling.

"This is creepy," Daniela says to Tomas. "Um . . . maybe we should leave."

Tomas hears her but he cannot leave. He is drawn to a doorway leading to another room. Daniela follows.

As they enter the other room, suddenly both of their hearts start pounding in their chests. They see an animal cage about five feet tall and are filled with inexplicable terror.

Daniela begins to cry, "Please Tomas, let's get out of here."

But she knows that even *she* cannot leave now. There is a force in their guts pulling them towards the cage. Everything is stone-cold quiet until abruptly, the children are aware of a faint sound coming from the cage.

Daniela can hardly breathe as she whispers to Tomas, "What's that?"

"Uh . . . uh . . . I, duh . . . don't know," Tomas stutters.

They reach the animal cage, and a faint red glow appears in the center. The sound becomes a bit louder and now they can hear it better. It is the sound of a child crying; a deep, mournful sound of the broken young spirit of a child who died a long time ago. She has remained in the same state of terror as the day she perished, and her spirit now haunts the rooms of this old, abandoned building.

Daniela and Tomas cannot hold back. They grab hold of the bars of the cage and instantly the spirit of a frightened child appears right before their eyes. She is a toddler, no more than three years old holding out her hands to Daniela and Tomas, shrieking with wild eyes of terror, *Mama! Mama! Donde estas! Mama! Donde estas! Mama!"*

Daniela and Tomas are engulfed in the same horror as the dying spirit of the little one. Their hearts fill with her terror, and they fall to their knees crying out, "Mama! Mama! Where are you! Mama! Where are you! Mama!"

The little one screams and screams until her little heart finally gives out. She falls down dead on the floor of the cage, wide-eyed, staring in terror. The red glow in the cage expands until it reaches the walls where it turns to blood, dripping down to the floor.

Daniela and Tomas are gripped with the death pain of the little one. They clutch their chests as they too can feel their hearts starting to give out. Struggling to breathe, Daniela looks at the terrorized death stare of the little girl. She reaches her hands out to the child and wails with unspeakable grief in a language that she has never heard before, "Perdóname, niña de mis ojos."[10]

Daniela and Tomas have witnessed the brutal suffering of this precious child of the past in the last torturous moments of her life. It is more than their hearts can bear and they collapse on the floor.

* * *

"THERE THEY ARE!" Suzie of the Seashells yells frantically at Rudolpho.

They see Sergio, Elena, Adam Mateo, Eve Sophia, and the old building below as the Cloudtransporter comes in for a landing. Rudolpho also sees the boa constrictor blocking their path, so he turns on his Metatron device preparing to *greet* Andre.

Suzie and Rudolpho charge down the ramp of their aircraft heading for the group.

Suzie calls out to them, "It's okay everybody, stay still. We will have that bad boy out of the way in a second!"

Rudolpho comes within a few feet of the boa constrictor, points the Metatron device at him and fires a laser blast at Bella's companion.

Andre is instantly fried to a crisp and within seconds finds himself back in Bella's arms in the bowels of hell.

* * *

---

[10] *English translation: Please, forgive me, my sacred, beloved child. (Literally: Forgive me, child of my eyes.)*

Turning sorrowfully to his mistress, gazing upon her with big, puppy-dog eyes, Andre snivels and whimpers, "OUCH!"

* * *

"COME ON!" Suzie shrieks at everyone and they all make a dash for the old building.

Upon entering the small room, Sergio and Elena rush to their children who are lying unconscious on the floor.

"My son! My son!" Sergio falls to his knees weeping.

Elena cradles her daughter in her arms and cries out to the heavens, "Help us! Great Spirit! Please do not take my Daniela from me!"

Adam Mateo and Eve Sophia come over to the fallen children and lift them up in their arms.

In a calm, gentle voice, Eve Sophia says, "We must go from this place, quickly."

They carry Tomas and Daniela outside and lay them on the ground, placing their hands on the chest and head of each youngster.

Sergio, Elena, Rudolpho, and Suzie stand holding each other as they look on anxiously. After a few minutes the Chrysalenes proceed to pick the children up and lovingly cradle them in their arms singing angel songs of healing. The dark sky begins to clear, and the young ones slowly open their eyes.

When Sergio and Elena see their children come back to life, they each hold a hand up to the heavens and cry.

Suzie of the Seashells and Rudolpho hold their hands up to the heavens and Suzie says, "Thank you, most kind and loving Great

Spirit. Thank you for bringing Tomas and Daniela back to us and thank you for bringing us all here together. May we move forward in the days ahead in Your Light and Your Love."

Sergio and Elena sit on the ground holding their children while the others sit with them.

"My son, what happened to you?" Sergio asks Tomas.

"I don't know papa. It was all so very horrible."

"And terribly, terribly sad," adds Daniela. "There was a little girl in that building who couldn't find her mama. She was so frightened! So very, very scared!"

Daniela is upset all over again as she recounts the tragic story of the little girl who died of loneliness and fear.

Eve Sophia lays her hands on Daniela to comfort her and says, "It was a very long time ago, long before the Council came to power. Border crossings like this one were quite different."

"How so?" asks Tomas.

Daniela dries her eyes and listens to the truth of a sad part of her people's history.

Eve Sophia continues, "People could not travel back and forth across the border as they do today. That is why this gateway is still standing. It was guarded and gated, and at times it was even closed. Sometimes people were told to go to that building over there," she says, pointing to the place where Tomas and Daniela were just rescued from, "and they might have been held for many, many days."

Tomas, Daniela, Sergio, Elena, Suzie of the Seashells, and Rudolpho all look at Eve Sophia in disbelief. Only Adam Mateo sees the truth, like Eve Sophia, through the heart of a Chrysalene.

Daniela wails, "But what about the child who could not find her mama? She was in . . . in . . . a kind of animal cage or something!"

Adam Mateo and Eve Sophia look at each other. Then they lower their eyes in sadness as Adam Mateo explains, "Sometimes little ones were taken away from their mamas and papas while they were being held here. They were put in cages and completely separated from their families. And sometimes they never saw their mamas and papas again."

Everyone is crying now, and Suzie clutches her seashell necklace. Memories of her own vision of the violent separation from her mother, is coming back to her. Suddenly a word comes to Suzie, and she knows why she was brought here and what she must do. Turning to the others who are lost in their grief over such tragedies of the past, Suzie says to the group, "It's all right, I know what we must do."

Looking at Tomas and Daniela, she says, "It is the reason why we have *all* been brought here."

Everyone looks at Suzie with a glimmer of hope as she points to the old, abandoned building and says the word that has just come into her heart. It is a word that she is unfamiliar with, but the voice speaking to her heart *is* familiar with this word, indeed. Suzie says, *"Sanctification, human creatures. You are to sanctify this building and make it a holy place, forever and ever."*

Everyone looks at Suzie of the Seashells and they all nod in agreement.

* * *

Eve Elli, Lord Emeka, and little Lady Bi come in for a landing at their estate in Johannesburg. With them are Liling, Dumaka, Mimi, and Ryan. Their priority is to contact the Chrysalenes at the Village of the Holy Ones and explain to them what is going on. As always though, Mama Eve Zula, Papa Adam Makena, and Eve Gerda already know everything, and they are waiting on the landing field to greet their returning friends.

"Hello, everybody!" Mama Eve Zula exclaims when they all disembark from the aircraft. "We feel so much happiness to see you all again! Truly we have missed you very much, especially the precious little one!" Mama Eve Zula says with great affection.

Baby Bi puts her arms out to the Chrysalenes and they all embrace her.

"Welcome home sweetie," says Eve Gerda with a smile, giving baby Bi a great big hug. The happy little one giggles with delight, and they all walk together to the big house.

The group gathers in the living room while the kitchen staff prepares a meal. Lord Emeka says to the Chrysalenes, "I guess you know what is going on then and what our assignment from Kookie is."

"Oh, yes," says Papa Adam Makena with a grin. "We do for sure. And we are all here and ready to serve. We are most happy to join you at the pyramid if you like."

"Thank you kindly, good people." Emeka responds. "Your presence at the pyramid will be most helpful, I'm sure. As always, we are most grateful for your service."

Eve Elli interjects enthusiastically, "And I should like very much for us all to go to the local Coffeehouse this evening."

"That's a wonderful idea," says Papa Adam Makena, "especially since the villagers from the Garden of Bi go there quite often in the evenings."

"Awesome!" says Ryan. "I would love to play my drum with those guys again!"

Mimi chuckles and says, "Well, honey, I would just love to join you all. I believe there are two drums that we left in our suite the last time we were here."

"You're on, my love," Ryan says, giving his wife an affectionate pat on the back.

Early in the evening the group arrives at the Coffeehouse. And the people of Johannesburg and the smaller surrounding garden communities come over and greet them warmly. Ryan and Mimi find their drumming buddies and start to play together, while little Lady Bi bounces to the beat on her mama's lap.

They are all having a good time catching up with their friends when a man comes over and introduces himself. He puts his hand out to Lord Emeka saying, "Hello, My Lord. I am so pleased to meet you. I have been staying at the Garden of Bi and one of the villagers here told me who you are when you walked in." He points to someone sitting at a table at the far end of the café.

"Well then," says Lord Emeka, extending his hand to the stranger. "It is very nice to meet you too." Emeka introduces everyone in his group to the man and then he says to him, "By the way, I did not catch your name, sir."

"Ah, yes indeed!" The man chuckles. "My name is Haitao. And my friend back there is Chen."

Emeka and the others glance at Chen and wave to her; everyone, that is except Liling, who is suddenly hit with a sharp pain in her side. Liling says nothing and does her best to conceal the pain. It subsides in less than a minute.

The woman called Chen is wearing a red cape with the hood pulled down covering most of her face. And in her hand, she is holding a wooden staff with the head of a serpent. Chen smiles at Master Commandant Haitao and the serpent winks at Chen.

From the bowels of hell Lucifer smiles as he observes the interaction. With his queen, and with Master Commandant Haitao, he is pleased.

* * *

The villagers of Chiconahui are filled with an unknown fear. They have not been out of their huts very much for the past few days, and were it not for the Chrysalenes, the crops would be in serious trouble. Fortunately, the Chrysalenes are unaffected by the inexplicable dark energy that has been looming over the villagers.

Phil and Doc are working fast and furious to make enough herbal preparations for everyone. What is calling to them most are the tree roots of the forest. Doc is sure that the grounding energy provided by the indigenous trees will help settle the disquieting feelings of everyone in the community. By the end of the day, the herbal tea that she and Phil have made has indeed been helpful in bringing people out of their huts. The mood has lifted somewhat and this evening they are gathering around the fire pit.

The Chrysalenes are overjoyed to see the villagers out of their huts and feeling a bit better. As they go around offering healing and love to the people, they begin to sing. And the beautiful sounds of their angelic choir fill the air around the campfire. Before long folks are smiling at one another again.

Doc goes back to their hut to make more herbal tea. As she gets to the door, she hears the familiar sound of a rattlesnake nearby. *Oops,* Doc thinks to herself. *Better wait a few minutes until that thing is gone.* As she listens the rattle sound fades away, and once it is gone altogether Doc feels safe enough to go inside. Gathering up the tree roots she begins to make another batch of tea, when something unfamiliar sitting on the counter grabs her attention. It is a glass jar of amber-colored liquid.

"Hmm," Doc says aloud, "I wonder where this came from?" Then she remembers something Phil told her about another mixture he was making to add to the healing effects of the tree roots. "Well, I guess this must be it."

Just to be sure, Doc holds the jar to her chest and asks what the substance is. "Is this what Phil left to add to the herbal preparation?" She hears a voice in her head saying: *Yesss, yesss indeed! Phil left thisss for you. It is the milky substance of the leaves of the same tree. Verrrry, verrry good for feeeeling better. Yesss indeed! Yesss indeed!*

"Okay," says Doc. "In you go!"

She empties the jar of amber-colored liquid into the boiling water along with the tree roots.

What Doc does not see is George standing outside the hut and watching her from the window. When he sees Doc pour the contents of the glass into the boiling water, George smiles.

Doc goes out to collect more tree roots. She is happy that their tea has been so effective in helping the villagers and wants to be sure that they have plenty of it on hand. While she is gone Phil comes back to their hut.

"Honey!" he calls out to her. "We'll be needing some more tea. Thought I'd come back and help you get it ready."

It takes a moment for Phil to realize that Doc is not there and that he is talking to himself. However, he sees the herbs cooking and knows she must not be far away. Watching the herbs for a moment Phil thinks to himself, *I guess I could use a bit of that myself,* and he picks up a nearby spoon to give it a taste.

Instantly, Phil is not feeling well. He is dizzy, light-headed, and starts to sweat. He becomes aware of a cold, numbness creeping into his body and finally realizes that he is having difficulty breathing.

He drops to the floor and hears a voice in his heart saying, *Do not fear, human creature. It is time for you to come home. You have just saved the entire village of Chiconahui from death by rattlesnake venom. The Great Spirit and your family are waiting to welcome you. They are all rejoicing knowing that you will be with them again very soon.*

At that moment Doc comes back and she sees Phil lying on the floor. She drops her bundle of tree roots and runs over to him. "Phil! Phil! Oh God! What happened?"

Phil is barely able to open his eyes as he says to his sweet wife, "Snake . . . venom . . . in . . . the tea . . . throw, it out! . . . Love you . . ." Phil closes his eyes for the last time with a peaceful smile on his face.

"*NOOOO!*" Doc screams.

The villagers and Chrysalenes sitting around the firepit hear Doc scream. They jump to their feet and run to the hut where they see Doc on the floor with Phil. She is cradling the body of her husband, rocking back and forth, stricken with sudden grief, and crying in agony.

The Chrysalenes already know what has happened and they sit down with Doc forming a circle around her. "Dear sister, Phil is at peace now. May we offer our comfort to you?"

Through her tears Doc says to the Chrysalenes and the villagers, "He never truly forgave himself for losing his entire family to the Ebola bioweapon, for being the sole survivor and not being able to stop their tragic deaths. And I know he must have found peace at saving this entire village."

Then her tears turn to rage as she yells, *"BUT I SHALL NEVER FORGIVE MYSELF FOR WHAT I HAVE JUST DONE! FATHER IN HEAVEN! WHAT HAPPENED? THE VOICE IN MY HEART HAS NEVER FAILED ME BEFORE!"*

Doc breaks down screaming at herself, *"I JUST KILLED MY HUSBAND! I KILLED THE MAN I LOVE! I TRUSTED THE VOICE IN MY HEART! AND NOW MY MAN IS DEAD!*

Eve Maria puts her arms around Doc and closes her eyes, calling upon the voice that spoke to Doc a little while ago. The Chrysalene hears the serpent's hissing voice and knows at once what has happened.

Eve Maria gently explains, "Dearest woman, it was not the voice of the heavenly host that you were hearing as you normally do. It was the voice of the serpent come back to the Garden, whispering lies to Eve. You must not be angry at yourself, good woman. Lucifer is quite the deceiver. And we have learned something very important through Phil's passing. He has truly sacrificed himself that we might learn this lesson."

Looking up from her husband's face which is now bathed in Doc's tears, she asks Eve Maria, "What lesson is *that?*"

The Chrysalenes look at each other as the villagers gather around and then they turn to Doc. Eve Maria says, "The deceiver is now a living presence who is here among us."

The villagers gasp, Doc stops crying, and she suddenly looks at everyone with a fierce anger burning in her eyes. "The serpent!" she cries out. Nodding and speaking sadly Doc says, "Yes, the serpent . . . Indeed!"

She takes Eve Maria by the hand, looks in her eyes and says, "I think I know who it is."

* * *

Emeka, Eve Elli, and their companions are winding down for the evening at the Coffeehouse in Johannesburg. Mimi is having a great time drumming with their old friends, and little Lady Bi is out like a light sleeping on her mama's lap. Even with all the stimulation from the drums, lights, and noisy atmosphere of the place, Bi is just snoozing away.

"Well," says Emeka to Eve Elli, "I guess it's time to take our little one home for the night."

Eve Elli smiles at her husband and says, "Yes, it is time for us to leave right now." Looking at Liling she quickly adds, "But some of us will not be leaving just yet. Let us say good night to the others and may the Monarch Angel and our Creator be with the High Lady Liling tonight."

Although Emeka does not know what Eve Elli is talking about, he does know that when his Chrysalene wife talks like that his job is to just smile, nod and get moving!

Eve Elli goes over to her Gramma Mimi and Grampa Ryan and says good night to them. Of course, Gramma Mimi must give just one more kiss to the sweet little bundle in Eve Elli's arms. And Mimi kisses Bi gently so as not to wake her.

The woman in the red cape and her companion seemed to have disappeared for a little while, but they return just as Eve Elli is leaving.

Emeka and Eve Elli wave goodbye to Dumaka, and Liling does not even notice when the others all slip out quietly. With Liling's highly developed intuition she knows exactly who has just returned, is sitting in the corner, wearing a red, hooded cape, calling herself Chen, and talking to the man who calls himself Haitao.

It is the same woman who in life murdered Liling's dearest friend, Lady Bi.

Dumaka is not sure what is going on, but he notices that his sweet wife has gone off into another dimension, hardly able to talk to him or focus on any of the activities going on around them. All her attention is suddenly drawn to Haitao and Chen.

"Are you okay, honey?" Dumaka asks his wife to which her response is a mechanical, "Sure."

Other people have also filed out of the Coffeehouse by now and there are only a few villagers left in the place as well as Dumaka, Liling, Haitao, and the woman in the red, hooded cape who calls herself Chen.

Liling finally stands up. Without taking her eyes off Chen she starts moving in her direction. Upon seeing this the woman pulls back the hood of her red cape fully revealing herself. Bella and

Liling are locked in each other's stare as Liling steadily approaches her.

Eve Elli's prayer was heard loud and clear. In a flash, Angel crosses the veil into the third dimension and her Monarch form, heading full speed for the Coffeehouse in Johannesburg.

Liling is now standing directly over Bella who is seated at the café table. With their gazes still locked on each other Bella whispers something to the staff in her hand. As she does so the staff begins to move taking on the live form of a boa constrictor. Suddenly, a Monarch Butterfly appears and crash-lands right on the serpent's head.

Liling hears the Monarch in her heart as the butterfly covers the boa's eyes with her wings declaring, *I don't think so, scaley creature!*

In an instant Andre is turned to stone and crumbles to dust. Bella jumps back and Angel says to Liling's heart, *You got this, sister creature!*

The Monarch Angel and the remains of Andre suddenly disappear.

Bella grabs her hand, wondering what just happened. Liling looks at her, smiling. Leaning forward, right in Bella's face, Liling says to the ghost of the cold-blooded killer of her best friend, "I will fear no evil."

Bella leans back, crosses her arms over her chest and gives Liling a sarcastic grin. "Oh really?" she says with a smirk, still locked in a staring contest with Liling. "And what do you think *you* can do?"

But before Liling can answer, Bella leans forward and snipes, "I'll tell you what you can do, High Lady Liling. You can do *NOTHING! ABSOLUTELY NOTHING!* Because you have no real power My *LADY!* You have nothing! Only that silly little gardener you married, *Dumaka,*" Bella says with venomous sarcasm dripping from her tongue.

Liling is now nose-to-nose with her adversary. Staring fiercely into Bella's eyes she replies, "What I have is something you cannot understand. Why your mother cared more for your sister Lady Bi than she did for you, Lady Bella, formerly known as Lady Chen. Why you have murdered so many others besides Bi, including Master Howard, and most likely your own parents in that alleged boating accident. It is why you discovered the power of material things and climbed on the back of Lucifer to ride all the way to the top as the evil ruler of One World, until it was Lucifer himself who took you down, yes down, out of this world and into his own."

In a rage Bella leaps up, grabs Liling's throat and yells, "And now it is *YOUR* turn to die."

With her eyes still fixed on Bella's evil stare, Liling says, "No, my sad sister, you cannot kill me with your bare hands. You are merely an apparition now, a ghost. And as long as I have no fear, you cannot harm me. You do not understand because you never had what *I* have with my simple gardener husband. It is the true power of this world, Bella. The one and only Absolute Power of the universe. And that power is called LOVE."

Bella tries to scream but the sound will not come out of her mouth. She tries to squeeze her hands tight around Liling's throat, but they remain limp.

Liling puts her hand up to Bella's face and says, "I command you evil spirit, in the name of the Kind One, to return to the Light! May you be washed clean and roam the earth no more!"

Bella seems frightened for a moment but then she simply laughs and disappears.

Master Commandant Haitao on the other hand, who has been sitting there witnessing the whole encounter is terrified.

The Monarch Angel is perched on a nearby window ledge and says to Liling's heart, *Well done, Liling creature! As long as you remember that LOVE is the strongest force in the universe, you will have no reason to ever fear evil.*

"Thank you, Angel," Liling says, and she watches the Monarch fly out of the window into the starry night above.

* * *

In the bowels of hell, a forlorn serpent turns to Lucifer and says *OUUUUCH!*

The beast looks at the peeved snake and starts laughing. Andre narrows his eyes and frowns at Lucifer with a *HMPH!*

* * *

In a little village near Moscow called the Garden of Suzie, Vi has just come in from the hothouse carrying a pile of fruits and vegetables. She hands them over to Yakov and Neely who are preparing to make an exquisite meal for the villagers, the Chrysalenes, and a new family who will be arriving later that afternoon.

Yakov and Neely are especially looking forward to the community meal this evening since they have just received the news about the new family. They are a couple with two sons, one who is 20 years old and the other who is 17. Originally from Euroslavica, they were displaced 18 years ago after the fall of the Council. Therefore, today's community meal will be a real celebration and welcoming of the new family, Slavic style.

The meal is ready, all the preparations have been made, and the sun is going down. The family has not arrived yet and the villagers are all quite hungry.

"Well," says Yakov to all who are gathered at the outdoor picnic area. "I really don't want to start without them but maybe they have been detained somewhere. Why don't we give them just a little bit longer and then we'll get started."

"Sounds like a good idea! You got it! Sure thing, Bratan!" the villagers agree.

A few minutes later, four autobikes pull into the Garden of Suzie ridden by four bedraggled looking people. Neely goes to greet them.

Seeing that they have had a rough time of it, the others, out of concern and respect bow to the newcomers and say "hello" in a toned-down manner.

Yakov says to them, "Welcome, good people, to the Garden of Suzie. We were just getting ready to have our evening meal. Would you all like to join us or do you feel like resting for a while? We can show you to your hut if you need some time to yourselves."

"Thank you kindly," the man says.

He takes one look at Yakov and Neely and bows his head low staring at the ground. He thinks he has seen Neely before, but Yakov looks especially familiar.

The man's wife speaks up, "We have not eaten for the past two days and are very hungry. If it is all right with you, we should like very much to eat something."

"Oh my! Yes! Please join us! Have a seat! There's plenty of food!" the villagers gasp, as they go to the family and invite them to the table.

Everyone begins to eat on a more solemn note, sensing that something has happened to the newcomers on their way over.

Yakov and Neely look at each other with trepidation. They both *know* they have seen this man somewhere before, a very long time ago.

Trailing behind the family another man is riding on an autobike headed for the Garden of Suzie. He senses someone coming up from behind him and stops. The man turns around and is startled to see Bella standing there. She is carrying her serpent staff which she gives to the man and says, "Here, Master Commandant Pasha. Take this staff."

At his hesitation she gives him a menacing grin and says, "Now, now Pasha. There is nothing to worry about. I have already put plenty of fear in Lord Viktor and his family these past two days. If there is one thing I remember about Viktor, my dear Pasha, is that he is protective of his family. I'm sure that he will do our every bidding.

"Now mind," Bella continues, "that you take good care of my darling Andre, here. His part in the Garden is *most* important. Don't you forget that, Pasha dear!"

"No, ma'am. I won't forget."

Bella kisses the snake's head on the top of the staff as she says, "Take care my pet. Mama will be keeping my eye on you."

Andre winks at her.

Bella looks off in the distance at the entry to the Garden of Suzie. "Yes indeed," she says. "Mama will be keeping an eye on *all of you!*"

Chapter 9 – Battlefields

ANGIE AND KOOKIE are about to land in Cavern Village, Wyoming. Looking down from the Cloudtransporter they see the fertile acres of farmland which have been transformed into a large garden community: The Garden of Tom.

Master Sam and Mistress Sheila wait for them on the landing field, along with a large gathering of villagers. Kookie is lost in sad memories about the last time he was here without his beloved Angie, not knowing if he would ever see her again. Angie looks at her man remembering how hard it was for her too, to be separated from him in such a way. But she also remembers what she learned from that experience.

"I know how hard it was on both of us, honey, but remember the big lesson we all learned from those dark times," says Angie.

Kookie looks at his beloved and says, "Yes, my love, I do. *With Love All Things Are Possible.*"

Angie puts her arms around Kookie's waist, and they kiss and hold each other in a tender embrace. When the portal opens the two disembark. They are greeted by the roaring sound of an adoring crowd, welcoming the return of their heroes of One Garden.

Kookie and Angie are about to join a feast in their honor. The villagers have been cheering non-stop as the couple make their way through the crowd, headed to the picnic tables.

When Master Sam and Mistress Sheila had announced to everyone that their heroes were returning, the entire garden community became excited, and started preparing. Everyone has been joyfully scurrying around including those who never met Kookie and Angie but heard all the fearless, self-sacrificing stories about them. Even the youngest villagers know how Kookie and Angie fought the dark lord and gave them the freedom they have today. The farmers of the Garden of Tom who lived through the Battle of the Cornfield remember that time well. Many of them are the former commandos who were sent by Lady Bella to murder the peaceful farmers during the dark time of her rule.

The Legend of Eve Elli and Commando Tom has been handed down to a whole new generation of villagers. Young ones sing songs of the faith and love of a three-year-old Chrysalene Eve Elli who gave healing love to commando Tom. He was then able to hear Kookie's message of freedom, resisting Lucifer's orders to murder little Eve Elli.

"Welcome, Kookie and Angie! Welcome! We love you! Thank you!" Words of love and gratitude are joyously exclaimed throughout the crowd as the heroes arrive at the picnic tables.

Master Sam calls everyone to join them and sit down. When they have all taken their seats Sam announces: "Friends of Tom's Garden, we are honored to have with us today the heroes of our new world, Kookie and Angie!"

Everyone stands, cheering and applauding. They go on and on getting louder and louder, until their cheers turn into chants, and chants into song. Master Sam puts his hand up and the crowd quiets.

He continues, "We would like to honor you both with a special gift. It is something that many of the villagers including the little ones, have been working on since we heard of your imminent arrival."

Kookie and Angie look at each other with great curiosity.

"Since we heard that you will be spending some time in the cavern, we thought that these would be especially useful."

Now they are *very* curious, indeed! Sam picks up a large box that has been sitting next to him on the ground. He brings it over to Kookie and Angie, placing it before them on the table. Finally, and with much affection Sam says to them, "We know how much you two love these, especially Kookie. Well … *ENJOY!*" he laughs, along with the rest of the crowd.

Kookie can stand it no longer as he tears open the box. Angie helps him pull out a rather large basket. When they see what is inside, they are both overwhelmed with joy and laughter. It is filled with cookies of every kind with little notes attached to each one expressing gratitude and love from the villagers.

Kookie stands up and says, "Thank you so very much gracious people of the Garden of Tom. You deeply honor Angie and me with such an outpouring of appreciation and affection. And looking at all the cookies here, I'd say that word has gotten out. I just *love* chocolate chips cookies! Or *any* cookie for that matter!"

Laughter erupts among the villagers followed by another round of applause.

A couple comes over to Kookie and Angie with their three children. The youngest is a little girl who appears to be about five years old who is dragging her mama by the hand over to their heroes.

"Pardon us please," says the woman lowering her gaze and bowing her head. "But my daughter here wants very much to meet you."

Angie smiles at the family and says, "Thank you, ma'am. The honor is all ours." Then she smiles at the child and says to her, "Hello, my name is Angie. What is your name?"

The youngster gives Angie a bashful smile, and her mama says, "Her name is Luna." Luna's mama points to their other two girls, "Our eldest is Ida and the middle one here is Vanya. Oh, and my name is Dakota and my husband's name is Leo."

Angie says to the young girls, "Hello there Luna, Ida, and Vanya!" And looking at all five of them she says, "So nice to meet you all!"

Then papa Leo explains to them, "My girls have each made a cookie for you. And we want you to know how very thankful we are for all that you have done."

Looking straight at Kookie, Leo continues, "You may not remember me but in the Battle of the Cornfield after the beast struck Tom down, I was one of Bella's commandos who followed Tom's lead. I picked up the broken corn stalks and put them in the wheelbarrow. The other commandos began to follow Tom's lead as well and when I asked the farmers where to put them, they came forward and helped us. It was the beginning of a new life of love, peace and understanding between us which we, the commandos, never knew before."

Kookie and Angie are overwhelmed with emotions and Angie puts her arms out to the whole family. They hug and express tears of joy and laughter, especially when Luna pulls her cookie from the top of the pile and hands it to Kookie. It is chocolate chip!

Master Sam has one more announcement to make before the food is served. He gets everyone's attention once again. "Since this was all very last minute, I have not had a chance to explain to you the purpose of Kookie and Angie's visit. I would like to give them the floor now so they can explain it to you themselves."

They look at each other and nod. In a subdued voice Angie begins, "As I'm sure you're all aware, throughout his lifetime my husband has been disturbed by what he considered to be one of the Councils' worst offenses against the people of One World, apart from turning us all into their slaves."

The crowd murmurs and nods in agreement.

"He was disturbed by the mind-control techniques that were used against us, as well as the way we were all denied the knowledge of our own past. Since the fall of the Council, we and many others including Lord Emeka have been working to restore libraries and the remembrance of our history and heritage."

More nods of approval and applause.

"Through our research we have discovered an ancient technology which helps us to remember things, both personal and global. Our son David has been helping Kookie and me develop a way of tapping into and enhancing this ancient technology."

A few soft murmurings of *whoa* vibrate through the crowd.

"The Monarch Angel came to me in a vision and told me that in order to complete the process we had to come here, to the nearby cavern, and find the Great Quartz Crystal of the Hidden Cavern."

Now the villagers have gone stone-cold silent, except for Leo who is still standing behind Kookie and Angie with his family.

"If you please ma'am," Leo says, "We are all familiar with the cavern over yonder. It can be a treacherous place if you do not know your way through it. And I have also seen the Hidden Cavern of which you speak. If I may, with your permission good lady and kind sir, I would like to accompany you and be your guide to find the Great Quartz Crystal."

Kookie and Angie look at each other and then at Leo.

Angie says to him, "Bless you, Leo. I did not know how we were going to navigate this trail on our own. Thank you so very much!"

"You are most welcome ma'am," Leo responds.

"Okay then," says Kookie tapping the tips of his fingers together. "We leave first thing in the morning."

That night as Leo, Dakota, and their three girls prepare for bed the youngsters express much excitement about their papa going with Kookie and Angie on their journey.

Luna says to her mama, "Is papa going into the cave to see the big crystal, mama?"

"Yes, honey!" Dakota chuckles as she tucks her daughter into bed.

"The REALLY big crystal?"

"That's right."

"The *REALLY, REALLY, BIG CRYSTAL?!*" Luna exclaims with wide-saucer-eyes.

"Yes, sweetie, the *REALLY, REALLY, BIG CRYSTAL!*" mama Dakota laughs, enjoying her daughter's enthusiasm.

Ida and Vanya are also giggling at their little sister as Vanya says to Leo, "Papa, when you are down there in the hidden cavern do you think you can find some big crystals to bring back for us?"

Leo smiles as he tucks his daughter into bed and says, "I'm sure I can manage that, malishka.[11]

---

[11] *Russian term for baby girl*

"Yay!" the girls all shout. Gradually, they settle down and fall asleep.

Young Luna finds herself in a dream of a long time ago. She is in a cozy shelter. It is small, round, and comes to a point in the center at the top. There is another child in the shelter with her and they are laughing together, playing under the blankets. Luna and the other child step outside the shelter where they are greeted by the warm sunshine, birds singing, and the sound of a nearby running stream. The two girls feel the warmth of the sunshine, the birds, and the stream, filling their hearts with so much love and peace.

Suddenly, there are sounds of loud and frightened voices coming their way. People are running toward the two children yelling, "Wasichu! Wasichu!"

A woman scoops up Luna in her arms and continues to run. Then she hears loud bangs, and as Luna turns around, she sees the other child fall to the ground. There are more people lying still near the fallen child and everyone is screaming and running. They are being chased by men with large sticks which make the loud bangs.

Suddenly, Luna feels a sharp, searing pain rip through her little chest, and the last thing she hears before leaving this world is the woman scream and cry out to her, "Wakanjeja!"

Young Luna wakes up wailing, "*MAMA! MAMA!*" Dakota, Leo, Ida, and Vanya all wake up and are by her side.

"What is it, honey? What happened? Are you alright? Did you have a bad dream?"

Luna is sobbing heavily. Dakota is holding her little girl and they all listen with much compassion as she relates the dream to her family. When she gets to the part of the little girl being shot in the chest, Leo and Dakota hold her tight, grief and sorrow filling their hearts. They both understand this to be something of the past of Dakota's people. They have only heard disputed rumors about such things, but within their hearts have always believed them to be true.

Luna looks at her mama with great sadness. Wiping her tears away she says, "What does that word mean, mama? The word that frightened everyone so much!" She thinks about it for a moment and then says, "wuh, wuh, wwwaah, sii, chuu."

Leo and Dakota look at each other and Dakota says to her daughters, "The word is Wasichu, and in the old days it was a word in Lakota used by my people, *your* people, the Sioux. It means, White Man."

Leo touches his wife's cheek as he lovingly says, "We are *all* your people, my darling. We are one people of Great Spirit's world of One Garden.

And high up in the heavenly realm a voice is speaking to the hearts of Leo, Dakota, Ida, Vanya, and Luna, saying, "*Amen, Sioux Creatures, amen!*"

* * *

In the Garden of Suzie, right outside the town of Moscow, everyone has taken their seat around the tables in the picnic area. Yakov raises his glass of water in his usual manner to bless the meal and the people, and to bless and welcome the newcomers to the garden community. However, since the new folks seem to be somewhat uncomfortable, he tones down the usual levity of such a moment.

Speaking in Russian he simply says, "Bless the new family who has come to make their home here. May they feel loved and welcomed by us all."

Everyone raises their glass of water and says, "Here, here!" to the family. When the four of them dig in and start eating they scarf down their food like ravenous wolves.

When he is finished eating, the man looks up and realizes that he has not introduced himself to the villagers of the Garden of Suzie. Slowly and carefully, he puts his bread down, stands up and addresses the group.

"Good people of the Garden of Suzie. My family and I are honored and humbled to be here."

He lowers his eyes for a moment and the group goes quiets. They can tell the man is having a hard time with something inside of him.

"I must tell you however . . ." he falters and grows fearful. "There is something that I must tell you . . ." But before he can say another word, he sees Master Commandant Pasha standing nearby holding Bella's serpent-headed staff. Pasha's eyes burn into the man's fearful glance, and he raises the stick. The man knows that he has a decision to make, right now, and that there will be no turning back.

Silence reigns and all eyes are upon him. He continues . . . "My name is Viktor, this is my wife Marie, and these are our two sons, Ivan, and Boris. For the past 18 years, since the end of the Council of One World, we have been living in different garden communities throughout Sinopacifica. We are always greeted by kind people such as yourselves, and hopeful that we can stay and make a life amongst you."

Viktor pauses again and this time looks at Pasha who has gotten much closer to him. "But then . . . they find me. And they threaten me . . . that I must do their bidding, or they will hurt the good people of the garden community where we live."

Now Master Commandant Pasha is only a few feet away from Viktor and he appears to be brandishing the staff like a weapon. The "weapon" begins to move in Pasha's hand and suddenly Viktor must spill the rest of his words quickly.

"I have never revealed my true identity to anyone, but I *must* do so now. *I am Lord Viktor of the former Council of One World, and one of only several survivors of the blast that incinerated Lady Bella and all the pro-Council Lords who died that day!*"

Gasps reverberate around the tables.

And then, just as Pasha reaches Viktor with a wriggling and writhing Andre in hand, Viktor points to the man with the serpent and shouts: *"THE ENEMY IS RIGHT HERE! AND I WILL COVER FOR THEM NO MORE!*

High Lord Yakov, former High Lord Commandant, sees the fangs of the serpent about to come down into Lord Viktor's flesh. Yakov's instincts as the highest-ranking military officer of the former One World kick in fast. He grabs the bread knife on the table in front of him and with one swift whack, decapitates Andre.

In the next instant Yakov grabs Pasha by the back of his hair and presses the serrated edge of the knife against his throat. "Well, well, Master Commandant Pasha! It's been a while," says Yakov, tightening his grip on Pasha's hair. "Now what the devil brings *you* here?"

Pasha does not speak but shoots a very frightened look at his former High Lord Commandant. "Or perhaps it *is* the devil that brings you here!"

"Puh . . . puh . . . puh . . . please, muh . . . muh . . . My Lord, Yakov," he stammers, "Luh . . . luh . . . let me explain.

Yakov motions to Viktor to set a chair in front of his former commando. Between the two of them they coax a very shaky Pasha to sit down.

"Okay then," says Yakov. "Explain."

"I'm sorry My Lord, she threatened me, too."

"Really?! And who might *she* be, commando," Yakov questions him warily.

Lowering his eyes to the ground Pasha says, "She is Lucifer's queen. In life she was Lady Bella. It is true that she died with the rest of them years ago, in the blast that Lord Viktor just mentioned. But her spirit roams the earth. She will stop at nothing to get what she wants; what *he* wants."

"And what is *that* commando?" Yakov is not at all convinced that Pasha is leveling with him.

Pasha looks directly at Yakov now as he says, "Lucifer wants absolute power. And Bella will stop at nothing to give her lord what he wants, and what she wants too."

Thinking for a moment Pasha adds, "She said something about a power of the pyramids, and how she and Lucifer will have absolute power if they gain control of the pyramids."

Yakov and Neely both glance at each other somewhat dismayed that Lucifer knows what they are up to. "What else did she tell you?" Yakov asks.

"I was told to pretend to be on your side, My Lord."

Lord Viktor is now the one who is wary as he says to Pasha, "Is that so? Then why did you come after me with that live weapon of yours?"

"I think that you of all people, know the answer to that one, My Lord Viktor. And it is why they will not leave you alone, is it not?"

Viktor is angered now as he gets in Pasha's face and says, "Are you trying to tell us, *Master Commandant,* that you truly wish to leave your associates behind, as I did, only you are too afraid to do so?"

Pasha simply lowers his eyes and does not speak.

Yakov looks warily at him and says, "Well then, former commando of mine, what am I to do with you?"

Yakov understands the influence that fear can have on those who feel hopelessly locked into their world of hell. He has seen many people try to pull themselves out of the world of darkness, only to give up and succumb to the less frightening way of remaining trapped in their own misery. He also knows what Viktor and those like him have gone through, fighting the brave battle against Bella and Lucifer. His guts are telling him to trust Pasha and try to help him.

Yakov is lost in thought and looks away for a moment. And as he does do, Pasha quickly pulls a gun out of his pocket and points it at Yakov.

Everyone around the table screams and Pasha suddenly turns the gun around. He hands it to Yakov and with a trembling voice says to him: "Please help me, My High Lord Commandant."

* * *

In the bowels of hell Bella offers comfort to her whimpering serpent. Rubbing the back of his neck she says to him, "There, there, my pet. Don't you worry about that bad boy who whacked off your head with a silly old bread knife."

Andre snivels and Bella continues, "Why the fool couldn't even do it right, with a machete!"

"OW! OW! OW!" wails Andre, blinking away his tears.

"Oh now, never you mind, sweetie. Mama Bella will kiss it *aaaalll* better!" she exclaims and starts pecking away on his neck.

Andre looks up at her with big, sad eyes and they smile at each other.

Lucifer looks at Bella, but he is not smiling. "Well then, my *PET!*" he says angrily. "What are you going to do with those bad boys *now*, since our *PASHA* has failed so miserably?!"

"Strategy, husband," Bella replies with a cheeky grin. "When a commandant fails, bring in a lord."

Chapter 10 – Decoy

PA, ES, AND SPA relax on the veranda overlooking the lush, tropical gardens of the Yucatan estate, waiting for their mid-afternoon meal to be served. The brothers sit in silence, lost deep in thought as they mull over their conversations of the past several days.

PA speaks up. "Brethren, have you considered all that we have discussed?"

"Oh, yes," says ES.

"Yes, indeed," says SPA.

"Do either of you have anything to propose regarding her ladyship?" says PA.

The three of them look at each other. PA and ES look bewildered, but SPA is staring with razor-sharp clarity at both as he replies, "Yes my brethren, I do indeed have something to propose regarding Bella."

But before SPA can utter another word Bella suddenly appears before them in the garden holding her serpent.

"Well!" Bella says, coming to the edge of the veranda, "And what might that be My Lord SPA, Highest of the Council of One World? You must tell me all about it. May I join you on your veranda?"

Without missing a beat SPA simply grins at her and says, "Why yes, Lady Bella! Do come in."

* * *

After Yakov's encounter with Viktor and Pasha, he knows that he badly needs the guidance of a Chrysalene, only there aren't any in the vicinity of the Garden of Suzie. So he decides to contact his bratan.

Kookie is just about to go into the cavern with Angie and Leo when he gets a call from Yakov on his Metatron device.

"Hey, Bro, what's up?" says Kookie. "Everything okay with you?"

"Not exactly," says Yakov. He knows that there is no use trying to make everything sound simple with his big brother. "Actually, I need a Chrysalene . . . *NOW!*"

Kookie's tone turns serious as he asks his brother, "What's the matter, Yakov? Got anyone in mind?"

Yakov continues, "Yes! Someone who can be here . . . you know . . . *NOW?!*"

"Sure thing. Would you like to tell me about it?" Kookie says more softly."

"*NO!*" says the younger brother with indignation. "I would not!"

"Well, okay then," says Kookie somewhat perplexed. "I'll get someone from the Village of the Holy Ones over to you right away. If Mama Eve Zula or Papa Adam Makena are not available, then I'll find someone else."

"Thanks, Bratan. Thanks!"

Yakov is already breathing easier knowing that a Chrysalene will guide him in the Light of Love through the difficult situation with Viktor and his family, and especially with Pasha. He also knows how much both men will benefit from a Chrysalene's counsel.

Yakov and Neely prepare to take a trip to the pyramid prior to Kookie's activation, with Vi, Viktor, Marie, and Pasha. Yakov figures it will be healing for them all to arrive there early and just sit there and meditate for a while. They have already discovered the calming benefits of listening to the voice of the Soul of the Stones in their heart.

Meanwhile, someone else has been listening in on Yakov from the bowels of hell. She communicates to her henchman ES, what is going on and sends him to the Garden of Suzie immediately. ES arrives with a plan and heads straight for Yakov.

"Hello," he says. "I hear you have a need for a Chrysalene."

"Uh, yes!" Yakov says thinking to himself, *that was quick*. Going over to the man he puts his hand out and says, "Thank you for coming. My name is Yakov. This is my wife Neely, and these are our friends Viktor, Marie, and Pasha."

Pasha turns pale and his eyes go wide, as he is the only one who recognizes ES. Suddenly he is in great fear for his life.

"And what is your name?" Yakov asks ES.

Smiling and bowing in Chrysalene fashion he says to everyone, "I am Adam Esau and I have come here to serve you."

Only Pasha sees the glare that ES throws at him. And Pasha realizes that they are *all* in grave peril.

* * *

In the village of Chiconahui, after Phil drank the snake venom Doc cried out that she knew who killed him, suspecting it was George. And George had his story all ready for her when she confronted him. He offered his sincerest condolences to Doc, singing Phil's praises and saying what a hero he was. And then he showed her the leaves that he had collected in his pouch which he claimed Phil told him were for the healing of the villagers. Doc knew that only she and Phil knew about the medicinal leaves, so she figured she must have been mistaken about George.

"The addition of the leaves to the tree roots in the tea have truly had a strengthening effect on the formula," Doc says to George, as she is also drinking the tea. "I am feeling as well as can be expected and appreciate your help."

"Glad to hear that, ma'am," says George with a slight grin.

Doc continues, "And the rest of the villagers of Chiconahui are also feeling much better."

George is satisfied that he is gaining Doc's trust as he brings her another cup of tea.

"Thank you, George," she says, taking the tea from him. "I just wish that I could reach my daughter Suzie. I really need to tell all our other friends what has happened, especially Mimi. But I just don't feel right about it without telling Suzie first."

"I know what you mean, Doc. It must be hard for you to not even know what is happening with Suzie right now, never mind not being able to reach her."

Suddenly Doc sits bolt upright, wide eyes flashing! *"WHOA!"* she yells at George. *"THAT'S IT!"*

"That's WHAT?!" George yells back, rather startled.

"Reaching Suzie!"

"What?"

Doc jumps up and shouts, "The pyramid!"

She grabs her Metatron device and is out the door in a second making haste to the pyramid. George tries to keep up with her, but

Doc is way ahead. And then he catches a glimpse of someone coming toward him. George slows down while Doc continues to dash ahead.

She reaches the pyramid and becomes thoroughly emersed in the business at hand. Doc remembers that there is a beacon sort of action connected to the 369-program on Metatron. If Suzie is away from her Metatron device and unable to be reached, Doc's Metatron device with 369, further enhanced by the pyramid, just might get Suzie's attention.

George stops when he sees the man coming towards him. He recognizes the man at once and is greatly confused. The man stops in front of him and smiles.

George looks at him warily and says, "What are *you* doing here, My Highest Lord PA?"

"I am finishing the job that you were sent here to do. Thank you for your service, Master Commandant George." PA puts his hand in his pocket, pulls out some leaves and quickly shoves them into George's mouth.

Doc does not see the struggle behind her as George gasps, turns blue and falls to the ground.

* * *

Tomas and Daniela are moved at the idea of sanctifying the old, abandoned building at the California border where so many people, especially children suffered so much. Sergio and Elena are honored to be a part of such a sacred ceremony. Suzie explains that once they have sanctified the building, they can turn it into a place where ceremonies can be held. It will be a way to remember and honor those who have lived through such terrible things.

"It will become a sacred ground," she says. The Chrysalenes are deeply touched at the compassion of their companions as they all prepare for the sanctification.

* * *

At the Pyramid of Chiconahui, Doc stands on one of the stones. The beacon system of Metatron is all fired up and ready to go. She holds the device against her chest and calls upon the voice of the Soul of the Stones . . .

* * *

Sergio and the group begin walking toward the old building when Suzie notices something off in the distance.

"Look!" she points out to everyone. "It's the Cloudtransporter. It's, it's, like *glowing* or something!"

The others see it too and are very perplexed.

Rudolpho turns to Suzie and says: "What in the world is that?!"

They look at each other with a sense of urgency and Rudolpho exclaims, "We better check that out, honey! Now!"

As they reach the portal, the light of the glowing Cloudtransporter has grown much stronger. "What the blazes *is* that?" Rudolpho cries.

"I don't know, honey!" Suzie exclaims.

Rudolpho says, "Well, I guess we had better go inside and find out *what the blazes that is!*"

"I guess so!" says Suzie although she is not so sure she wants to.

They open the portal, and a stream of Bright White Light comes pouring out of the craft, almost knocking Suzie and Rudolpho backwards off their feet.

* * *

Doc cries out, "Soul of the Stones! Help me please, help me! I must reach Suzie! I must speak to her! Please help me talk to my Suzie!"

And Doc hears a voice calling out from the very center of the pyramid. It is a faraway voice sounding like a dream.

"I hear you, mama! It's Suzie! I can hear you! Are you okay? Where are you? Oh, mama!"

* * *

From the Bright White Light inside the Cloudtransporter, Suzie hears Doc saying to her, "Something has happened, and I need you to come back here just as soon as you can."

Suzie becomes anxious and calls out, "What? Mama! What happened?"

There's a pause, and Doc gets weepy as she tells her daughter, "It's your papa, sweetheart."

Suzie is listening quietly now as she starts to get weepy too.

"Your papa passed. He is with his Creator now."

Both mother and daughter break down crying together in the fourth dimensional opening of the pyramid.

Suzie finally speaks and asks her mama, "Where are you now?"

"I'm at the pyramid of Chiconahui!"

Wiping her tears Suzie says to Doc, "We are still at the California border, but we'll be done here soon. Can we come and get you, mama? We can take you to see Judy if you like."

"Oh, honey! I would love that!" Doc says through bittersweet tears.

Suzie looks at Rudolpho who nods at her, and she says to Doc, "We will be there very soon. Get ready to leave, okay?"

"Thank you, honey. Thank you."

Suzie and Rudolpho go back to the old building and tell the others what happened. They all knew Phil as a wonderful father figure, and they are feeling his loss deeply.

Eve Sophia puts her arms out to Suzie saying, "I am *so sorry*. Your father's people, the Sioux nation, were also hurt by the conquerors. May we add his name to the sacred memory of this building?"

"Oh, thank you, Eve Sophia. My mama will love to hear that. We must go back to Chiconahui and pick her up just as soon as we are done here. Thank you, thank you," she says, brushing away her tears. "Would you and Adam Mateo lead us through the ceremony?"

Adam Mateo and Eve Sophia look at everyone with much compassion. They bow and nod to the little group, motioning for them to follow. As Tomas and Daniela enter the old building, this time they are not afraid.

Daniela says to Tomas, "It's not scary anymore, is it?"

"No," he says somewhat surprised. "It's not scary at all."

Sergio, Elena, Rudolpho, and Suzie also notice a peacefulness in the building that was not there before, as they enter the room with the cage. Only the cage is gone. It is just a small empty room now. There is a window in the corner which the children had not noticed before and a soft ray of light streams in.

On the window ledge is a Monarch Butterfly. Eve Sophia and Adam Mateo go to the center of the room where the cage with the little girl was, and everyone gets down on their knees. They all close their eyes and Eve Sophia says:

"Great Spirit, there was so much suffering in this place at one time. We know that many souls left the earth right here in this room. We know that they are at peace now, and we ask that You sanctify this room and this building in their honor and in Your Holy name. We would also ask You to consecrate this spot in the name of our friend Phil, and his people of the Sioux nation. Finally, we dedicate this spot to the little girl who died here, whose spirit came to Daniela and Tomas. If You would kindly let us know her name, we will say blessings to her and to all the children who suffered as she did."

The little group goes quiet for a moment as they become aware of a glowing light in the room. They open their eyes and see the Monarch Angel growing right before them, transforming into an Angel of the Lord. Her sparkling wings are orange, yellow, and gold, and everyone stares at her in wonder. Angel speaks to their hearts saying:

"Bless you, human creatures for your most loving hearts. That you may always cherish and honor the memory of the children who suffered here, the little one who came to you was called Lucia. Her spirit will rest now. Phil is here to take her home where she will be with her mama again."

The Light in the window suddenly becomes very bright and Suzie sees her papa Phil standing before them. He puts his arms out to his Little One and says to her heart, *"Wakanjeja, I love you. And I am so proud of you today, my daughter. You will always be my Little One."*

Suzie is beside herself with tears as she says, "I love you too, papa, and I will always be your Little One, your Wakanjeja, Suzie of the Seashells."

Daniela and Tomas get wide-eyed with wonder as they see little Lucia materialize and run to Phil. She is laughing and happy as can be, as Phil scoops her up in his arms. He looks at Suzie one last time, waves to everyone and turns to the Tunnel of Light.

And as they ascend through the bright Tunnel Angel says to everyone, *Little Lucia is at peace now. She knows that she will be back in her mama's arms real soon."*

The Light dims, and Angel becomes a Monarch Butterfly again, perched on the ledge of the window.

Adam Mateo finishes the ceremony. "Thank you, Great Spirit, and bless you Phil and Lucia on your journey home. And now this place where we are kneeling has been made Holy, in Your name."

There is a warm sunlight coming in from the window. Angel turns to the smiling faces of Sergio, Elena, Rudolpho, Suzie, Tomas, Daniela, Adam Mateo, and Eve Sophia.

The Monarch pours love and sunshine into their hearts and says, *"The Creator truly does love His human creatures. And so do I. Now hop to it! Doc needs you right away in Chiconahui. Beware the one who calls himself Paul!"*

And with that the Monarch flutters away.

They all heed Angel's warning and get right back to the Cloudtransporter. Loading up everyone's autobikes and camping equipment, Suzie and Rudolpho set their course for Chiconahui.

"After we pick up Doc," Suzie says, "we will continue up the California coast and visit Judy. I will get a message to Judy now, let her know what has happened, and ask her to gather our California and Oregon friends together in memory of my papa."

* * *

Doc is getting ready to leave Chiconahui and head for California as soon as Suzie and Rudolpho come to pick her up. She goes to the village to make sure that everyone has enough herbal tea. She also leaves instructions with them about where to find the tree roots and leaves, and what they look like.

Everything seems to be well in order and Doc explains to the Chrysalenes, "I will be gone for a little while. I badly need to reconnect with my friends in California and share our grief over Phil."

Eve Marie reassures Doc, "My dear lady, the people of Chiconahui are feeling much better. They understand your needs and we bless you on your journey of healing and love to be with your friends."

"Thank you, Eve Marie," Doc says as she and the Chrysalene hug each other.

Doc starts walking back to her hut when she realizes that in her grief and rushing around, she has not seen George around for a while. *Hm,* she thinks to herself, *I wonder where George is?*

* * *

Packing a few things Doc finds one of her old journals. She comes across the notes she made of her impressions of Phil when she first met him at the Center Coffeehouse in Arbor Vista, California. Doc closes her eyes and takes a deep breath which she lets out with tears rolling down her face.

Lost in thoughts of her beloved husband, Doc hears an unexpected knock on the door. "Come in," she says, wiping her tears away.

In walks an unfamiliar elderly gentleman who appears to be in his 80s, or so.

"Ma'am?" the man says to her. "Are you the one they call Doc?"

"Yes, I am," she says. "And who are you?"

PA looks long and hard at Doc thinking over everything that he, ES, and SPA have talked about and rehearsed before they left on their individual assignments. He thinks about how he managed to *dispose* of George while Doc was at the pyramid contacting Suzie and how he has been stalking Doc, listening to her talk about her plans.

He smiles at her and says, "My name is Paul. I was contacted by my villager friend George who said that there were some problems here and that a good woman by the name of Doc needed my help."

"Oh," Doc says somewhat bewildered, "And where *is* George?" she asks Paul.

"He was needed back at our village, so I have come to relieve him."

Doc accepts this as a reasonable answer and says to Paul, "Well, I thank you for coming, sir. It is probably a good thing to offer your help to the villagers. I will be gone for a few days and do not really want to leave them at this time."

With a sigh Doc adds, "They are only just starting to feel better and I'm sure that they could use your support."

"I shall do my best to be of service ma'am," Paul says bowing graciously to Doc. "Rest assured that they will be in good hands until your return."

"Thank you," Doc says.

She can see the Cloudtransporter outside coming in for a landing and says to Paul, "Well, I shall be off now." Then with a sorrowful smile she adds, "It will be a comfort to me knowing that the villagers will be looked after by someone kind."

Doc nods respectfully at Paul. Then she takes her things and goes out to meet Suzie and Rudolpho at the Cloudtransporter.

* * *

At Lord Emeka's estate in Johannesburg, the sun is just rising. The morning meal is being prepared for Emeka and Eve Elli's guests, and they are all planning to leave right away for the Garden of Bi.

Liling has not told anyone what happened the night before regarding her encounter with Bella at the Coffeehouse. Her husband of course was there, so he witnessed everything. And when they left the Coffeehouse the terrified Master Commandant Haitao bolted out of there, so they have no idea what happened to him.

Everyone files into the dining room and Emeka says to his friends, "I talked to some of the villagers at the Coffeehouse last night and they agreed to meet us at the pyramid. I think it would be a good idea to spend a little time there this morning, meditating and connecting with the ancient energy."

Ryan is amazed at the whole concept of pyramid power and asks, "You mean like, *talk* to the stones or something?"

"Yes, that's exactly right!" says Emeka. "She is called the Soul of the Stones and when we connect with her, we can really hear the voice within speaking to our hearts. Of course, we will not activate the full power with Metatron until we get the go-ahead from Kookie, but meanwhile we can connect our own energy with the place and see what it has to tell us."

"Wow!" Ryan exclaims. He is impressed. "I can hardly wait to connect emotionally with a pile of ancient rocks!"

Mimi chuckles at her husband and pipes in, "I can remember when I first met Doc and she introduced me to all this energy stuff with nature. I thought it was really weird too!"

"You got that right, honey!" Ryans laughs.

Liling and Dumaka give each other a knowing glance. They decided not to tell anyone about Bella and Haitao just yet, but to keep a sharp eye out for anything suspicious when they get to the pyramid.

Eve Elli has been tuning in to her own inner voice when she announces to everyone, "Mama Eve Zula, Papa Adam Makena, and Eve Gerda are almost here."

"Aha!" says Emeka pointing his index finger in the air, a habit he picked up from being around Kookie since he was five years old. "I suppose we had all better get ready to leave then!"

"Sure thing!" Dumaka exclaims and the others nod in agreement.

The group leaves the Big House and runs into the Chrysalenes who are just arriving.

"Hello there!" the Chrysalenes call out to everyone.

"Hello! Hello!" the group responds.

Emeka says, "We are headed to the Cloudtransporter."

Glancing at Ryan he adds, "And we are all excited to connect emotionally with a pile of ancient rocks this morning!"

They all share a laugh and head to the aircraft.

The villagers of the Garden of Bi who Emeka spoke to the night before at the Coffeehouse have already arrived at the pyramid. They were intrigued when Emeka shared a little bit about what they were planning to do there. And now they are waiting for the group from Emeka's estate to arrive. The villagers have perched themselves on the stones, and with their eyes closed, deep in meditation, they feel the pyramid's soothing energy in their hearts.

Relaxing in the morning sun and enjoying the peacefulness of the stones and nature around them, no one notices another person arrive who was also at the Coffeehouse the night before.

Emeka finds a clearing nearby and lands the Cloudtransporter. As they all disembark, the group sees the pyramid before them with the villagers meditating.

Little Lady Bi's eyes go wide when she sees the large stone structure up ahead and coos, "OOO!"

"Yes, sweetie! OOO!" Mimi chuckles. "It is *very* impressive!"

They reach the pyramid and Emeka calls out to the folks he spoke to the night before, noticing that there are quite a few more villagers who apparently also decided to turn up. "Hello there! Good morning, everyone!"

"Hi there! Good morning to *you*, Lord Emeka!" reply the happy people sitting on the pile of ancient rocks.

Emeka's friends are all eager to join them and none more so than Ryan who eagerly climbs to the top of the pyramid. Looking at his little great-grandbaby and wanting to impress her, the otherwise shy Ryan begins beating his chest as he wails, "OOO!" to little baby Bi.

She lets out a big, baby, belly laugh at her silly great-grampa.

Liling asks the villagers, "How are you all doing this morning?"

"Okay! Great! Wonderful vibes!" they call out to her.

"It's amazingly calm and peaceful just sitting here, My Lady," one of the women of the Garden of Bi says to Liling.

"Well, we're going to join you all and see what happens," Liling adds.

The others climb onto the pyramid and choose a rock to settle upon. As they close their eyes and begin to meditate, they all experience the same soothing energy the villagers feel.

All that is, except Dumaka who goes into a deeper meditative state. The voice of the Soul of the Stones is speaking to his heart:

Earth being and kind-hearted friend, I Am giving you this vision that you may know what has happened to your people in the past and share it with others, that ALL of you may learn from it. It is even more important that you learn this lesson now as you are about to move into a higher frequency of love.

Dumaka opens his heart to the vision from the Soul of the Stones.

He sees himself about to embark on an old-time shipping vessel. There is a large group of people boarding the ship with him; men and women, most of them young adults looking very fit and healthy. The sun is shining, and it is a beautiful day. The seamen on board are waiting to escort them to the deck below.

Suddenly, everything goes black, and Dumaka realizes that he is encased in a wooden box. His arms, legs, and neck are shackled, and he can hardly move or breathe. He can hear muffled cries and assumes that they are the others he came on board with, all laying there in the same torturous situation. The seamen are yelling at the captive people, taunting them. Sometimes he can even hear laughter amongst them. Dumaka is seized with terror.

At one point he is aware that many days have gone by, and the muffled cries are now few and far between. There is a bad odor suffocating him as he lies in his own excrement. He can hear the seamen talking about how many of the people have died already, and how they had to throw their bodies overboard. The terror he feels is indescribable.

Finally, the ship docks and the box is opened. Dumaka sees himself standing on a block on the pier where several men stand around looking at him. They are talking to one of the seamen. One of the men takes Dumaka and motions that he is to get into another vehicle, which looks like a larger box with horses in front of it. Finally, Dumaka sees himself in a small hut, similar to the one he lived in as a gardener in Johannesburg prior to the fall of the Council. And he realizes to his horror that the slavery they were all freed from has happened before.

Dumaka is shaking as he opens his eyes and sees his beloved wife looking at him.

"Are you all right, honey?" Liling asks him.

"No, my darling. I have just had a dreadful vision of our people of the past."

He looks sadly at Emeka and Eve Elli. They come over and Dumaka shares the vision with the three of them.

"I just can't believe that we have been down this terrible road before," he says. And then with a burst of anger Dumaka shouts, *"This must NEVER HAPPEN AGAIN!"*

They all nod with solemn expressions. Eve Elli agrees, "That is why we are activating the pyramids, kind Dumaka. So that humanity does not have to keep learning these same terrible lessons over and over again."

She bows her head to him and says, "I am so sorry Dumaka, so sorry for the suffering of your people."

"Thank you," Dumaka replies, feeling a glimmer of hope.

All of a sudden, out of nowhere, Liling feels a sharp pain in her side as if someone has just kicked her. She turns around with a start and recognizes Haitao seated nearby. He looks straight at her with an eerie grin. Liling pales and has difficulty breathing from the sharp pain in her side while Haitao's gaze bores into her.

Dumaka sees what is happening and recognizes the man who was with Bella at the Coffeehouse the evening before. He jumps up and yells, "Leave my wife alone!"

Everyone else startles and looks up to see Liling collapse. Dumaka goes after Haitao who tries to run away and yells, "Stop that man!"

Haitao does not get far. Another figure emerges from behind the trees whom no one has noticed. He catches Haitoa who appears relieved but surprised to see him as he says to the man, "I sure am glad to see you, SPA. But what are *you* doing here?"

SPA just smiles at Haitao and says, "I am taking over from you. Oh, and thank you for your service."

Then SPA suddenly shoves something into Haitao's mouth and within seconds he begins to gasp and turn blue. As Dumaka catches up with them, Haitao falls to the ground and dies instantly.

"Whoa!" Dumaka shouts at the stranger. "What happened?!"

"Turn around and you will see," SPA says.

Dumaka spins around and sees Liling sitting up, appearing to feel much better. He runs back to his wife howling, *"Honey! Are you okay?!"*

"Yes," Liling declares, rubbing her side which now feels completely better. She is able to breathe again. Everyone else gathers around Liling greatly relieved that she is all right.

Liling stares at the stranger coming toward them. There is an uncanny familiarity to him although she is sure that she has never seen his face before.

During the time of the Council, PA, ES, and SPA remained unseen by the Lords and Masters, appearing only as voices on a blank screen. That way they were able to keep their identities concealed.

SPA comes to where Liling is sitting. With a friendly smile he says, "Are you all right, ma'am?"

"I think so," she says, although not quite sure. "And who might you be, sir?"

Bowing, he says, "My name is Sam. I am new to these parts. I saw what you all were doing on the pyramid, and it aroused my curiosity. I sure am glad to see that you are feeling better."

Then he looks at everyone with a warm smile, bows again and says, "I am happy to serve you in whatever way I can."

Ryan interjects, "But what happened to that man over yonder?" he asks, pointing to Haitao.

"Why, I just don't know. He was running towards me and suddenly grabbed his chest. Then he just keeled over and stopped breathing altogether. Poor man!" Sam says with mock sympathy.

"Wow!" Ryan exclaims and the others nod.

As the friends try to understand what has happened, Eve Elli comes over to Sam. And with the knowing smile of a Chrysalene she says to him, "I am Eve Elli, and this is my child, Bi." Pointing to her husband she says, "And that is my husband, Lord Emeka, son of the Late Lord Ekene."

For a split second, Sam/SPA's eyes grow wide as saucers, but he pulls himself together as quickly as he can.

Eve Elli continues with much compassion, "Yes, I do believe that you have come here to serve."

She smiles and bows her head as she says to the one whom she recognizes as SPA, "And I do hope you have already decided, kind sir, which master it is that you are going to serve."

Chapter 11 – Deception

SPA LOOKS DEEP INTO the eyes of the Chrysalene, and Eve Elli looks deep into the soul of the old man. He knows that he cannot fool or hide from her. SPA knows that Eve Elli sees him exactly as he is, who he was meant to be and who he has become.

She sees SPA, ES, and PA's grandfather as a young man growing up in a powerful family. The man started out with great ambitions to serve people and make the world a better place for everyone. He started a business that grew quickly and became a worldwide conglomerate. He had a son who grew up in the lap of luxury and power, who forgot the ideals of his father. Greed took over SPA, ES, and PA's father's heart along with the fear that he might lose it all. He did not trust anyone and grew further and further away from the grandfather's beliefs; the original high ideals that the grandfather of PA, ES, and SPA had for humanity.

SPA, ES, and PA's father divided his family and had his three sons sent to three different continental territories where they were raised by family servants who taught them the greedy and fearful ways of their father. They brothers were renamed after the continental territories that they were raised in, adopting the language and customs of that territory. This way, their father felt that his sons would never trust each other enough to grow into their own power and challenge him for control.

He was, therefore, able to maintain total control of One World. They were all given Universal Translators. But, when the three brothers spoke to each other through their communication devices they became adept at reading each other non-verbally.

Lucifer saw what was going on in the family. He seized the opportunity and approached PA, ES, and SPA's father. Lucifer promised him the security, power, and wealth he craved. The father made a deal with the devil, which rapidly led to the decline and fall of the people and the rise of a new world order ruled by the Council.

The Council and the Upper Crust became obsessed with the idea of people "needing" them; needing their protection, needing to be taken care of, needing their lives to be dominated and controlled by the superiority of the Council and the UC. And that was the world of power, greed, and corruption that PA, ES, and SPA were raised in as the "Highest" rulers of One World.

What the Council and the UC did *not* see however, was something that Eve Elli *does* see as she looks deep into the soul of SPA. She sees how fear was implanted in his heart at a young age, that the only way to control people was to manipulate their free will in whatever way they could. This involved all forms of mind-control including separating people from their history, the knowledge of their past, dividing the people from each other, and ultimately separating them from their true selves.

The fear grew in the hearts of PA, ES, and SPA and it opened the door further for the voice to creep in, the voice of the beast that took over their father's soul. The more they listened to the voice of the fallen angel, the less they could hear the voice of the heavenly realm that was also calling to them. All the brothers could hear was fear, hate, confusion, and separation from that which is kind, loving, and good. The fear grew bigger and uglier in the hearts of PA, ES, and SPA until love and kindness were shut out altogether. However, Lucifer is a destroyer, and he eventually took control of the souls of SPA and his two brothers.

Eve Elli looks into the soul of the old man and sees the final blow that was dealt to him and to his brothers by the beast. To survive their long captivity under ice she sees them slaughtering, one by one, those who were buried with them, the techies and members of the High Overlord Council. And then Eve Elli sees the broken, beaten-down, buried-beneath-the-ice brothers, eating their slaughtered inmates to stay alive.

Finally, she sees SPA's son Ekene and how he died while trying to murder Kookie and his friends. She sees his grandson, her husband Emeka, and his great-granddaughter, the Chrysalene baby Bi, who Eve Elli is holding in her arms right in front of him.

SPA has learned all about the Chrysalenes as he looks at Eve Elli and his great-granddaughter, baby Bi. He knows that *she* knows everything about him and that he cannot deceive her.

A Chrysalene cannot hate, fear, or feel anything other than love and compassion for all living beings. As Eve Elli connects with the soul of her daughter's great-grandfather, who turned human beings into slaves and cannibalized his friends in captivity, her eyes sparkle and radiate with the Light of Heaven.

She smiles and says to SPA, "An Angel of the Lord has appeared before you and said, *'Come, Follow Me.'* May I be of service to you, sir, in helping you find that way."

She smiles, bows to Sam, turns, and sits with the others on the pyramid.

The rest of the group sits there not knowing what to make of it all. But they do feel the familiar peaceful healing of Eve Elli, especially when she lights up and glows with the Light of Heaven.

A few of the villagers go to the fallen stranger, Haitao, and tend to his body. And the rest of them invite Sam to join them as they are about to connect emotionally with a pile of ancient rocks.

* * *

In California, Judy has just heard the news of Phil's passing. She immediately sends word through her pigeons #9 and #10 to the Major at Howard Pharmaceuticals, and Lisa and Kenny at Bear River Garden. Judy also lets everyone know that Doc, Suzie of the Seashells and Rudolpho will be joining her shortly. Lisa, Kenny, and the Major are on their way.

The Major decides not to let Kookie and the others know about Phil until they have completed their mission at the pyramids. He realizes that it is best for them not to be emotionally distracted with grief at this crucial time.

"We are almost there," Rudolpho announces.

As they look out the window of the Cloudtransporter they can see all the new, thriving garden communities below. For Doc, it is a beautiful testimonial to Phil's life, as Judy, Kenny and Lisa worked hard together with her and Phil to help bring those communities to fruition.

Judy now sees the Cloudtransporter coming in for a landing. "Oh, my goodness! They're here!" Judy exclaims to her pigeon buddies #9 and #10, who are nestled snuggly against her neck.

Judy gets excited and heads out to the landing field to meet her dearest and oldest friend Doc. Adam Tate sees Judy and joins her.

Doc is the first one to emerge from the portal, and when she sees Judy coming toward her the two old friends can hardly get to each other fast enough. Judy and Doc embrace each other and both women release tears and grief.

"Oh, honey, I'm *so* sorry!" Judy laments. "Come inside the cottage and let me make you comfortable. Then Adam Tate can sing the healing song of angels to you."

"Thank you, Judy," Doc cries. "I just need to stay here with you folks for a little while."

"You are most welcome to stay here for as long as you like," Judy assures her. "I have already fixed up one of the guest cottages for you."

Doc manages a smile through her tears and Suzie of the Seashells is the next one to collapse in Mama Judy's arms.

The group makes their way to Judy's cottage where the Major, Lisa and Kenny are already waiting.

"Doc," the Major says gently," I'm deeply sorry about Phil, and I'm even more sorry to have to ask you questions at this time. I just have this bad feeling that something is still very wrong there."

Doc looks at him rather puzzled as she says, "You know, I have this strange feeling in the pit of my stomach that you may be right. I have not really been able to think straight since Phil's passing, but now that you mention it something *is* still going on there, isn't it?"

She tells the Major exactly what happened to Phil, from the moment she found him dying and he told her that there was snake venom in the herbal tea, to the encounter that she had with the stranger who showed up out of nowhere.

"And then there's the disappearance of George," Doc says with a shudder. "You're right Major. Something *is very wrong.*"

Sergio, Elena, Suzie, and Rudolpho are listening and have the same gut reaction. Rudolpho says in a solemn tone, "I guess we were all so caught up in Phil's passing that we just haven't been able to hear that other voice inside of us. What do you think we should do, Major?"

The Major looks at all of them gravely. "I think you should all stay here for now, and *I* shall be paying someone a visit at Chiconahui. What did he say his name is, Doc?"

"He said his name is Paul."

Suddenly, Suzie, Rudolpho, Sergio, and Elena look at Doc and then at each other.

Suzie says, "Isn't that the warning we got from Angel? Didn't she say we should beware of Paul?"

"Yes! She did!" the others exclaim.

The Major is very clear now about what he must do and arranges to leave for Chiconahui.

* * *

Yakov and his group are walking to the pyramid near the town of Moscow with their new companion Adam Esau. The mood is somber, and they walk quietly, not really knowing quite what to say.

Yakov finally speaks up and says to Adam Esau, "We are truly grateful sir, for your presence here. I'm afraid that I am not familiar with you though. Did Kookie send you?"

"Not directly," says Adam Esau, "but I did hear from the other Chrysalenes that there was a need. So here I am ready to serve you."

This is a plausible explanation to Yakov and the others since the Chrysalenes are telepathic.

Adam Esau continues, "Might I enquire, gracious sir, what your need is so that I may serve you well."

Yakov, Neely, and Vi look at each other and sigh. "It is a long, complicated story," Yakov confesses. "I just don't know what to do with our new arrival over there," he says, pointing to Pasha.

ES looks at Pasha with the best expressionless face he can muster, and Pasha looks away petrified.

Vi looks at Adam Esau warily. Her intuition is flaring. "And since you are a Chrysalene I'm sure you already know what our predicament is, Adam Esau."

"Uh, yes, ma'am!" says ES, remembering what Bella told him. "Indeed, I do."

ES gives Pasha a sly grin that the others cannot see and again Pasha turns away in great fear. He knows the brutality that the former members of the Council of One World are capable of, and Pasha is thinking that he probably does not have much longer to live.

"I am looking forward to your council then," Yakov responds. He is relieved to think that Adam Esau will give them good advice regarding what to do with Pasha. Remembering the time when Viktor helped the Alliance defeat the Council and their allies, Yakov also wants very much to help Viktor, Marie, and their two sons.

The group arrives at a clearing and standing before them is an ancient pyramid. It is covered in vegetation and eroded from the effects of the elements. The villagers from the nearby town have already gotten there and are peacefully meditating on the ancient structure.

Neely looks at the others from their group and says, "It is so exquisite, is it not?"

Marie is overcome with emotion as she agrees with Neely, "It just takes your breath away!"

They all approach the ancient stone structure and find a place to sit. Breathing in the energy of the Soul of the Stones, Yakov, Neely, Vi, Viktor, and Marie instantly feel at peace. The only ones who stop before reaching the pyramid and stay just out of hearing range from the others are ES and Pasha.

Finally, ES puts his hand in his pocket, looks at Pasha one more time and says to him, "Well, Master Commandant Pasha. Now what indeed *AM* I to do with you?"

But before Pasha can say anything or ES can pull anything lethal out of his pocket, a woman's voice is heard right behind them saying, "Hello there, my good men. I was told that you are in need of a Chrysalene. My name is Eve Gerda."

Smiling and bowing humbly before them she continues, "May I be of service to you?"

ES lets go of the poisonous herbs, removes his hand from his pocket and looks at her with a blank stare.

The others all see and recognize Eve Gerda and Vi calls out to her as she walks over, "Well hello, Eve Gerda! I'm *so* happy to see you! Won't you come and join us at the pyramid?"

Smiling and bowing to Vi, Eve Gerda says, "It is an honor to see you again dear Vi. So happy that I can be of service to you."

"We are most grateful to have you, holy woman." Vi glances at the two men standing there who appear to be frozen in time. She says to them, "Well, are you both joining us then?"

Of course, *ES* knows that the Chrysalene Eve Gerda knows exactly who he is.

* * *

In Cavern Village, Wyoming, Kookie, Angie, and Leo have just entered the cave in search of the Hidden Cavern and the Great Quartz Crystal. Kookie and Angie are grateful to have Leo along as they enter the underground maze of dark chambers. Kookie turns on his Metatron device to see what kind of reading he gets. The earth frequencies in the cave have an unknown effect on anything electronic, and Kookie knows that he will be out of contact with the outside world while he is in there. But as far as the Great Quartz Crystal goes, he is curious to see how the energetic hook-up works with Metatron and the pyramids. He must also track the time it takes them to get to the Hidden Cavern so he can go back outside, contact the others, and tell them exactly when to turn on their Metatron devices.

"Just follow me," Leo says. "It shouldn't take us more than 20 minutes or so to get there."

Kookie and Angie are excited as they descend into the underground world of crystals.

Leo is thinking about what Kookie explained to him regarding the energy of the pyramids, and the purpose of connecting them with the Great Quartz Crystal.

They stop for a rest and Leo asks, "So Kookie, what exactly do you expect to happen here once everything is all hooked up to Metatron?"

Kookie grins as he taps the tips of his finger together. "Ah!" he exclaims pointing his index finger in the air. "It's really quite simple. Rocks, crystals, and stones are ancient as are their memory and wisdom of all things related to our planet."

Angie interjects, "They have a soul and a deep love and respect for all life on earth, as do the trees." She smiles tenderly at Kookie for a moment, reminiscing about her captivity in the underworld and the wisdom she received from the tree roots. "I once got to spend some time among the tree roots, and they told me the most amazing things about our past."

Leo goes wide-eyed when he hears this. "Wow! What did they tell you?"

"Well, the most important thing," Angie says, "is that they shared their feelings with me about how sad *our* suffering makes them feel. They truly are most compassionate and will do anything to help people."

"Whoa! No kidding!" Leo exclaims, and asks, "Is the connection with the pyramids a way that can help us?"

"Yes, it can," Angie replies, "by helping us remember our past. But we humans have a tendency to forget, especially those things that are too painful to remember. The activation of the pyramids all over the world will help us to not only remember the darker parts of our history, but most important, to *learn* from them."

Kookie adds, "Unfortunately that is something humanity does not, as a whole, do very well."

Leo is thinking about his own past as a mercenary commando, sent to do Bella's bidding. He says, "But what about those memories that are painful? Maybe we bury them down deep for a reason. What will happen when those horrible things come to the surface?"

"Yes, we are concerned about that," acknowledges Angie, "And also, after activation, what will happen to those with bad intentions? Will they learn even more devious ways to control people?"

"Whoa!" Leo cries out. "We certainly don't want the bad guys to have absolute power again! We *know* the damage that can come of that one, and what One World became under the control of PA, ES, and SPA!"

"But this time," Angie says, "the Light of the Spirit will illuminate the souls of all those who follow the path of love. And as those souls fill with clarity and divine purpose, to quote the Monarch Angel," (Angie poses and flutters like a butterfly) "*"We shall see who wins, human creature!"*"

Leo and Kookie laugh and nod in agreement.

"Well," says Kookie, pointing his index finger in the air, "if you two have had a good rest let us continue to the Great Crystal, shall we?!"

And up above in the heavenly realm a voice giggles, *Hee, hee, hee! Nice one, Angie creature!*

* * *

Eve Elli, Emeka, and the others at the pyramid near Johannesburg have settled down comfortably on the stones. Sam has joined them too, although he is decidedly *not* comfortable.

After the commotion with Haitao and Liling they are all a bit frazzled, so Eve Elli sings a healing angel song to everyone. Her sweet sounds fill the air with soothing, healing energy, and soon the group feels much better.

Even Sam notices that he has relaxed a bit. He closes his eyes and allows the experience to wash over him. It is not long before the Soul of the Stones speaks to the hearts of everyone present.

Beloved beings of the earth and light, hear me as I speak to your heart. Know how very loved you are by the Infinite and all His ancient creations. We rejoice in your happiness and weep in your suffering. We understand the pain of your lessons not learned.

Beloved beings, we know that for most of you gathered here, those hard lessons have already been learned and that you already have much Light from the Heavens around you. It is for this reason that you are already more powerful against the forces of the underworld than you realize. The activation will raise your vibration which is already quite high and cause much happiness.

However, for those who have not already learned the life lessons you have, their experience will be quite different. Depending upon how far down the dark tunnel they have fallen, their reactions can be very frightening. But you will all be there to help and guide them as you begin to truly know and experience Divine Love. And with your sudden transformation, remembering your connection to Spirit and who you truly are, you will be able to lead the rest of the world into a higher state of love and compassion. The doorway of wisdom and love will remain an open portal for all those who seek knowledge in generations to come.

I AM here bringing Light to your spirit and hope to those who have greater lessons yet to learn.

The voice of the Soul of the Stones recedes, and everyone opens their eyes. An inexplicable peace fills the hearts of Liling, Dumaka, Mimi, Ryan, Emeka, the Chrysalenes, and all the villagers of the Garden of Bi. They are all smiling, chuckling, and sighing with relief.

Dumaka says, "Wow! That was great! If that is how we are going to feel after the activation, bring it on!"

Eve Elli smiles and responds, "Remember that Angel will be here for you, too. And so will I."

Everyone feels blissful and ready for the big activation; everyone that is, except one.

SPA hears the voice of Lucifer in his head, and he is trembling with terror.

YOU FOOL! *DO YOU DOUBT MY POWERS?! WHEN THIS ACTIVATION IS DONE, IT IS **I** WHO **WILL HAVE ABSOLUTE POWER!** AND IF YOU EVEN THINK ABOUT RESISTING ME, **YOU WILL EXPERIENCE MY FULL-BLOWN WRATH! FOR ALL OF ETERNITY!***

Sam/SPA collapses, and everyone rushes to him.

Eve Elli puts her hands up to stop them. "This man's lessons have already begun. First, he must decide which way to turn and then he must reach out and ask for help," she says to everyone.

Eve Elli Looks at SPA, unconscious on the ground. She leans over him, speaking tenderly to his soul in a voice that no one else can hear:

"Those of the Light are standing by, ready to step in and help you." Then Eve Elli kisses his forehead as she whispers, "And so am I . . . Grandpa SPA."

Chapter 12 – Activation

THE MAJOR KNOWS there is not a moment to lose. He has just arrived at the Village of Chiconahui and Eve Maria is there to greet him.

"Hello there, holy woman," the Major says as Eve Maria smiles and bows her head before him. "It's good to see you, ma'am."

"You are most welcome here Major. Bless you, kind sir. I am Eve Maria, and we are all so happy that you have come."

"Uh . . . hm . . . the Major stutters and then pauses, breathing deep. "So, where *is* everybody then, Eve Maria?"

"They are all in their huts," she explains, "and the Chrysalenes are taking care of them."

"Is there . . . uh . . . something wrong, Eve Maria?"

"Not too long ago," she elaborates, "the villagers were doing rather poorly just as they are now. Then Doc and Phil came and made them an herbal tea. They spread much love around along with their tea and the people improved rapidly."

"I see," says the Major. "So then, what is happening now?"

"Well sir, since the passing of Phil, and Doc's departure they seem to be doing poorly again. In fact, they are not doing well at all."

"How so?"

Eve Maria lowers her eyes and says, "As much as we have tried to help, sir, the villagers seem to be descending to a place from which they cannot find their way out. We have kept them fed and nourished but their will to live looks to be almost completely gone. We have been losing them a little bit more each day."

"I don't understand," says the Major. "Can't you Chrysalenes help with your healing?"

"It is one thing to help with healing, and yes we can do that," explains Eve Maria. "But it is another thing entirely to interfere with the will of any living person. As the Creator has given His people free will, all we can do is help each other to heal and feel better. However, if there is a force that is taking the will to live away from someone then we are powerless to stop it."

The Major is beside himself now, scratching his head with confusion and frustration. "Do you know what this force is? The force that is taking the villager's will to live away from them. And why didn't the Creator call on someone to come here and help the villagers with all this? Especially since you guys aren't allowed to do anything without messing with free will?!"

Eve Maria gives the Major a big smile as she says, "But the Creator *did* call on someone, kind sir. And here you are!"

"I . . . uh . . . Oh!" the Major stammers a bit embarrassed and befuddled. "So then, this is all *my* job?"

Eve Maria chuckles as she replies, "Yes sir! Indeed, it is, kind Major! Come, let me show you what's happening."

Eve Maria takes him to the pyramid. Along the way the Major remembers when Eve Elli was little and how frustrated the three-year-old girl was, not to be allowed to explain certain things to her Gramma Mimi. Mama Eve Zula explained to little Eve Elli that people must always learn their own lessons and that those who are divinely gifted such as the Chrysalenes, are not to interfere with the lessons of others. Eve Elli had to learn at a very young age the difference between helping people and letting them grow.

Eve Maria echoes the Major's thoughts. "The lessons of humans are considered sacred, my friend. It is a person's direct connection to the Creator. So, if we try to help them too much then we are actually coming between them and the Creator. It's a fine line, but one that every Chrysalene must learn not to cross."

"Wow," says the Major. "That really does make sense when you put it like that."

They have arrived at the clearing of the Pyramid of Chiconahui and Eve Maria turns to the Major. "Well sir, there is the problem."

The Major looks at the pyramid and sees an elderly gentleman sitting on the stones.

"*That's* my problem? That old guy sitting over there?" the Major asks in surprise. He is unable to imagine that some old guy is the cause of all the trouble that Eve Maria is talking about.

"Yes, sir. That he is. And I'm sure you will do just fine," she says with a smile. "To quote a dear friend of the Chrysalene's, '*Go for it, human creature, and we'll see who wins!*'"

She chuckles and heads back to the village.

The Major is left standing there by himself. "Well," he says out loud, "I guess I had better go over and introduce myself to this guy and find out who he is. And what he wants."

* * *

"We're almost there!" Leo exclaims to Kookie and Angie.

The three of them have been walking in silent wonder, taking in the magnificence and beauty of the crystalline formations. The deeper they go into the caverns the more magically surreal the underground panorama becomes, and the more intense the energy feels. Finally, they reach the passageway that leads into the Hidden Cavern and all eyes go wide. Their voices rise in an awestruck chorus: *"WHOA!"*

The Hidden Cavern is covered in clear quartz crystals from top to bottom and all around. When the soft light from Metatron flashes on the crystals it radiates a shimmering glow of all the colors of the rainbow. Kookie, Angie, and Leo feel as if they have stepped inside a gigantic kaleidoscopic prism. The colors dance all around them and at the center is the largest and most spectacular crystal they have ever seen: the Great Quartz Crystal.

Kookie's jaw drops. "Wow! I feel like I've just stepped into another world!"

Angie adds, "And another time!"

They tip-toe around the crystals on the ground to get to the spectacular centerpiece. Angie is the first to reach out and put her hands on the enormous energizer and she shrieks with delight. *"YEEHA! HUZZAH! YAHOO!"*

The men laugh and Kookie says to her, "That good, eh honey? Lemme have some!"

He puts his hands next to hers on the giant crystal. *"OH YEAH! OH, HONEY! OH BABY!"* Kookie cries out. Then, as an afterthought, "Oh, sweetie! I *wish* I had brought my tuba with me!"

Angie giggles and goes over to their gear. She reaches into the large bag, and to her husband's great excitement pulls out his tuba. Then she digs around further and finds the mouthpiece and Kookie is sure that he has just died and gone to tuba heaven. He begins to serenade his wife as the gentle echo of soft, pastel tones from Kookie's tuba bounce off the crystal walls of the Hidden

Cavern. Angie, Kookie, and Leo are entranced by the beauty and intensity of the power flowing through them.

A thought occurs to Kookie, and he stops playing. Looking at Leo and Angie he says, "You know, I feel like I just need to keep going with this."

The other two nod in agreement and understanding.

Then Kookie turns to Leo and says, "Do you think you can go back outside and message everyone on Metatron for me? I just need to be sure that they are all ready to go and we can set a time for activation."

Leo says enthusiastically, "Absolutely! Just show me how the thing works!"

"Great!"

Kookie proceeds to show Leo how to use the Metatron device for communication. They need to be all set and ready to go, activating the pyramids near Moscow and Johannesburg, tying them into the already activated pyramid of Chiconahui.

"Thank you, Leo. Now I can stay here and keep playing to my darling Angie, and when you come back the rest of it will all be very simple."

"You got it, my man!" Leo says as he scurries off to the mouth of the cave.

* * *

At the pyramid near the town of Moscow, the villagers of the Garden of Suzi along with Yakov and his group are settled down on the stones, enjoying the peaceful atmosphere. Vi is happily escorting Eve Gerda to the pyramid when Yakov and Neely come over to greet her.

"Well, hello there, Eve Gerda! So good to see you again!" Neely exclaims.

She is very happy to see a familiar Chrysalene face. Vi is not the only one who feels a bit suspicious of Adam Esau. Neely and Yakov look warily at ES who is off in the distance with Pasha.

Yakov's Metatron device goes off. He looks at it and says to everyone, "Hey! It's Kookie!"

He accepts the incoming message and Leo appears on the screen. "Hi there, this is Leo," he says, introducing himself to Yakov. "Kookie is at the Great Quartz Crystal of the Hidden Cavern, and he asked me to get in touch with everyone. He wants you all to know that he is ready for activation!"

"Whoa!" exclaims Yakov. "You mean, like *now?*"

"Yes, sir! Just as soon as you can."

"Well," Yakov thinks about it for a moment, "we are at the pyramid now, so I guess we're all set and ready to go!"

"That's great!" says Leo. "I will get a hold of the others and confirm an exact time for activation. Since the devices are already synchronized with each other, all you will have to do is hit the button on your end at the exact same time as everyone else."

"Thank you, bratan. I shall be awaiting further instructions."

Leo and Yakov disconnect, and everyone gets excited.

"Here we go!" Yakov exclaims.

Vi, Neely, Yakov, and Eve Gerda, climb onto the pyramid and find a comfortable spot. In their excitement they seem to have forgotten their suspicions regarding Adam Esau. ES glares at Pasha as he puts his index finger to his lips, indicating that Pasha needs to keep quiet . . . *or else*! The two men climb onto the pyramid along with the others and find a place to sit. Eve Gerda leads everyone in prayer and meditation and Yakov anxiously awaits Leo's call.

From the bowels of hell Lucifer sends a message to ES, who is also anxiously awaiting his master's call.

Hear me, fool! This is my command! At the moment of activation, you are to kill Pasha. It will strike fear in the hearts of everyone there. This will cause the dark energy of their fear to spread, instead of the energy of the light. I shall receive that fear and send it to all humans around the world. YOU WILL NOT FAIL ME, ES! **YOU WILL NOT FAIL!**

* * *

At the pyramid near Johannesburg, Liling receives an incoming message from Leo. He explains to her what he just told Yakov and asks when they think they can be ready for activation.

With SPA lying unconscious on the ground and Eve Elli having just told them all to leave him be for the moment, Liling, Dumaka, and the others become agitated.

Liling turns to everyone with an imploring look and says, "Well, what do you all think?"

They, in turn, look to Eve Elli, who closes her eyes and listens for the call of her messenger and guide. Then Eve Elli says, "The message is quite clear: *Hop to it, human creatures!*"

Everyone chuckles with relief and each one says in turn, "Okay! You got it! Yes, ma'am! Thanks, Angel!"

With eager anticipation they get positioned on the stones and Eve Elli leads them in prayer and meditation.

With her Metatron device ready to go, Liling waits for the word from Leo.

* * *

The Major approaches the old man sitting on the Pyramid of Chiconahui. PA looks up, smiles, bows his head, and nods.

Thinking back to the last conversation he had with Doc regarding Angel's warning about a guy named Paul, the Major looks at the man and says to him, "Hello there, I am Master John, son of Master Howard of Howard Pharmaceuticals. Although most people call me the Major. Are you by any chance the one they call Paul? . . . Sir?"

"Indeed," the man says.

The Major is on his guard, so he decides to change his tactics with Paul.

"Ah!" the Major exclaims putting his index finger in the air, imitating his bro. "Do tell, Paul, sir. You must be a truly great man to have lived to such a ripe old age! Would you be willing to share your secrets with me, Wise One, regarding your longevity?"

PA searches his memory for information about this man. He remembers Master Howard of Howard Pharmaceuticals and his complicity with the Council back in those days. He now wonders if this foolish-sounding man can also be bought for a price.

PA looks at him sternly and says, "So, you are the descendant of Master Howard and current Master of Howard Pharmaceuticals. Yes?"

"Oh, yes! Yes indeed! Indeed, I am!" The Major replies, trying to look, sound, and act, just as stupid as he possibly can. He thinks to himself, *I wish Vi could see this!* which almost causes him to laugh out loud. He quickly pulls himself back into character and says, "I have come here to serve, my good man. Is there any way I can be of service to *you?*"

Suddenly, PA drops his guard and says to the Major, "Yes son. There is a way in which you can be of service to me."

The Major looks at him with expectation and PA says, "You can tell me all about this *activation thing* that is supposed to happen."

"Oh that!" the Major snickers. "That's something my friends are playing around with. I don't even know what it's all about. I guess they just like to have fun with their games being the geniuses that they are, and all."

The Major sees that he has PA's undivided attention, so he goes in for the kill. He leans into PA, looks around as if checking to make sure that no one is listening, and whispers, "I would be ever so grateful, Paul, sir, if you could help me with this thing. You see, someone is supposed to contact me soon and tell me what to do. But all this technology has me freaked out, if you follow what I'm saying. I mean I'm just not the genius that those guys are, if you know what I mean."

"Yes indeed, Major, I *do* know what you mean!" PA's thought of what he can do to this fool is beyond his wildest most ecstatic dreams. Which is exactly where the Major wants him.

"Okay, so when I get the message, I would really appreciate it if you could enter the code and frequency for me. I get so confused with this stuff. And I *really* don't want to let Kookie, Yakov, and Liling down."

Hearing the names of his old enemies throws PA into an internal rage which he tries with all his might to conceal from the

Major. He says as calmly as he can while glaring into the Major's eyes, "Just tell me what to do, son."

The Major gets up and starts looking around acting as if he is "checking out" the pyramid. He is muttering to himself about where a good place will be to sit for the activation and other such things that come into his head. He is playing for time until he hears from Kookie, hoping that "Paul" does not catch on to the set-up.

And then the message comes in. It is Leo giving the Major the same instructions that he has just given everyone else. They agree on a time and the Major pretends to be pressing a few buttons.

He looks at Paul and says, "Now, when the timer goes off, I will need you to enter the code for me. Thank you *soo* much, my good man!"

"Glad I can be of some help, son of Master Howard," Paul says with a wary grin. For one moment, PA thinks that this may all be a bit *too* easy. This guy just can't be as ridiculous as he sounds.

* * *

Leo returns to the Hidden Cavern and announces, "Everybody is ready!" Looking at the timer on the Metatron device he says, "Twenty-one minutes and 14 seconds to go!"

"Thank you, my good man," says Kookie who has been meditating with Angie.

"So, what happens now?" Leo asks.

Tapping the tips of his fingers together, eyes still closed, smiling in a state of pure bliss, Kookie says, "Oh you know, we just wait."

"Oh . . . *kay!* And *then* what?" Leo inquires with a trace of impatience.

Angie chuckles and points to the Metatron device that Leo is still holding. "When the timer goes off, we hold Metatron against the Great Quartz Crystal and push this button right here. The folks at the Pyramid of Chiconahui, and the pyramids near Moscow and Johannesburg will also put their devices against one of the stones and press this same button at the same time. The codes are all preset, so the energy from the crystal will go to Chiconahui first, connecting with the energy of the activated pyramid. Then it will transmit to Moscow and Johannesburg, activating those pyramids. Finally, the triangulation effect will kick in and all other pyramids around the world will be activated as well."

Angie sits back and taps the tips of *her* fingers together, smiling, in a state of pure bliss. She tells the amazed former commando, "And that will all take place in about a one-second window of time!"

"Wow!" Leo exclaims.

"Yes, wow!" Angie agrees. "And that is why we all must be in perfect sync with our timers.

* * *

The Major looks at his timer which shows only 10 minutes till activation. At the same time, he watches Paul carefully and can see that the old man is not 100 percent sold on the "Helpless Fool" yarn that he has been spinning. *If this geezer catches on things could go seriously wrong. Better do this now.*

He hits a few buttons.

"Aha!" exclaims the Major. "One minute to go!"

He reaches over to Paul and hands him the Metatron device. "If you hit that button there and scroll down, you should see the numbers 777. When the timer goes off, hit the 777 immediately!"

PA looks at him with definite suspicion. The Major sees the wariness in Paul's eyes, so he quickly hops off the pyramid and starts jumping around howling, "Ooo! I'm so nervous! I can't stand it! No! No! *NO!*"

PA just shakes his head and looks back down at the device. The timer goes off. PA presses the button on the numbers 777.

The Major stops jumping and howling. He looks at his companion, catches his eye, smiles brightly, and shrugs his shoulders as the thought goes through his head, *Gotcha!*

Suddenly, fear grips PA as he looks at the Major and a memory comes flooding back to him, screaming in his head: *THE DEVICE! THE ONE WE COULD NEVER FIND!* ***KOOKIE'S SECRET WEAPON!"***

In a flash, PA throws the Metatron device to the ground and the Major runs to pick it up. "Thanks, bro!" he says with a big smile.

He pushes a button on the device and rejoins the countdown with Kookie. Five minutes to go and the Major is about to get back on the pyramid when he sees the change that has already started to come over his "buddy" Paul. PA sits with his eyes glazed over as if in a trance. There is a trace of a smile on his face.

The Major goes over to PA and escorts him off the pyramid. "Why don't you just sit yourself down right here on the ground, bro. I'll be right back. Then you and I can have a *real* conversation."

PA's smile brightens a little and the Major smiles back. Then he jumps back on the pyramid and gets ready for the activation.

* * *

Yakov holds his device against the pyramid near Moscow.

Liling holds her device against the pyramid near Johannesburg.

The Major holds his device against the Chiconahui pyramid and chuckles at his buddy on the ground, who is now grinning from ear to ear and waving at him.

Kookie holds his Metatron against the Great Quartz Crystal of the Hidden Cavern. The timer hits zero and everyone presses their button.

Suddenly, there is a flash of light in the sky. It bursts into a myriad of kaleidoscopic patterns and a rainbow of colors, lighting up the triangulation and extending to all the other pyramids around the globe. There is a radiant, glowing warmth covering everyone at the activation sites and in the nearby garden communities.

In the village of Chiconahui, the villagers who were feeling deeply depressed suddenly feel a cloud lifting from their spirits, and those in the immediate vicinity of any pyramid around the world feel inexplicable elation.

Kookie and his group buzz with exhilaration as they head for the mouth of the cave. He can hardly wait to talk to the others and see how they are all feeling.

Yakov, Neely, Vi, and Pasha feel the same ecstasy, hugging each other and laughing at nothing until tears roll down their cheeks.

ES is confused and deeply troubled. He has suddenly forgotten what he is supposed to do. In fact, he cannot even hear the voice of Lucifer who is screaming at him.

Eve Gerda approaches ES and says, "Well, hello there, Adam Esau."

He looks at her with a growing suspicion in his heart. He thinks, *She MUST know who I am. Will she tell the others?* Fear begins to take over and he realizes that he must get away from there as quickly as he can.

Eve Elli has been sitting next to the comatose body of SPA. Little Baby Bi is in her arms, and she is the first one to see SPA stir.

"OOO!" Bi says, pointing to SPA.

Liling, Dumaka, and the rest have been laughing and hugging each other, and now they see what has caught Bi's attention.

"Oh, my goodness!" exclaims Liling as she rushes over to the man who calls himself Sam. His eyes open and he sits up. Liling says to him, "Can we help you, sir?"

SPA is groggy and confused. He looks around at everyone and is suddenly gripped with terror. He forces himself to rise, his movements jerky, his eyes wide like a frightened woodland creature.

He starts to run.

The Major suddenly feels blissful and jubilant. He looks at Paul who is sitting on the ground and smiling, happy as a clam. The Major goes over and slaps him on the back. "Hey there, bro! How's it going?"

"Oh, Major!" PA says, "I'm feeling simply wonderful!"

"Glad to hear it, Paul. I'm feeling rather thunderstruck myself! Ha!"

PA looks confused for a moment and says to the Major, "Paul? Who's Paul?"

"Why I thought that was your name, my man. At least that is what you told me when I asked."

"Oh! Ha, ha!" PA says, "Yes, I remember now. I have been called other things in my life, too. My name is PA, Highest Lord of the Council of One World. Can you imagine? And my two brothers are called ES and SPA. Yes, indeed! We were named after the Continental Territories that we ruled over. Of course, that was daddy's idea. Can you imagine anything so silly?" PA slaps his knees and lets out a great big guffaw.

The Majors eyes grow wide as saucers. He is frozen in shock and his jaw has dropped to the ground. He is unable to stop staring at one of the three brothers who the Alliance defeated, freeing the people from mind-control and bondage, and who, along with his brothers, went missing and was presumed dead 18 years ago.

The Major cannot take his eyes off PA and is barely able to move his hand to reach for Metatron and send out an urgent message to Kookie, Yakov, and Liling.

* * *

Deep in the bowels of hell Lucifer is in a rage. *"Queen Bella! You will come to me! NOW! And bring that infernal serpent with you!"*

Bella appears in an instant with the infernal serpent draped around her neck.

"Why husband," she says, *"You seem distraught. What is the matter?"*

Narrowing his eyes at her the beast goes into a screaming rage. Andre is quaking and Bella is confused. The beast bellows at her, *"THOSE THREE IDIOTS HAVE FAILED ME!* ***AGAIN!"***

"WHAT?!" shrieks Bella. *"What do you mean they failed you? All they had to do was feed the poisonous plant to George, Pasha, and Haitao, gain the enemies' trust, and then feed the plant to any one of them. Just one, between the three of them! Then the energy transfer from the activation would have reversed and sent everyone into a state of extreme fear, hate, and paranoia, giving YOU absolute power! How could they mess up something that simple?! WHAT HAPPENED?!"*

"I TRUSTED WEAK-MINDED BUFFOONS! ***THAT'S WHAT HAPPENED!***

"But not anymore, my dearest Bella. YOU will go there and DESTROY THOSE THREE! I WANT THEM HERE! IN HELL! NOW! You will make each one of those mindless creatures commit a crime against one of Kookie's companions; one of betrayal, deceit, and murder. And when they are caught in the act, you are to kill them! That will bring them straight to me. And THEN I shall have my way with them FOR ALL OF ETERNITY!"

Lucifer adds with an evil grin, "And then my dear, you can whip them with your most exquisite passion for ever and ever."

Bella licks her lips and moans with pleasure, "Oooo yeees, my lord! Yeees! I shall not let you down!"

PART 3
ABSOLUTE POWER

Chapter 13 – Grace

KOOKIE, ANGIE, AND LEO return to the mouth of the cave with crystals they gathered from the Hidden Cavern. Their pouches are filled with the divine treasures of the earth. As they compare their crystals with each other, Leo imagines how his wife and daughters are going to love these.

"Oh, look!" Leo exclaims holding up a crystal as big as his hand. "Isn't this beautiful?!"

"Yes, it is," Angie agrees. "And if you hold it against your chest, you will hear the voice of the crystal speaking to you heart!"

"No kidding!" Leo proclaims with wonder as he proceeds to listen to the crystal.

Kookie remembers that he must check in with the other groups. He goes into Metatron's message system and to his consternation sees red lights flashing from Liling, Yakov, and . . . *The Major? Now what the blazes is the Major red-flashing me about?*

Kookie listens to his messages as they walk back to the Garden of Tom. As he is hearing all the details from everyone, his eyes grow wider, and his pace slows.

Suddenly Kookie stops short, and yells, *"HOLY SCHMOLLY!"*

Angie and Leo stop, and Angie looks at her husband like he has suddenly lost his mind. "Honey?" she ventures in a hesitant voice.

"WHOA!" Kookie wails and looks at his wife. He howls, *"We gotta go! Right now!"*

"What? My husband! What is going on?"

He catches his breath and says, "PA, ES, and SPA are alive!"

"WHAT?!" Leo and Angie both cry out.

"They are back from the underground ice palace where they were trapped all this time. The spirit of Bella is giving them their orders from Lucifer, and between the three brothers and Bella they have amassed an army of mercenaries!"

"WHAT?!"

"A whole battalion of former Major Commandants of One World are awaiting further instructions at their Yucatan location, the former estate of Lord Josef who also died in the blast that killed Lady Bella. And it is not far from Chiconahui!"

Leo is outraged. *"INSTRUCTIONS?! FROM WHOM?!"* he growls.

Kookie's voice calms down. "Instructions from PA, ES, and SPA."

Angie is dumbfounded. "Are you sure? I mean, how did anyone find out all of this?" she asks.

"Do you remember the 777 program we created and installed in all the Metatron devices?"

"You mean the one that reverses the polarity of the duality as you are always so fond of saying in geek double-talk?" she snickers.

"Yup! That's the one, honey!" Kookie exclaims pointing his index finger in the air. "The Major encountered PA without knowing his identity at the Pyramid of Chiconahui just prior to activation. He was told by one of the Chrysalenes there that this guy was causing *some kind of problem* among the people. When the Major realized she was right and that this guy was up to something, he decided to zap him with 777."

"Really? No kidding!" Angie quips. "So, what happened?"

"PA was turned inside out upside down and backwards, in a manner of speaking," Kookie replies.

Angie laughs and Leo shakes his head. Leo finally says, "You wanna let *me* in on this?"

Kookie is tapping the tips of his fingers together as he says, "It means that whatever PA was before, he is now his own polar opposite!"

"WHOA!" they both exclaim, somewhat amused.

"In his newfound state of Mr. Nice, he has just revealed all their plans to the Major. And the Major has shared everything with Yakov and Liling regarding ES and SPA showing up at *their* locations! From what Liling and Yakov are reporting, two men who they believe to be ES and SPA, took off in a state of panic after the activation. Seems like they have become paranoid or something. But Yakov, Liling, and the gang want us all to meet up as fast as we can at Judy's Garden and figure out where we go from here."

Turning to Leo he says, "That is one of our safehouses and it is where they are all headed now."

"But, honey," Angie says to Kookie in a serious tone. "As I recall isn't the 777-effect temporary?"

Kookie sighs, "I'm afraid so."

"Well then," Leo queries, "how long do you anticipate that PA will remain Mr. Nice?"

"I honestly do not know," Kookie admits. "I only just invented the thing. You could say that this is a test run."

"Good grief!" exclaims Leo.

"Exactly," says Kookie. "And that is why we have no time to lose. We must be off to the Garden of Judy immediately!"

Leo starts to fidget and asks, "Well . . . um . . . I don't suppose you would mind if I come along with you? I'm sure Dakota and the girls will understand."

Kookie says, "It would be my pleasure to have you, my good man. We must leave as soon as possible though, so after you let your family know Angie and I will be waiting for you at the Cloudtransporter.

"Thank you, thank you, Lord Kookie! I shall be very quick indeed!" Leo exclaims with great excitement as he rushes off to tell his wife.

* * *

The Major talked PA into leaving Chiconahui and coming with him to the Garden of Judy and they are the first of the group to arrive. He introduces his companion as Paul and does not explain to Judy who he is, only that they met at Chiconahui.

"Hello, Paul!" Judy exclaims as she gives him a big hug with #9 and #10 snug up against her neck.

The pigeons joyously flap their wings and Paul exclaims, "My goodness! Aren't they the friendly sort!"

Judy laughs, "Indeed they are! Go ahead and put your hand out to them."

Paul looks very perplexed as he extends his hand to the birds. And to his amazement they extend their feet to shake hands.

"WHOA!" Paul exclaims and giggles with delight.

The Major, however, has to cover his face to stifle a huge guffaw. "Well Paul, looks like you've made yourself a coupla new little friends!"

To himself he is thinking, *of all the genius programs Kookie has created, this 777 thing is something else! Take a former murderous global dictator who enslaved all of humanity, and turn him into a giggly puddle of mush over two pigeons! NOW DON'T THAT BEAT ALL!*

He shakes his head and smiles in disbelief.

"BWAHAHA!" The Major cannot hold it in. Judy and Paul just look at him and they all laugh together, having a grand old time with #9 and #10.

Adam Tate and the other Chrysalenes hear the exuberant commotion and come over to join in. Of course, the Chrysalenes already know everything about PA and are just as amazed at his transformation as the Major.

"Welcome, brother," Adam Tate says to Paul with a great big grin. "May we, and the pigeons, be of service to you!"

* * *

When ES left the Pyramid at the Garden of Suzi, he took off as fast as he could for the spot in the woods where he left the Cloudtranporter. He is now safely in the air and on his way back to the estate in the Yucatan.

SPA, however, lost all sense of reality. He ran off into the nearby forest in Johannesburg where he is now cowering and trembling in fear. Paranoia is deepening and he cannot move. He has lost the ability to speak, crouching on the ground and shooting quick glances around at every noise he hears, both real and imagined.

Then he sees someone in the distance who is coming towards him. At first SPA jumps up and starts to run away, but then he senses a familiarity to the woman in the red cape. She is holding a staff with the head of a serpent.

Bella smiles as she approaches him. "Well, hello there, SPA," she says calmly. "You seem to have lost your way."

SPA's fear decreases as he looks at her. He allows Bella to come right up to him as she says, "There, there, brother SPA. No need to fear me. I will help you feel better . . . much better . . . *all* better," she says with a smile. "Would you like that? Do you want my help? If you do just put your hand out to me."

SPA looks down and gives Bella a slight nod. He extends his hand to her.

And deep in the bowels of hell Lucifer lifts his head, closes his eyes, grins, and hisses, *Aaah, yesssss!*

ES is about halfway across the ocean headed for the Yucatan when he is suddenly aware of a voice in his head speaking to him with great urgency saying, *Your brother is in trouble. He needs you. Go and get him. I will program the coordinates on your craft.*

And low and behold, ES sees the numbers on the screen in front of him changing. His destination is now a forest near Johannesburg.

* * *

Judy has made the announcement to all the garden villagers, the Chrysalenes, and the visiting guests that Kookie, Yakov, Liling, and all their companions are on their way over. "They will be here very soon!" Judy exclaims.

"Great!" the villagers call out as everyone is anxious to hear what happened at the pyramids.

Doc comes over to the Major. She looks at him with tears welling up and says to him, "Soon it will be time to let everyone else know about Phil."

He puts his arms around her and says, "We are all here for you Doc."

The Major is thinking about both men they have recently lost. With Doc weeping on his shoulder, he looks up to the heavens and says, "Bless you, Phil and dad. We will always love you."

PA walks around the garden community with Adam Tate and enjoys the sunlight, the fruit and vegetable gardens, and the healing company of the Chrysalenes. He shares the story of his younger years with Adam Tate as he did with the Major. And while they are walking around something catches his eye off in the distance.

"My, what a beautiful garden! Would it be all right if we go over there, kind sir?" PA asks Adam Tate.

"It is my pleasure to serve you, Brother PA. And it is especially a great honor to take you to that particular garden."

The two men walk over to Henrietta's Rose Garden. It is blossoming with roses of all assorted colors and the fragrance emanating from the flowers is beautiful and soothing.

As they are about to enter the garden, PA stops, closes his eyes, and puts his hands on his chest. He says, "I feel a great energy coming from this place. I can feel great love here."

His expression turns to one of confusion as he opens his eyes looks at Adam Tate and says, "That's strange. I'm seeing a worm!"

Adam Tate laughs and tells him the story of Master Howard and the worm, and how he planted the rose garden out of love for his wife, Mistress Henrietta.

PA is greatly moved. He walks into the garden with gentle steps and gets down on his knees. Adam Tate kneels beside him, and PA is overcome with emotion.

"You know, sir, when my brothers and I confiscated all those books many years ago there were some that talked about this thing called a Creator. I do not know what that is but somehow, I feel it is something I need to learn. Can you teach me how to talk to this Creator, kind sir?"

Adam Tate puts his hands out to PA and says, "It is something you already know, brother. It is about calling out to the spirit within your heart which is speaking to you all the time."

"Really? But what do I say to the spirit within my heart?"

Adam Tate smiles. "Close your eyes and feel yourself in the presence of the Creator of the universe. If there is one thing you want to say to the Creator, what is it?"

"I want to say that I have never felt as happy and at peace as I do right now. I want to say that I do not know why I have been given this feeling of love in my heart, but I am sure that I do not deserve it. But most of all," PA gets emotional as he says, "I do not ever, ever want to return to the cruel and evil person that I was.

"And I do not want to be called PA anymore. I wish to be known from now on as Paul."

Adam Tate smiles with great joy. He proclaims to the man on his knees in front of him, "Then it is already done!"

At that moment, Paul looks up and sees a light in the sky. It is coming down to him, forming a shape with brilliant shining colors of orange, yellow, and gold.

Everyone in the Garden of Judy sees the light and the shape of brilliant colors. They come to the rose garden to see what is happening. The form materializes into the Monarch Angel, and she speaks to the heart of everyone present:

Human creatures, from this day forward, this man before you is to be known as Paul. From now until all of eternity, bless you Paul, our friend and brother!

Paul holds his hands up to the Monarch Angel and bows his head in greatest humility. "Thank you, thank you. May I be worthy of the name of Paul, and the life that I have now been given."

With that, Angel ascends to the clouds and returns to the heavenly realm.

Everyone watching is filled with love, although they do not know yet who Paul is, or what his former name was. They are about to find out very soon though, as three Cloudtransporters come within view making their descent to the Garden of Judy.

* * *

In the bowels of hell Lucifer bows his head in silent disgrace. He has just lost one of his most prized souls for all eternity. A seething rage boils inside of him as he considers the other two brothers, ES and SPA.

Looking up to the place where he was once a prized angel himself until he fell from grace, Lucifer shakes his fist and screams:

*"I **SHALL** HAVE POWER! **ABSOLUTE POWER!** I SHALL RULE AND HAVE DOMINION OVER THE EARTH AND ALL OF THE PEOPLE! THEY ARE **NOT***

*YOUR PEOPLE! THEY ARE SIMPLE-MINDED SHEEP WHO WILL FOLLOW **ANY** COMMAND, **MY COMMAND!***

HAVE THEY NOT DONE SO? ALWAYS?

WHEN I TOLD THEM TO HATE, THEY HATED!

WHEN I TOLD THEM TO BE CRUEL, THEY TORTURED EACH OTHER!

WHEN I TOLD THEM TO MOCK EACH OTHER, THEY BECAME DIVIDED!

AND WHEN I TOLD THEM TO KILL, THEY DID SO WITH A VENGEANCE!

WHOSE PEOPLE DO YOU THINK THEY ARE?

WHOSE VOICE DO YOU THINK THEY ARE FOLLOWING!

I AM THE ONE WITH ABSOLUTE POWER! NOT YOU! AND I SHALL HAVE THE SACRED PYRAMID ENERGY THAT THEY HAVE RELEASED AND TEAR THE FOOLS TO PIECES! ONE AT A TIME!

A voice from on high says to the fallen angel:

As fear is your fuel, the energy you produce will always fail. All that you have brought forth will ultimately be destroyed.

You were left to rule the underworld, that the precious human creatures might discover through their trials and tribulations who they truly are. Their journey through the dark side will ultimately lead them to the Light. The Creator loves his human creatures and will never, ever forsake them.

Lucifer is not about to let the Angel of the Lord have the last word, as he says, *"WE SHALL SEE ABOUT THAT!"*

And Angel replies, *"Indeed! And we shall see who wins, beastie creature!"*

* * *

Kookie, Liling, and Yakov can hardly wait to see each other. As they disembark from their Cloudtransporters they rush together, throw their arms around each other, and revert to their old, childhood greeting.

Holding their hands up in the air, they say, "Ni Hao, Privyet, Hey!" and fling their hands down.

To this day it still brings a smile and chuckle to the high lords and lady when they say hello in each other's languages.

Then Judy approaches all of them with the news they have not yet heard. "I'm sorry, but we thought it would be best to share the news with you guys after you accomplished your mission at the pyramids."

Angie looks worried and says, "What is it, Judy?"

Judy goes over to Doc and puts her arm around her. She then turns to everyone with great sadness and says, "Our dearest friend Phil has passed."

"Oh no! What happened!" They all gasp and cry out at once.

Doc tells them the story of the snake venom and George's deceit. "But worst of all," she says, and begins to break down weeping, "I was the one who put the venom in the tea. The voice of Lucifer whispered to me, and I could not tell the difference between him and the Kind One within my heart!"

Kookie and Vi lower their gaze as they totally relate to the guilt that Doc feels.

Vi speaks up. "It was like that for me Doc, when I realized that I was the one who unknowingly administered the Ebola bioweapon to so many people and worst of all to a little girl named Suzie."

Walking over to Doc, taking her by the hand and looking deep into her eyes, Vi continues, "And when I gave the necklace of my innocent victim to Phil for his little one who had no name, he honored us all by giving her the name of Suzie of the Seashells."

Vi is now smiling at Suzie and says, "It was the beginning of my journey of self-forgiveness and healing. And I have Phil to thank for that."

Suzie comes over, they all embrace and have a beautiful release of tears together.

Mimi goes to Doc and Suzie and gives them a warm comforting hug. "I'm so sorry," she says.

And Kookie, Angie, Yakov, Liling, and all the others follow, taking turns offering love and comfort to mother and daughter.

"Thank you," Doc replies, wiping away her tears. "Judy and the Chrysalenes have been so very kind and supportive. Henrietta and I have been consoling each other, too. In fact, she has been teaching me her exquisite baking tips and I have been teaching her about herbal teas and remedies."

The two old friends, Mimi and Doc, smile at each other and sit down for a quiet chat.

At Judy's cottage, Henrietta, Elena, and Sergio have been preparing a feast. Judy announces that the meal is ready, and they all gather around the table, sofas, floor, or wherever they can find a spot.

Pasha and Leo, who are new to the group, are introduced to everyone and given an extra warm welcome.

Kenny and Lisa arrive with a pair of pigeons sitting on each of their shoulders. The birds are just as blissful as their people.

The food is brought out and everyone ooos and aahs at the yummy spread of fruit, veggies, pastries, quiche, and salads of every description.

Finally, Kookie stands up with a glass of water in his hand and gets everybody's attention.

"My friends, thank you all for your participation in what is sure to become the most significant thing that we have done since freeing One World of mind-control and slavery."

"Here, here!" They all nod and agree, raising and clinking glasses together.

"I would like to share with you that I have been receiving reports on Metatron which are already coming in from all over the world, about significant changes people are noticing in their mental health and emotional well-being, just as we have all noticed among ourselves!"

Glowing smiles and nods of appreciation go around the room as many have indeed been experiencing great happiness and inner peace.

Kookie continues, "However, before I get too specific about all of that, there is a very important announcement that I have to make about someone here."

He motions to Paul and says, "This man sitting here is no stranger to us although none of us have ever seen his face before. He and the Major only just met at the pyramid of Chiconahui. I will tell you who he is and then I would like for him to tell you his story and what happened to him at the activation."

Everyone is mystified. Kookie pauses for a moment and says, "My friends as you will recall, just before the downfall of the ruling class of One World, the three leaders known as the Council, PA, ES, and SPA, suddenly disappeared without a trace. They were presumed dead. Well, the Major and I only just found out that they were buried alive in their underground ice palace in the northern regions and survived for the past 18 years. And recently when the ice melted, they were set free."

"Whoa! Oh, my goodness! Really?" several people exclaim.

"PA, ES, and SPA have been staying at the late Lord Josef's estate in the Yukatan, together with a mercenary band of like-minded Master Commandants. Each one of the brothers has been sent on a mission to infiltrate our people and subvert our benevolent actions, specifically to regain power and control of the world, in the name of Lucifer. This man seated here with us is one of those brothers."

"No! It can't be! Oh, my goodness!"

Kookie continues, "He was sent to the Village and Pyramid of Chiconahui, and I will let him tell you the rest of his story."

Motioning for Paul to stand up, Kookie slowly looks around at everyone and says, "My friends, this was the Highest Lord of the former Council of One Word, PA. Now he is our new friend and brother, Paul."

A stone-cold, silent shock wave goes around the room. Eyes pop, jaws drop, and everyone freezes in a state of suspended animation. Everyone, that is except for three people. The Major is shaking his head with an ear-to-ear grin, rubbing his hands together. Kookie is smiling, tapping the tips of his fingers together.

And Angie is rolling her eyes, shaking her head, and smiling at the two of them.

Paul stands up and all eyes and ears are upon him. He glances around the room, closes his eyes, lowers his head, and says, "It is with deepest appreciation that I stand here before all of you good people, receiving that which I most decidedly do not deserve . . . your friendship."

The mood of the friends in Judy's cottage begins to relax a little.

"But before I tell my story I must say that this is the most excellent meal I have ever been invited to. My goodness, what marvelous looking pastries! I can hardly wait to taste them!"

Everyone chuckles and Henrietta smiles. She is truly touched.

Paul proceeds to tell them about his life as a young man, how the brothers' power and wealth continued to grow, and how the three of them became more and more corrupted by all their power until eventually they succumbed to the voice of the beast within.

As Paul looks around the room at his new friends, he solemnly states, "Nobody can handle absolute power for very long. If you try to wield it, it is the surest way to bring you to your knees. And that is what happened to me and my brethren."

He continues to tell them about everything that happened from the time they were released from the polar palace, Lady Bella's evil spirit, and how they were coerced into compliance with Lucifer once again. Then he explains about meeting up with the Major, the Metatron device, the energy of the pyramid, and how it changed him. And, last but not least, he shares what happened at Henrietta's Rose Garden and the Monarch Angel, which some of them were there to witness.

Kookie and the others heard about it after they arrived, but now everyone is hearing the whole story from Paul himself. And they are all filled with compassion for their new friend and brother, Paul, the former PA.

Paul finishes with, "I do not know what I am supposed to do now or what has happened to my brothers ES and SPA. But I do know that I wish to be a part of your world and serve you in whatever way I can. Thank you kindly for listening and for welcoming me into your fold."

The smiles and warm expressions say it all, as one by one everyone comes over to Paul, hugging him, patting him on the back, and blessing him.

Eve Elli and Lord Emeka are the last to step forward putting little Lady Bi into the arms of Paul. Eve Elli says, "Dearest brother Paul, this child is my daughter, Lady Bi, who is also the daughter of Lord Emeka."

She turns to her husband who looks into the old man's eyes, and Paul is struck by a familiarity to that name.

"Yes," Eve Elli continues with a smile as she sees his recognition, "Lord Emeka is the son of the late Lord Ekene, the son of your brother SPA."

Suddenly tears well up in Paul's eyes and his lips start quivering as he beholds the little one giggling in his arms.

With much compassion, Eve Elli says softly, "This is your great-grand-niece."

Words do not come to him, only an avalanche of tears as he hugs baby Bi tenderly. And his precious little great-grand-niece blesses her uncle with a shower of baby kisses all over his face. Eve

Elli and Emeka put their arms around Paul and Bi, and Paul now has something he has never had in his life . . . a sweet, loving family.

* * *

In the bowels of hell, the seething beast is erupting with rage as he spews with venom, *OH NO, PA! I SHALL **NEVER, NEVER, NEVER,** LET YOU KNOW LOVE. BUT I **WILL** LET YOU KNOW DEATH! VERY SOON! YES INDEED! VERY SOON!*

* * *

That evening, Kookie, Yakov, Liling, and the entire group go out into the field of Judy's Garden. One of the things that Phil and Doc did for the past several years in their efforts to help garden communities get started, was to encourage people to build outdoor firepits. Phil shared the significance of campfires in a community, and how at one time such gatherings were important to his people, the Sioux. He showed villagers how to build them, and then he would lead discussions about life while sitting around the campfire smoking a peace pipe together.

Judy has not had one built yet, so in Phil's honor she asks everyone to help dig out a pit, find some good rocks from the nearby wooded area and build a firepit.

Adam Tate and several of the other Chrysalenes fetch the rocks while Paul, Viktor, Pasha, and Leo dig and smooth out the pit. Henrietta, Judy, and Lisa bring the dessert pastries from their meal with a few jugs of water. And Kookie has brought the peace pipe along with sage and sweetgrass.

When all is prepared, the large group gathers around the firepit, and a campfire is started. Food and water are passed around as Kookie prepares the pipe.

"Okay everyone," Kookie says. "Let us begin by honoring and giving thanks for all the blessings the Creator has given us today."

He lights the peace pipe, takes a few puffs, and waves the smoke over his head with his hand. Then he says what is in his heart. "Peace and love to our brother Phil who has gone home to the Great Spirit. Thank you, my brother, for being a loving inspiration to us all through the dark times and helping us move forward into a courageous new world.

"And thanks to all of you for helping activate the pyramids around the world today, so people everywhere can choose to open their hearts to a higher, divine love. May we all continue along the path of love, service, and unity as One People, in One Garden." Pondering this for a moment, Kookie adds, "in *His* Garden."

Everyone says, "Amen," and the peace pipe passes on to the next person. As it continues around the circle, everyone expresses the same sentiments: the need to love, to serve, and to remember.

When it is Paul's turn, he expresses the need to remember and to learn from the past. He says, "The damage my brothers and I did to humanity was to exploit the human frailty of fear, and not making amends when we were wrong. And as a result, we ended up encouraging that way of thinking among the Lords and Masters of the Upper Crust. We became afraid of taking a good look at the darkness within as well as the evil that exists in the world.

"By being afraid of looking at our wrong doings, we ended up being even worse to our fellow humans. By the loving grace that has been given to me on this sacred day, I wish to help give back the memories, the history, and the dignity that my brothers and I took away from people. And may we all realize how truly powerful and beautiful we truly are."

The outpouring of heartfelt love continues around the circle with good food, good conversation, and one Loving Great Spirit.

And all over the new world of One Garden, people gather and express words of love and compassion, lifting the hearts of people everywhere.

Chapter 14 – Fallen

DEEP IN THE BOWELS OF HELL the beast paces back and forth muttering to himself, *I SHALL have it! I SHALL HAVE ABSOLUTE POWER! DO YOU HEAR ME?* He shakes his fist upwards at the heavenly realm that he was once a part of. *I shall NOT allow the return of YOUR world! Not now! Not ever! It was I who destroyed their garden of paradise and I shall NOT let it return!*

Bella has also been eavesdropping on PA's transformation as she listens to her husband rant. And a plan is beginning to unfold in her evil genius mind as to how she can give the fallen one what he desires most, absolute power over the people of the world.

Lucifer continues to rage. *I shall tear down all those gardens with fear and hate! You know I can do it! I have been dividing people for thousands of years, ever since the beginning.*

I SHALL NOT LET THEM HAVE THEIR GARDEN OF EDEN! NOT EVER AGAIN!

Bella interrupts the fallen one and says, *Lucifer. . . Husband!*

AAAAHHHH! he yells at her. *You dare to speak to me when I am yelling at the One up there?!*

Indeed! Bella exclaims with a cheeky grin. *I believe I know how to give you that which you most desire.*

Lucifer is quiet now as he sneers at Bella.

I have been listening to PA and . . .

AAAAHHHH! YOU MENTION THAT NAME TO ME! THAT TRAITOR! I WILL CRUSH HIM IN A TERRIBLE DEATH! I WILL . . .

Bella grabs a hold of Andre and suddenly decides that she has listened to enough whining and blubbering. So, Bella does what Bella does best. Holding up her serpentine whip she slams down on Lucifer's head with a thunderous, sharp whack that sends him reeling.

She looks at Andre and says, *Open wide, sweetie pie!* And with a guttural growl Bella yells at Andre, *Let's give papa a GREAT, BIG, GRIN!*

Andre is happy to oblige Bella's request. He bares his fangs and Bella screams, *AAAAHHHHH!!* coming down on the still reeling Lucifer with the force of a mountain. Bella and Andre have impaled her hubby leaving him in several pieces on the ground.

The pieces tremble and move towards each other, reconnecting Lucifer as one evil whole. As he pulls his bad self back together, Lucifer shakes his head and looks at his queen with renewed affection.

He says, *We can play with each other later! Now what were you going to say about that idea of yours?*

That's better, Bella quips, and lays out her plan of action. *I heard PA talking about what changed him. A program called 777.*

Lucifer sneers, *Not another one of Kookie's inventions!*

Yes indeed, Bella replies. *It changes energy to its polar opposite. I think that if we can RE-activate the pyramids with 777, we can change those annoying good feelings that are spreading everywhere to, well, just the opposite! And then my dear the world will be your oyster!*

Lucifer realizes what his queen has envisioned, and he is thrilled to his evil core. He shouts, *MY QUEEN! YOU ARE AS BRILLIANT AS YOU ARE BEAUTIFUL!* ***NOW*** *LET'S PLAY!*

Bearing his chest to her with a passionate grin he shouts, ***WHERE'S THAT SERPENT?!***

* * *

The Cloudtransporter carrying ES and SPA is coming in for a landing at the late Lord Josef's Estate. Both men are badly shaken, and SPA's paranoia seems to be getting worse.

ES says to SPA, "I heard that you had a visit from Lady Bella. What did she say to you, brother?"

SPA can barely speak. He is quivering in a corner, staring at the floor as he manages to say, "She will help . . . help us . . . feel better.

The craft lands and the brothers step outside. Unlike their earlier arrival at the estate which was filled with fanfare and adoration from the Master Commandants, no one greets them. There is an eerie stillness to the place as if it is deserted, although ES and SPA know that the others are all inside. They go into the house and head for their quarters when one of the servants appears.

"My Lords," greets the servant in a somber tone, "it is very good to see you both."

ES and SPA nod as they continue to their quarters.

The servant follows cautiously and inquires, "I say, do tell me where your brother PA is? Will he be arriving shortly, then?"

"We are waiting to hear from him," ES replies beginning to fear over PA's whereabouts.

"Well then, Your Highest, is there anything I can get for you? A meal perhaps?"

"Sure," says ES. They are at their quarters now. He turns to the servant and asks, "Excuse me but where are all the Master Commandants?"

Looking down at the floor, the servant is hesitant to reply. Finally, he speaks. "I am afraid that something happened here a little while ago. The other servants and I do not know what to make of it."

They are standing at the doorway of ES and SPA's quarters. ES stares into the man's eyes with apprehension.

"Just tell us what happened!" ES spews in irritation.

"Very well," the servant says nervously. "Everything seemed normal today. The men were doing their daily runs and exercises, as well as their other usual morning routines. Then suddenly, there was a strange flash of light. It seemed to be coming from all over, but it was moving from one end of the sky to the other. There were many colors that moved about too, like a kaleidoscope or something. And immediately after that it happened."

"What exactly happened? What are you talking about?"

"Well, the men sort of got. . . well. . .scared. For no reason. And then they just up and went crazy. Started to yell and scream and attack each other. Also, for no reason."

"And what about you," ES demands. "You seem okay."

"Yes, well, that is another strange part of all this. We the servants seem to be just fine. In fact, if truth be known *we* are feeling very well indeed! I'm sure we would all be feeling even better were it not for the Master Commandants and what happened next."

"WELL THEN?!" ES is irritated by the servant's apparent hedging. *"WELL? SO, WHAT HAPPENED NEXT?"*

"My Lord," the servant says fidgeting, "suddenly they all just started. . . um. . ." he can hardly get the words out as he fears ES and SPA's reaction. Then he just blurts it out. "They started to *seriously* attack each other."

SPA listens and comprehends all of what he hears although he is unable to say much.

ES is completely dumbfounded. "*Seriously* attack each other? What on earth are you talking about?"

"What started with their hands and fists got rapidly worse." After a brief hesitation the servant continues. "They got their knives out and finally their guns."

"*WHAT?!*" shrieks ES and this time SPA yells too.

"*SO, WHAT HAPPENED TO THEM? WHERE ARE THEY NOW?!*" ES howls in a fit of hysterics.

The servant bows his head in sadness and says to the two brothers, "Come along My Lords, and I will show you."

ES and SPA follow the servant out to the back garden of the estate, where, to their horror they spy the bloody aftermath of a violent battle scene. The servants have dug out a trench and are busy filling the mass grave with the bodies of the Commandants who have perished.

ES cries out, "*ARE THERE ANY SURVIVORS?!*"

"Yes, My Lord. Twelve Master Commandants became terrified after the light display in the sky and ran cowering to their rooms. They are still there shaking with fear. A few of the servants and I have been doing our best to tend to their needs."

ES and SPA look at each other, feeling defeated and forlorn. They wearily hang their heads and ES says to the servant in a subdued tone, "We will go to our rooms now."

As they turn to leave the servant asks, "Would you care for some dinner, My Lords?"

"Yes servant. That would be fine," ES replies.

The brothers head for their quarters. When they arrive and open the door, they are greeted by another unwelcomed bombshell. Standing with their mouths hanging open, Lady Bella says, "Well, My Highest Ones. Are you going to just stand there at the doorway gaping at me or are you going to come in?"

ES and SPA approach Lady Bella with much fear.

"*SIT DOWN!*" she commands.

They sit.

"While you two fools took off and ran from your assignments, *DO YOU KNOW WHAT HAPPENED TO YOUR BROTHER PA?!*" Bella howls as she cracks her Andre-whip.

ES and SPA flinch with fright as they cautiously and timidly shake their heads, *no*. They fear for their lives and anticipate hearing the worst about PA. Leaning forward, Bella gives them the yarn that she and Lucifer agreed upon as part of their plan. "Your brother, the Highest PA, is a traitor! He has betrayed your people of the Upper Crust, he has betrayed your father who created the World that recently disintegrated, and most of all he has betrayed the two of you, his very own brothers."

ES and SPA are in total shock. They cannot believe what they are hearing.

"Yes indeed, Highest Lords of the Council. Your brother was easily persuaded to join the other side when the Major approached him at the pyramid of Chiconahui."

Bella sees the fear in ES and SPA turning into anger as she continues, "The Major told him that the people of this new foolish

Garden world of theirs were easy to dupe; you know, the old mind-control thing that the three of you found worked so well with the people of One World in the past."

The anger in ES and SPA grows as Bella keeps talking. "Well, the Major offered to make a deal with PA handing him Metatron, the device that you were looking for and could never find."

Their anger is now palpable as they ball up their fists and their faces turn red.

"It seems the Major told PA that with the Metatron Device the two of them could join forces and rule One Garden together!"

"NO!" ES and SPA jump up together and scream.

"Oh yes, My Lords. Oh yes indeed!" Bella is ready for the final command when she sees the rage burning in the eyes of ES and SPA. She walks over to them, gets right in their crimson faces, and says, "You will fetch the servant with whom you were just speaking. The three of you will then go to the Garden of Judy and follow my plan *exactly!*

Bella lays out the details ending with, "And you will then return to the estate with Lucifer's two prizes. First is the Metatron device with the 777-program. And then, *you* SPA will murder the Chrysalene Eve Elli and *take her nasty little child, baby Bi! The one they named after my foul sister!*

"As soon as you are all on board, the craft will automatically bring the device and the child back here to the estate. You will then be given further instructions."

"IS THAT CLEAR, HIGH LORD ES, AND HIGH LORD SPA?!"

ES and SPA are alternating between seething hatred for their brother PA and abject terror of Bella.

They answer, "Yes! That is most clear, Bella, queen of the underworld."

"Good," she says with a wry smile. Bella picks up Andre, and as her form begins to fade, she says to the angry and frightened brothers, "The Cloudtransporter is ready and programed. Take the servant and leave immediately. There is no time to lose. DO IT NOW!"

And Bella is gone.

ES and SPA head down the hallway to look for the servant who was helping them. ES realizes something. "We had better ask the servant his name."

"Why is that my brother?" SPA inquires.

"Because we ought to show him a little kindness. That is, we would not want him to suddenly decide to join forces with them and betray us too like our miserable brother!" ES snarls.

"Yes," says SPA, his faculties are returning to him fueled by the hatred growing in his heart for his brother. "We must be very careful about that."

"Truly, brother, we must!"

"Yes indeed!"

They are at the servant's quarters and begin to look around. SPA says, "Now where is that slave? I mean, that *servant!*" he says sarcastically.

Presently they find him coming out of the room of a suffering Master Commandant.

ES calls out to him, "Servant! Come here!"

"Yes, My Lord," the servant replies.

"We have an assignment for you servant and will need you to accompany us on our mission." ES gives SPA a sly look and continues addressing the man. "We have discovered the hideout of the traitors and their device which helped them destroy One World. It is the same device that has caused the destruction of the men you are now witnessing."

"Dear me!" exclaims the servant.

"Yes indeed!" says ES, "And we will need your help retrieving the device so that this horror can never happen again."

"Oh, yes, My Lord, indeed! Just tell me what you want me to do."

ES and SPA smile at each other. They turn to the servant and say, "Be prepared to leave immediately with us on the Cloudtransporter and we shall explain it all to you on the way."

"Yes, yes, My Lords! Immediately!"

"Oh, and by the way," ES continues. "DO tell us your name, servant. With these treacherous people we will need to know who you are."

"Yes, My Lord. My name is Jonah."

* * *

Early in the morning at the Garden of Judy in California, the Chrysalenes are up and tending to their seedlings, plants, fruits, and vegetables.

The youngest Chrysalene among them, little Lady Bi is out with her mama Eve Elli, taking care of the seedlings. Meiling and Beth have decided to join them. They are both taken by baby Bi's loving on the seedlings. And the little one truly has a heartfelt, joyous effect on both young women.

The girls have been pondering a curiosity, and this morning they have decided to ask Eve Elli about it.

Meiling begins, "Eve Elli, ma'am, Beth and I have a question we would like to ask you, if it is all right."

Eve Elli smiles with delight and says, "May I be of service to you both in answering your question."

The young women look at each other, nod, and Beth asks, "Ma'am, why is it that little Bi is called Lady Bi? Isn't she the daughter of a Chrysalene and therefore one herself? And you are also a Lady since you are married to Lord Emeka. But you call yourself Eve Elli rather than Lady Elli, or Lady Eve Elli, or something."

Beth feels a bit embarrassed and looks to Meiling to continue.

"Um . . . meaning no disrespect, ma'am," Meiling says, "We were just curious about how come you are called Eve Elli and your baby is Lady Bi."

Eve Elli chuckles and replies, "Why that is a most thoughtful question, and I am very happy to explain it to you."

Beth and Meiling can hardly wait to hear the explanation for something that has been bothering them for quite some time.

"You see, it is really quite simple. As a Chrysalene, I have but one Lord and Master. He is not of this earth but of the heavenly realm. And while I do love my husband Lord Emeka very much, I serve my Lord in Heaven first. There is an expression which goes, *you cannot serve two masters.* So, by calling myself Eve Elli, I always serve the Master above."

The young women are pleased at this response as they nod and say, "Ah!"

Eve Elli continues, "And as for my sweet little one here," she gives her baby a loving cuddle as Bi giggles and snuggles back, "'Eve' is the name we female Chrysalenes call ourselves once we recognize the One who has granted it to us. Once Bi recognizes who she is and who she was born to be she will call herself by her true name. Little Bi will have the free will to decide which master she chooses to follow just as we all do."

"Wow!" Beth and Meiling exclaim. "That's really nice!"

Eve Elli smiles at her precious little one and says, "Yes, the Spirit in all of us truly is beautiful."

Meiling has another thought. "Oh, just one more question ma'am!" she begs, pointing her index finger in the air. "When you say that little Bi will call herself by her true name once she recognizes who she is, well . . . um . . . is that the same for all of us?"

Eve Elli's smile brightens so much she is now doing her Chrysalene glow. "Why, yes! My goodness, you girls are so smart! That's one of the big lessons we were all put on this earth to learn."

"Wow!" Beth and Meiling exclaim with great enthusiasm. "So, what are the other big lessons?"

"Well, a matrix has been created from the activation that is the basis of the higher energy that we are all receiving. Day by day the energy intensifies, until those of us who are living in the light will be able to shift with the earth into a higher love frequency. The lessons we are learning and the ability for each one of us to shift into the higher love, is all based on what we learn from our suffering and painful life situations.

"Right now, those lessons are forcing us to really take a look at who we are, why we are here, and what we are supposed to do. For a Chrysalene it's about being of service to others. But, dear young ladies, we can *all* be of loving service to others in whatever we do."

Beth and Meiling are mystified by Eve Elli's words. And they look at little Bi with renewed hope for the future.

Just then little Lady Bi reaches out to the seedlings and starts petting them. "OOO, ooo!" She giggles and squeals with delight. Bi starts glowing and throws the seedlings a kiss, "Mwah!"

David joins the women and greets them, "Good morning, ladies! How are you all doing today?"

They giggle and Beth says, "Fine, David! And yourself?"

Tapping the tips of his fingers together he replies, "Wonderful! We are having a gathering this morning at the firepit. Just wanted to let you know. It will be starting shortly." He pauses and then adds, "We will be having our morning meal there, too."

"Thanks David," Beth says, and she turns to Meiling. "Perhaps we should go to Judy's cottage and help with the food preparations."

"Sounds like a good idea," Meiling agrees. Then she says to Eve Elli with a warm smile, "Thank you for our talk this morning. See you and little *Eve Bi* at the firepit!"

Eve Elli smiles, bows her head, and says, "It is a pleasure to serve you."

Kookie, Angie, Liling, Dumaka, and Doc each have disquieted spirits this morning. Their super-sensitive intuition tells them that something is going on and they need to be on the alert. They wait for the others at the firepit trying to figure out how to make sense of their feelings and what they are going to say to their friends.

Liling turns to everyone with a knot in the pit of her stomach. "It's really strange to feel this way," she says, "especially since we have all been so peaceful and happy after the activation."

"This is true," says Angie, "But remember that the activation is making us hyper-sensitive to *everything* and some of what we are going to experience will be challenging."

Dumaka adds, "And as long as we have each other the Kind One will help see us through whatever comes down."

Liling smiles affectionately at her husband and nods in agreement.

Kookie listens to what everyone has been saying and considers his own thoughts. "It seems to me that once a pathway for great love has been opened the opposite is also bound to happen."

Angie says, "You mean like your whole concept of the *duality of the polarity*, honey?"

"Yes, sweetie, it is exactly that!" he chuckles, pointing his index finger in the air.

Doc asks Kookie, "What do you think this *negative polarity* is all about, or what form do you think it will take?"

"I honestly don't know," Kookie admits. "But one thing I am fairly certain of is that we are going to find out," he pauses and looks at everyone, "very soon."

Everyone nods in agreement. And the rest of their companions begin to arrive at the firepit.

Lisa, Neely, and Judy bring out the food, assisted by all the young folks. The others and several of the Chrysalenes are seated around the firepit waiting for the gathering to begin. The food is passed around, Adam Tate says the blessings, and Kookie brings the meeting to order.

"My friends, I wanted us to gather this morning to discuss a feeling that I, and some of the others here have become aware of. Perhaps there are those among you who have been feeling the same thing. With all the joy we experienced at the activation of the pyramids, we are feeling that some form of darkness has also been activated. This was anticipated, as darkness will come to the surface when a light is shone upon it. I do not know what form this darkness will take but I am feeling its energy.

"I believe it is the final lesson we are all being called upon to learn before we can make the great shift to Divine Love. And once we do, we will surely be able to enjoy and move forward in our garden communities of paradise, without threat of destruction by the forces of the fallen one. I believe there will always be challenges from the dark side, but there does not have to be a threat to the very existence of humankind anymore."

Everyone is quiet as they consider Kookie's words. They feel peace surrounding them with the matrix of the pyramid activation growing in their hearts. The loving forces of the natural and spiritual worlds are also enjoying the energy from Kookie's words.

The Monarch Butterflies are resting comfortably in Eve Elli's hair and there is now one nestled in little Bi's hair as well. Kenny has brought 12 pigeons with him from Bear River Garden, added to Judy's little buddies, and the ones perched on the shoulders of the youngsters. The birds are all joyfully hopping from one person to another, snuggling against every neck they perch upon. The people close their eyes with faces held toward the sun and the Chrysalenes begin their angel songs of healing.

A voice speaks to the hearts of one and all saying: *Gentle human creatures, remember how you are feeling at this very moment. Remember the love you all share. Remember that I Am always here and will never, ever desert you.*

A stronghold of love surrounds everyone gathered at the firepit of Judy's Garden.

Suddenly, Angie's serene thoughts and feelings are interrupted as she opens her eyes and looks off into the distance at the wooded area. She notices a young man walking toward them, and immediately speaks up to the others, interrupting their blissful state. "I wonder who that could be?"

The young man seems to have come out of the woods from nowhere. He walks straight over to everyone seated around the firepit, smiling, and waving at them.

"Hello there!" the stranger says. "I am new to these parts. Mind if I join you?"

The others all look at each other and nod. Kookie says to the man, "Not at all, brother. I am Kookie. What is *your* name?"

The young man stands in front of Kookie and broadens his smile. Extending his hand he says, "Hello, Kookie. My name is Jonah."

Chapter 15 – Lessons

KOOKIE OFFERS JONAH his hand in return saying, "Welcome, brother. We were just having our morning meal. Would you care to join us?"

The others give a warm welcome to the stranger, patting him on the back, shaking his hand and offering him food.

"Thank you kindly! I am indeed most hungry!" Jonah sits down next to Kookie, and Lisa brings him a plate of food.

"Please," she says, "help yourself. There is plenty of everything."

Jonah expresses much appreciation as he partakes of their meal. While he eats, he studies the faces around the campfire. Yakov has a wary feeling about him. Viktor, Pasha, Leo, and even Rudolpho have a vague sense that they have seen this man somewhere before.

The Major speaks up, "So where are you from my good man?"

Jonah has a story prepared for them. He mentions a small fictitious garden community that he allegedly stayed at for several years. At the rate the garden communities are growing it is virtually impossible to keep track of them all, so no one questions him.

However, Yakov, Viktor, Pasha, and Leo are not completely buying his story. Yakov asks, "What made you decide to leave?"

"Well," Jonah replies, "since the strange lights appeared in the sky, I have been hearing voices inside of me."

"Really? Wow! No kidding."

Suddenly, he has the group's full attention, including Yakov and the other Slavic men who remain skeptical.

Sergio and Elena are interested, considering what they just went through at the California border, as well as in their village of Chiconahui. They look at each other, mutter something, and then Sergio says to Jonah, "What have the voices been telling you, my friend?"

"That there are dark forces amassing in the world which do not want us to prosper and be happy. That I am to travel from one garden community to another and share my thoughts and feelings to see if others are experiencing the same thing. Then I am to see if there is any way that I can be of service."

Everyone is now fully engaged in what Jonah is saying as he pauses and then continues. "I am also told to stay close to the Chrysalenes. And since there are none in the community that I have been living in, I remembered hearing about Judy's Garden. The one called Judy is quite a legend you know, as well as Adam Tate and the other Chrysalenes."

Judy giggles with delight and the others all nod and chuckle in agreement. Numbers 9 and #10 snuggle closer against Judy's neck, as they couldn't agree more.

Kookie looks at the man seated next to him and says, "Well, as a matter of fact, brother, we were just talking about that very thing when you showed up."

"Really?!" Jonah gasps with feigned surprise. "I *knew* those voices were leading me in the right direction!"

"Indeed!" says Yakov. He isn't buying this at all, though he can see that most of the others are.

As Jonah surveys the group assembled around the campfire, he suddenly notices two people. Although he only got to see PA from a distance when the highest ones first arrived at Lord Josef's estate, he clearly recognizes him now. Besides, ES and SPA told him the outlandish story of PA joining forces with the Major so Jonah is expecting to find him there. However, he can tell from Paul's blank expression when they look at each other that PA does not recognize Jonah at all. But a few others still look at Jonah with vague recollection.

Viktor thinks, *hm . . . I know that guy!*

* * *

Deep in the bowels of hell Lucifer and Bella watch the scene unfold. Lucifer sneers and smirks at Jonah and says to his wife, *You do remember that man, do you not my queen?*

Bella furrows her brow and nods in the negative. She does *not* remember Jonah.

Lucifer lets out a maniacal laugh and says, *Well, I certainly do!* Then he turns to his unsuspecting queen and roars at her with words of venom:

FOOLISH WOMAN! EIGHTEEN YEARS AGO, LORD JONAH WAS ONE OF THE CONSPIRATORS ON THE BOAT WITH VIKTOR AND THE OTHERS AS THEY RAN AWAY FROM YOUR ISLAND JUST BEFORE THE BLAST! DO YOU NOT REMEMBER?

Bella's eyes go wide as she lets out a loud shriek. Then Bella starts screaming, ***WHAT?! WHAT BOAT?! WHAT OTHERS?! LORD VIKTOR DID WHAT?! HE RAN AWAY FROM ME?!"***

Lucifer continues to fiercely laugh out loud. He is greatly amused when he realizes that Bella has no idea what he is talking about.

Well of course you don't know about that, my Bella! How could you! You were so busy entertaining all those lords and ladies. What with your strutting around like a peacock in that outlandish outfit, he points to Andre, *including that infernal serpent draped around your neck. You never even saw the treachery that was going on right under your nose!*

BWAHAHAHA!

Lucifer cannot contain his mirth and Bella loses it completely. She grabs the infernal serpent, and in a flash, screams and impales her misbehaving husband, once again. This time there are a few more pieces that come quivering back together.

OOO! My dear! the beast says in a lustful tone, *save that thought for later. Right now, we must stay on top of the situation at hand. ES and SPA must NOT fail!*

* * *

Liling has an idea that she presents to the group. "My friends, we knew that activating the pyramids would bring forth many things, including memories of our personal past as well as various events in history. And we know that there are many forces out there dedicated to helping us. So, my idea is to continue expanding our memories of the past and learn what we can, while, at the same time taking precautions."

Yakov keeps a watchful eye on Jonah and very much likes the idea of taking precautions. He says to Liling, "What kinds of precautions do you suggest, sister?"

Liling looks at Kookie, Angie, David, and Rudolpho, and takes out her Metatron device. "Well, for one thing there are the precautions that our resident geniuses can do for us with their various programs of Metatron."

Everyone chuckles.

When Jonah sees the device, it takes all his willpower to stifle a gasp. *Good grief! That's it!* he thinks. *That's the device that caused the Master Commandants at Josef's estate to kill each other! That's the device that I am supposed to take!*

Several other people take out their Metatron devices and start looking at them leaving Jonah absolutely flabbergasted. *They've ALL got one?! And all I have to do is steal any one of them?*

While Jonah revels in how easy that is going to be, he also realizes that the other part of his assignment is most definitely NOT going to be so easy. But that is where ES and SPA come in, although they must remain hidden for now inside the Cloudtransporter in the clearing behind the wooded area.

Jonah knows he cannot waste any time, so he asks a seemingly innocent question. "Oh my, that does look interesting. I've never seen one of those things before." Pointing to the Metatron he says, "What is that device called, and what do you all do with it?"

Mimi proudly holds her device up to Jonah and says, "Well, we call this Metatron. It is named after the angel Metatron because he is so strong and of heavenly energy. Metatron does so many things that it is really hard to describe. But let's just say that it is a great protector, among other things."

Remembering back when Metatron first saved her from harm, she looks at Doc, Vi, Angie, and Ryan and adds, "One of the first times we used this it actually helped us to cross the California-

Oregon border without being seen. That was not an easy thing to do either considering how guarded that place was at the time."

It's all Jonah can do to stay calm and *not* jump out of his skin. "You . . . you . . . you mean like it made you *invisible* or something?!"

Mimi, Doc, Angie, Vi, and Ryan chuckle as they say, "Or *something!*"

Then Vi tell Jonah about one of her favorite subjects, self-cloaking. She recounts how, combined with Metatron, they were all able to seemingly disappear in front of the guards and walk past them.

Jonah is having an internal fit while remaining outwardly calm and casual. "Um . . . hm . . . *echem*" he clears his throat. "Do you think you can show me how that um . . . you know . . . thing works?"

They all laugh because they know how much Vi and the others love to teach self-cloaking to people.

Ryan says, "Well my man, you have certainly come to the right place for that!"

"Are you ready for your first lesson?" Vi asks Jonah joyfully.

"*Suuuure!*" Jonah says with incredulity.

"Great!" Vi exclaims as she turns to the others. "Why don't we take Jonah into one of the guest cottages and teach him a thing or two about self-cloaking?"

They all nod in agreement deciding that this would be a most fun thing to do. And Jonah tags along, his proverbial jaw hanging on the ground. He thinks, *Well, I now see how I am going to carry out the other part of my assignment too.* His eyes narrow as he looks at baby Bi and he follows the others to the cottage.

* * *

ES and SPA have been watching everything from the Cloudtransporter through a small device they implanted on Jonah. SPA looks at ES and rubs his hands together. "Oh, my goodness, brother! This is almost too delicious for words! I expect we shall have both of our prizes very shortly!" he says.

"Indeed!" ES responds. "We must be ready to take off the instant Jonah returns. We do not want to arouse any suspicions before we are safely away from here."

"That is certain," SPA agrees. Pondering the situation he says, "Remind me what Bella said about how we are going to avoid their detection once we get back to the estate. My brain was still rather fuzzy when she explained all that, but thankfully I am feeling much better now, as if a cloud has lifted."

"Most excellent my brother," ES comments. "I am so glad to see that you are back to your old self again."

The brothers snicker and ES explains the plan to SPA.

"Lord Josef was a technical genius. I wouldn't say he was on the same level as Kookie and Yakov, but certainly on par with Rudolpho. He was also, shall we say, rather paranoid and invented all kinds of protective devices and programs of his own."

ES thinks about it for a moment and chuckles. "Actually brother, Lord Josef was frightened of *US* and the advanced surveillance system we created to keep an eye on all the lords. How ironic it is that an invention of Lord Josef, designed to protect himself against us, is the very thing that we are now going to use to *help* us!"

ES and SPA do find this rather amusing. They rub their hands together, snort, chuckle, and sneer.

ES continues, "As soon as we get back to Josef's estate, we will go into the security system. It is located on a panel right inside the front door. Bella has given us the code to enter and once we do, the sequencing will start. In less than a minute we will, how shall I say, *Shape-Shift* into another reality."

"Huh?!" SPA says, bewildered. "Where was I when her infernal Ladyship explained all this to you? Was I in a coma or something?!"

"Well dear brother . . . in a manner of speaking, *YES!*"

"Gracious!" exclaims SPA getting irritated. "So, what is this business all about then? What exactly does it mean to *Shape-Shift into another reality?* Is it like the thing Kookie's friends are teaching Jonah how to do, that self-cloaking, or whatever it's called?"

"Oh no, not at all. Self-cloaking is only a way of making yourself unnoticed. It is not at all the same thing as being completely invisible which our friend the late Lord Josef has created a program for."

Now SPA is getting angry as he realizes the extent to which his mind was affected after the pyramid activation. He spews out, "WELL? So what the *BLEEP is it then?!*"

It is with great pleasure that ES explains to SPA, "Shape-shifting is about changing actual physical form. As you may recall we learned about that in our youth regarding indigenous cultures and their beliefs."

SPA nods as he does indeed remember learning about such things.

"While there are beings of the higher realms that are able to change their form, there are also beings of the underworld that can do the same. Lucifer is a shape-shifter," ES continues, "And for those who embrace the lord of the underworld such powers may be granted to them for a price."

"Dear oh dear!" exclaims SPA. "What are you trying to say then, my brother? Did the late Lord Josef pay that price?"

"I suppose he did," ES says as he shrugs his shoulders. "No different from us though, don't you think?"

SPA looks down for a moment and ponders this. He doesn't feel comfortable with the thought that they have indeed paid a high price to Lucifer for their power and wealth.

ES continues: "Thanks to the higher education program of the people developed by Lord Emeka while we were gone, there are supporters of ours who have become expert themselves at management and development of this level of technology. We will need these people once we have the Metatron device in our possession, to figure out how to work with Kookie's 777-program. Bella is locating those people while we are here capturing the prizes."

"Very efficient of her Ladyship, my brother," SPA says.

"Most efficient indeed! Anyway," ES continues, "once we activate the shape-shifter program the entire estate, plus everyone in it will shape-shift into another reality. And the reality that Bella and Lucifer have decided for Joseph's estate, which would be the perfect disguise for us, is a garden community!"

Upon hearing this SPA is dumbfounded. Suddenly, he has another recollection from his childhood that he shares with ES. "It seems to me that there was another story we heard when we were young lads. Something about a pumpkin turning into some sort of vehicle and rats turning into men to navigate the craft."

"Yes, that does ring a bell, brother. There was also the business about a woman's shoe appearing and disappearing in that story."

They consider this for a moment and then SPA says, "So am I to understand that Lord Josef has somehow managed to recreate all that? And all we have to do now is flip a switch, so to speak, and our entire operation at the estate, including all of us in it, will turn into a garden community?!"

"Indeed!" says ES. The brothers are suddenly amused by all this, and they laugh out loud.

"There is one thing I must do though before Jonah gets back with our *prizes,*" ES says while gloating. "I must send a message to the other servants at the estate and prepare them for the shift into a garden community as soon as we get back."

"Good," says SPA. "You do that, brother. And I shall look in on Jonah and see how our servant is doing with his self-cloaking lessons."

* * *

Jonah and his companions have been practicing self-cloaking all afternoon and they finally emerge from the cottage. He is amazed at all he has learned from Vi, Doc, Mimi, Ryan, and Angie. "Thank you so much for the wonderful self-cloaking lessons. I am sure it will help me at some point to avoid trouble."

"You are most welcome," Vi says, and the others nod. "We must all help each other as best as we can.

"Yes, indeed we must," Jonah replies with an underlying sinister tone that no one picks up on.

"If you will all excuse me for a little while I should like very much to wander around Judy's Garden and enjoy the loving, peaceful energy I feel here. I also want to find a spot where I can meditate and consider what Liling said this morning about remembering things from the past. I do believe that this is a very important part of being of greater service to the people of One Garden."

"I couldn't have said that better myself," says Ryan, who is quite happy to hear Jonah's words.

As SPA watches Jonah on the monitor, he is also quite happy to hear Jonah say that. "I couldn't have said that better myself either! Good job, Jonah!"

With a sly grin that is almost imperceptible, Jonah puts his index finger against his chin as if lost in benevolent thoughts. He looks around and without wasting any time knows what he must do next.

"Hm . . ." Jonah says to the others. "That rose garden over there looks like a very nice spot."

"Yes, it is," says Angie. "Well, you have a nice time and do let us know what ideas you come up with about helping people."

"I sure will. Thanks again!" Jonah says as he takes off for Henrietta's Rose Garden.

Angie turns to the others and says, "Lisa and Kenny have a great idea about a group going with them back to Bear River Garden. They want to do something with all the pigeons and will need some help."

Angie snuggles #3 and #4 against her neck. "Yes, my little sweeties, your predecessors have certainly come to the rescue for us in the past."

Scratching their little heads, she looks at everyone else and continues, "I guess we should go find Kenny and Lisa and see about helping them organize a group. I believe they are at Judy's cottage."

* * *

Jonah arrives at the rose garden where he finds Henrietta tenderly clipping a few roses. Beth is showing all the young men how to trim the bushes, and Meiling is showing Daniela how to water the bushes from a nearby rain barrel. Liling and Dumaka are sitting and meditating at the stone that Adam Tate placed there in memory of Master Howard.

Jonah looks around at everyone and seizes upon an opportunity to capture a Metatron device. He makes his move. . .

Prize #1 is in his pouch.

Then he looks up and notices Eve Elli off in the distance. She is on her knees in a patch of freshly tilled earth, blessing it before planting the new seedings. Little Lady Bi sits next to her mama also blessing the earth, and mother and child are praying and glowing together.

Prize #2 is in sight.

His thoughts turn to the clearing just behind the wooded area where ES and SPA are in the Cloudtransporter, patiently waiting for him and their "prizes."

SPA turns to ES and says excitedly, "I think this may be it! Jonah might be making his move on the Chrysalene at any moment! I had better get ready to jump in!"

"Yes indeed!" exclaims ES. "This truly is most exciting, brother!"

SPA gets ready to leave the craft as he looks around and says, "My brother, where is that pouch filled with the poisonous herbs?"

"Here it is," ES replies. He hands the pouch to SPA who grabs a handful of the crushed leaves and stuffs them in his pocket.

SPA watches as Jonah goes over to Eve Elli and little Bi. He crouches down in front of them and is about to speak.

SPA looks at the screen, puts his hand in his pocket, touches the poisonous herbs and says, "Ready whenever you are, Jonah!"

* * *

Eve Elli has a trace of a smile on her face as she watches Jonah approach her and little Bi. There is a ray of sunlight breaking through the clouds above, shining down on their angelic faces.

Little Bi is giggling away as she holds her hands up and says, "Da Light! Da Light!"

Jonah stands right before them as he says, "Yes, little one, that is the light."

Looking at Eve Elli he says to her, "Chrysalene, you must know why I have come."

Eve Elli bows her head and says to Jonah, "Yes, I know why you have come."

He looks at her a bit mystified saying "And you do not fear me?"

A Golden Light descends through the clouds filling the hearts of Eve Elli and little Bi. The Light is unseen by Jonah but is seen and felt by the Chrysalenes. Suddenly, little Bi opens her heart with elation and ecstasy. Her eyes go very wide and she gasps, lifting her arms to the heavens and proclaiming with great joy: "Eve Bi! Eve Bi!"

Her mama begins to radiate bright as a star and with overwhelming passion pronounces to her daughter, "Yes! Oh yes, my little one! You are Eve Bi!"

Eve Bi has just claimed her birthright as a Chrysalene. She has chosen to serve her Master of the Light.

Eve Elli's heart is overflowing with divine love. She turns to Jonah and declares, "We are Chrysalenes. We fear no evil."

Jonah is momentarily taken aback when he gazes into the eyes of love in its purest human form. He cannot comprehend what he is witnessing but nevertheless, knows what he must do. Staring into the heart and soul of Eve Elli, Jonah slowly extends his hand to her. There are no words spoken between them. No words are necessary.

Eve Elli takes his hand and rises while holding Eve Bi in her other arm. And Jonah motions for them to go with him into the wooded area. Glowing with the Light of Heaven, Eve Elli and Eve Bi go to meet their destiny.

SPA is at the portal of the Cloudtransporter in a flash. He pats his pocket full of poison, winks, and smiles at his brother saying "I shall be right back!

Jonah walks through the wooded area with Eve Elli and Eve Bi. As they approach the clearing, SPA appears coming towards them. When Jonah sees SPA, he stops and waits. Eve Elli watches as her daughter's great-grandfather approaches. And in her heart, she hears only one voice repeating over and over, "Have no fear for I AM with you."

SPA reaches Eve Elli and Eve Bi. He says to Jonah, "It's okay, you can go now."

The Chrysalene looks deep into the eyes of a man who has given his will over to the lord of the underworld; a man who must follow the command of his master Lucifer.

As Eve Elli and Eve Bi connect with SPA's heart, their glowing increases to an intensity that is almost blinding. SPA cannot gaze upon them for long. Averting his eyes, he puts his hand into his pocket and takes out the bundle of herbs. He blinks while glancing at Eve Elli's mouth, which is radiating with the Light of the Lord.

In his head SPA can hear only one voice, repeating over and over, "*DO IT! DO IT! DO IT!*"

His head begins to throb, and his hand starts to shake as he moves closer to Eve Elli, now within inches of her face. SPA raises his hand, holding the herbs in front of her mouth.

Deep in the bowels of hell Lucifer is fit to be tied! In a screaming fit of rage, he begins to thump and pound on the lost soul of his henchman:

DO IT! DO IT! DO IT!

SPA feels the pounding in his brain of the thunderous roar of the beast and the blinding Light of the Chrysalenes. It is more than he can handle.

Suddenly, SPA drops the herbs and falls to the ground.

Eve Elli and Eve Bi gently kneel down before him as they put their hands on SPA. And mother and child sing the angel songs of healing to Eve Bi's great-grandfather, SPA.

* * *

Jonah enters the Cloudtransporter and ES asks him anxiously, "Well? Did you get the device then?"

Reaching into his pouch, Jonah smiles and says to ES, "I would not disappoint you, My Lord."

He pulls out a little black box and hands it over as ES grabs it greedily.

"My goodness, man! How did you do get a hold of this? We didn't even see you do it!"

Jonah laughs and says, "Several years ago after the fall of the UC and my disappearance from that world, I became one of the people of One World. It was during that time that I discovered a talent within me which came in rather handy."

"Do tell!" ES exclaims, his eyes going very wide indeed. "What talent is that?"

Jonah chuckles and says, "It is called pickpocketing, My Lord, sir!" ES sits stunned as Jonah reminisces with a smile. "Actually, I was rather good at it. And when I realized that so many of them in this group carry this thing around with them, I knew it would be quite easy to nab one."

ES is bemused at how easy it was to finally get a hold of this device after so many highly strategic failed attempts to do so.

And while the two of them sit there chuckling about it and inspecting this highly prized piece of equipment, neither of them has been watching SPA, Eve Elli, and Eve Bi on the screen. They also do not hear the sound of the cargo door closing, on the exterior portion of the Cloudtransporter. A moment after that however, they do hear the portal open as SPA walks in. He is carrying little Eve Bi in his arms.

"Well, here's prize #2."

Turning to Jonah he says, "I take it you were successful in retrieving prize #1?" SPA inquires as he notices the little black device ES is holding. "Ah, there it is! Well brother, let's get out of here, then. Shall we?"

"Indeed!" ES agrees as they take off for Lord Josef's Estate in the Yucatan.

Chapter 16 – Wings

KENNY HAS DECIDED that he can best serve the people of One Garden by having a fully assembled pigeon's air support squadron ready for deployment at a moment's notice. He has called for a meeting at Judy's cottage, asking for volunteers to help with the mission and a very enthusiastic group of young folks show up.

Kenny is very grateful and encouraged when he looks at the group and says to them, "Thank you all for volunteering!"

"You bet, Kenny!" Meiling exclaims.

"You couldn't keep me away from those guys!" Charlie chimes in, and the rest of the youngsters smile, chuckle, and nod in agreement.

Kenny continues, "I would like to go over with you what we are going to be doing with the pigeons just as soon as we get back to Bear River Garden. I know that all of you now have pigeons of your own, except for Ivan and Boris, that is."

Turning to the sons of Viktor and Marie, Kenny says, "For you two guys this is going to be a new experience. And I'm sure the others will help you to catch up quickly and learn how to work with the pigeons."

Ivan calls out, "That's okay Kenny, we can handle it! We are here at your service, *sir*!"

The others all chuckle and say, "You bet Kenny! We *all* got this! Ready to roll, *sir*!"

Kenny is pleased as he goes over some of the basics of pigeon-handling, including how to write messages on the scrolls and place them on their feet.

"Here's the important thing," Kenny explains. "The birds are intuitive little creatures and they have saved us a number of times in the past. So, whatever we have in mind for them, you can rest assured they will cover our backs and act on their own when the time comes."

"Wow!" Ivan and Boris exclaim. They are looking forward to making new little friends and working with so many snuggly, fun little airmen.

"So, when do we leave?" Beth chimes in enthusiastically.

Suddenly, Lord Emeka bursts into the cottage. Mimi and Ryan are right behind him. Everyone in the cottage, including Judy stops what they are doing when they see the frantic look on Emeka's face.

"Emeka?" Judy says cautiously, coming over to him. "What's wrong, honey?"

He can barely stumble the words out, "My . . . wife . . . and, uh . . . my baby . . . are . . . m-m-muh . . . missing!"

"WHAT?!" everyone suddenly cries out.

Mimi can barely contain herself. She is holding onto Ryan who is trying his best to comfort her despite his own fear.

Judy puts her hands out to Emeka and says, *"Dear Lord! What are you saying?!"*

Tears well up in Emeka's eyes. But before he can say anything else, Kookie, Angie, Liling, and Yakov burst into the cottage.

And Yakov blurts out with indignation, "Jonah is missing, too!"

"What?!" Judy wails. *"What does that mean?"*

"I'm not sure," Yakov exclaims, "but right now we must find Eve Elli and little Bi. All of you, please come to the firepit immediately!"

* * *

ES, SPA, and Jonah have just arrived back in the Yucatan at Lord Josef's Estate.

"Hurry!" ES cries, "We have no time to lose. With their technology and intuition those guys can probably find us and be here in no time!"

SPA has been holding on to Eve Bi the whole time. She has been giggling, touching his face, and playing with his hair. She has even planted a few baby kisses on his ears.

As the portal opens, SPA puts Eve Bi down in a little seat and straps her in. He feels something stirring inside of him that he has never known or felt before. SPA goes to the portal, turns around and looks at her. There are tears trying to form in his eyes, but he swallows hard, burying those feelings deep down inside. SPA gazes upon his great-granddaughter little Eve Bi one last time.

He knows that he will never see her in this life again.

* * *

In the bowels of hell Lucifer and Bella have been watching as the lord of the underworld is about to claim his two prizes. But he is watching SPA with caution since he has not followed Bella's exact instructions with the Chrysalene child.

What are you doing fool! Lucifer snarls. *You were supposed to bring the child inside! And why did you not take care of the other one the way you were told?!*

Bella reassures him. *What difference does that make? Your men now have the device and Absolute Power of the World is within your grasp!*

Lucifer looks at Bella with hatred emanating from his evil soul as he yells, ***I WANTED THE CHILD FOR MYSELF! MY PRIZE! MY CHILD!***

Bella rolls her eyes with impatience as she says, *What's the matter with you, husband?! When you have Absolute Power you can take her, or whatever child you want for that matter, to be a part of your dominion!*

But Lucifer's lust for power is insatiable and nothing will ever be enough for him. He yells out, *I WANT HER NOW! I WANT TO SHOW THE ONE ABOVE THAT A LITTLE CHILD IS **NOT** GOING TO GET THE BETTER OF ME!* ***NOT EVER AGAIN!***

Well, says Bella, *do not forget the stowaway who came along for the ride. Perhaps you will now have a chance of taking them both!*

Bella has her own agenda with "the stowaway" as her hatred for Eve Elli has been growing. She is remembering the gratification it gave her to inflict all that suffering on her own sister. And Bella is now thinking to herself, *Oh yes . . . dear . . . sweet . . . Chrysalene. Come my dear! Come to mama!*

Andre is draped around Bella's neck, feeling her arousal throbbing passionately through her jugular veins. It is causing Andre some degree of titillation as he leans over, extends his long-forked tongue and licks Bella's face.

* * *

"Come on brother! Let's go!" ES yells out as he sees SPA still lingering at the portal.

SPA turns and goes down the ramp to join ES and Jonah, who are at the entrance of the estate impatiently waiting for him. As they open the door and step inside the house the cargo door of the Cloudtransporter also opens.

The servants and remaining Master Commandants are all waiting inside for Jonah, ES, and SPA. There are also two older women, the techies, who have arrived. They are Bella's recruits.

Jonah calls out to everyone, "Are you all ready?!"

"Yes!" they answer in unison.

"Good!" Jonah exclaims as he takes his place among the servants.

ES and SPA standby as the techies open the panel on the inside of the front door. The techies turn everything on and look at the Highest Lords of the former Council of One World. ES gives the nod and one of the women presses the button.

* * *

All the friends and Chrysalenes at Judy's Garden are gathered around the firepit. Kookie, Yakov, and Liling know that every moment is critical. They also know that they need the most intuitively gifted and experienced among them at the helm, so Liling and Angie step forward.

Angie says to Emeka and the group, "Dearest Emeka, Mimi, Ryan, and all our friends gathered; remember, our love is greater than their fear. And I know for certain that we will find them!"

Paul hangs his head in shame because he is certain his brothers are behind this.

Addressing Emeka, Angie says, "Do you have it with you?"

"Yes," he says in a forlorn voice. Emeka goes over to Angie and gives her what he is holding. It is one of the three Monarch Butterflies that are usually nestled in Eve Elli's hair.

Liling and Angie gently cup their hands together over the Monarch as the wings begin to flutter.

Kookie quietly motions to the group to hold hands and close their eyes, while Angie and Liling close their eyes and tune in with their hearts to the message from the Monarch.

As they are about to begin, another Monarch suddenly makes her presence known. Her beautiful transparent wings fill the sky, calming the spirits of everyone. And they all hear the voice of Angel whispering to their hearts:

Fear not, human creatures. Though Lucifer is poised to take your freedom away, yet again, remember what Angie creature has just told you.

LOVE is greater than fear!

Your time has come to rise, human creatures. And rise you will!

Hop to it now!

Everyone smiles a little and their hearts fill with hope. The vision of Angel fades, but her spirit remains within the hearts of all.

Angie and Liling close their eyes and listen to the message that is coming to their hearts. They see Eve Elli in the garden, and begin:

Liling: "Blessing the seedlings." She smiles, "So happy."

Angie: "Jonah comes. Butterflies in hair must find Emeka."

Liling: "Wooded area. Fear no evil. SPA. Poison."

Everyone gasps. Emeka clutches his heart.

Angie: "Angel healing songs." She smiles briefly, then the smile fades, "Cloudtranporter."

Angie and Liling both see the numbers 777 appear in their mind's eye. But it makes no sense to either of them, so they simply dismiss it.

Liling: Look of confusion, "Cargo hull?"

Angie: "Yucatan. Estate."

The voice and vision fade. Liling and Angie open their eyes, seeming to be perplexed. In a state of confusion, they look at each other, shrug their shoulders and speak the last word out loud that they heard as the voice was fading: *"WINGS?!"*

* * *

As the techie pushes the button everything on Lord Josef's estate transforms in an instant.

Eve Elli and Eve Bi suddenly metamorphose into a state of pure exhilaration. The Cloudtransporter disappears and is replaced with a small mesh "house." Inside the mesh house is a little Monarch Butterfly, joyously fluttering her baby wings and giggling with delight. Another Monarch appears just outside the mesh house. She flutters over to her little one trapped inside and says to her baby's heart, *Mama is here, my darling. I will not leave you.*

The techies were told by Bella to program the estate to a garden community, and baby Bi was to come inside the house with SPA and remain unchanged. The Cloudtransporter was to be shape-shifted into a child-sized cage which SPA would then put Bi into. However, without SPA consciously knowing why, something to do with gentle hair-tugs and little ear-kisses, he chose not to follow Bella's orders.

ES, SPA, Jonah, the two techies, the servants, and remaining Master Commandants of the estate see the entire big house disappear around them. ES and SPA now see four huts and several vegetable gardens. They do not see anything of the 12 Master Commandants and four servants. However, they do see a flock of 16 pigeons sitting on the soft earth they are all now standing upon.

The techies have turned into two younger women with completely different appearances. They look nothing at all like their older selves and are, in fact, exceptionally attractive. The two women look at each other and smile with a nod of approval. Then they look at ES and SPA who are staring at each other. The brothers are both surprised and greatly disappointed at what they see. They have not changed at all!

"Brother!" ES cries out completely flummoxed. "You look exactly the same!"

"So do you!" SPA yells. "What happened?!"

* * *

In the bowels of hell Lucifer is having a good laugh. *Simple minded fools!* he says while enjoying the brothers' discontent. *Why do you think they call me Trickster?! Do you really think that I would allow the two of you to have any pleasure with me? Oh no, my henchmen, oh no. I have something much better in store for you.*

Licking his lips Lucifer says, *You will both find out soon enough!*

Turning to his queen Lucifer says, *It is time for you to go up there again, my dear, and give those two nitwits the rest of their instructions.*

Bella simply smiles and looks at Andre. She is smoldering over her own agenda. *Come now, honey. You heard papa.*

* * *

Paul speaks up, "I'm sure that my brothers have something to do with this and if they are in the Yucatan now, that means they are at Lord Josef's Estate.

The Major ponders this and remarks, "Didn't you say that the place where you came from was not far from Chiconahui?"

"Yes, but I never set the coordinates for getting us from one place to the other, so I really can't tell you exactly where it is."

"That shouldn't be a problem," Doc chimes in, "I know the area very well. If a group of us go back to Chiconahui, it seems to me that all we have to do is comb the vicinity from the air in a Cloudtransporter until we see a big house. I mean, a lord's estate should be visible for miles and stick out easily in a place like that, don't you think?"

Sergio considers his own knowledge of the area combined with his heightened awareness since the pyramid activation. He looks at Elena who appears to be thinking the same thing as they nod at each other and smile. Sergio says, "I'm sure that a group of us from Chiconahui can help in the search for Lord Josef's Estate."

Kenny also has an idea. "We can send out 144 pigeons."

Looking at the young folks he says, "That is, each one of you can work with your own group of pigeons. You can send them to garden communities and villages in the Yucatan, letting people know what has happened. And if anyone has any idea where the estate of the late Lord Josef is located, that would be most helpful!"

"Whoa!" the young folks reply. They are all ready and keyed-up for deployment.

Kookie says to Kenny, "Sounds like a great idea, my good man. And I shall leave a Cloudtransporter for you to come and join us in Chiconahui when you are ready. "

"YES!" the youngsters exclaim. They are all excited to be part of the rescue mission for their beloved Eve Elli and little Bi. And they are all doing their best not to show any fear.

Judy and Henrietta decide to remain at Judy's Garden and pray for Eve Elli and little Bi with the Chrysalenes. And Lisa says that she will do the same with the Chrysalenes at Bear River Garden.

Leo shares his idea. "I would like to go back to the Hidden Cave of the Great Quartz Crystal." Looking at Kookie he continues, "From there I can connect the Crystal with Metatron like you did last time, so we can send even more power to the Pyramid of Chiconahui and the surrounding area."

Kookie exclaims, "That is an excellent idea!"

"Yes, and there is another reason I would like to go." Turning to Pasha, Viktor, and Marie, Leo says, "I would like very much to take you with me, my friends, back to the Garden of Tom in Cavern Village, Wyoming. There is a story I must tell you that I can explain in detail on the way."

The others have a pretty good idea what Leo is referring to and they are all touched.

Leo continues, "My brother Pasha, I understand that many years ago you were a commando in the mercenary group led by Master Commandant Mikhail, one of Lady Bella's warriors."

Pasha's eyes widen as Leo explains, "And that you were not one of the commando's chosen for Mikhail's final assignment. It was the assignment which took his life as well as the lives of most of the other commandos."

Pasha now turns pale, and he sits down.

"It is all right, my friend. In fact, I was one of those commandos who *did* go with Mikhail and survived the battle. I now live with my family as one of the farmers at the Garden of Tom."

Turning to Viktor and Marie he says, "And I also know of your plight these past 18 years as a displaced, on-the-run, Slavic lord family. Many of the former commandos of Tom's Garden are also Slavic, and I just know that you would all be welcome to make your home with us, if you wish."

With much love in his heart Leo says, "Would you all like to come and join us?"

Pasha puts his face in his hands and Viktor and Marie hold each other in a tight embrace, as they all begin to weep. Leo puts his hands on their shoulders and says, "I am sure you will be most welcome there."

With their heads held down in awe at the grace they are receiving, Pasha, Viktor, and Marie, slowly nod *yes*. Ivan and Boris are excited listening to their plans and know that they will finally have a place to call home.

Everyone looks on with compassion and love. And the rest of them decide to go to Chiconahui in search of the nearby Yucatan estate of Lord Josef.

Pondering everything, Yakov is furious with himself for not acting on his instincts sooner. "I knew there was something wrong with that Jonah!" he admonishes himself.

Viktor speaks up. "I remember now! Jonah was one of the lords who escaped with us from the Isle of Bella just before it blew!"

Paul suddenly remembers and says to everyone, "Yes! I saw him, too! He was one of the servants at Lord Josef's Estate. Good grief!"

"Kookie looks at Yakov and says, "Well, bratan, I wouldn't take it too much to heart. Let's just move forward from here quickly. Okay? As the Monarch Angel says, "Hop to it!"

Yakov forces a smile and nods at his big brother.

* * *

Leo, Pasha, Viktor, and Marie have left for Wyoming. Kenny, Lisa, and the young folks prepare to leave for Bear River Garden. And everyone else is just about ready to leave for Chiconahui.

They are boarding the Cloudtransporters when Kookie reminds them, "Make sure to have your Metatron devices with you at all times. We will need to stay in touch as we go off in different directions."

As an afterthought he adds, "We will also need the protection of the Metatron programs."

They all agree and begin to board their aircraft, when suddenly Liling is frantically searching through her pouch.

"Where is it?!" she wails, getting very frustrated.

"Where is *what*, my love?" asks Dumaka.

All at once, Liling is hit with the realization and full severity of what has happened and she starts to shriek, *"NO! OH LORD! NOOO!"*

"What?! What is it?! Oh my goodness, Liling! What happened?!" Dumaka, and several of the others cry out.

Liling looks at everyone as she cries out, *"MY METATRON DEVICE! IT'S MISSING!"*

She collapses in agony on the ground. Dumaka, Emeka, Mimi, Yakov, Kookie, Angie, and all the others are around her in minutes.

Dumaka takes her in his arms and holds her gently saying, "What happened, my love? Please tell me."

Stricken with grief Liling tells them, "There is something else I kept getting while we were having the visions with Eve Elli's butterfly. But it didn't make any sense to me, so I just dismissed it."

"What is it?" Angie asks, holding Liling's hands.

"I kept seeing the numbers 777."

Suddenly Angie's jaw drops, and she says, "Me too!"

Liling is beside herself with agony. Dumaka tries to console her, and the others all turn to Kookie. He and Yakov look at each other in horror knowing the full implications of what can happen now. They try not to sink into the gloom of the moment when suddenly, Angie has a thought.

"Listen, everybody!" she says. "Remember what the Chrysalenes and the Monarchs keep telling us. Whatever those guys have we have each other. And remember our biggest lesson from the downfall of the Council and the end of Bella's would-be reign of terror. With Love all things are possible! And THAT, my friends we have . . . lots and lots of love!

"Amen Sister!" Everyone exclaims.

Angie looks at Emeka and says, "Can you hand me that butterfly again? I think I have an idea."

Liling stops sobbing when she hears this and feels in her heart that Angie is on to something. Emeka comes back with the butterfly and places it in Angie's hand again. She motions to Liling and once again they cup their hands around the Monarch. Angie and Liling close their eyes, this time speaking to the Monarch out loud so everyone can hear what they are saying.

"Precious little being of Light and Love," Angie begins, "Please tell us, or show us, what you meant just a little while ago by the word *WINGS.*"

The Monarch starts to flutter in their hands and Angie and Liling can feel its joy. Then they start having a vision and share it with the others:

Liling: A little mesh container.

Angie: Like a house, or a cage.

Liling: Baby Monarch Butterfly inside.

Angie: Mama Monarch Butterfly outside.

The two women suddenly go wide-eyed and yell out together: *EVE ELLI AND EVE BI!*

"*What?!*" Emeka, Mimi, and several of the others cry out. "*EVE* Bi?!"

"YES!" Angie and Liling howl with delight. And Angie explains further, "Little Bi has claimed her birthright! That means we now have *two* Chrysalenes working on the inside over there! And in the form of Monarch Butterflies!"

Everyone is flabbergasted, but none more than Emeka and Mimi who are overcome with emotion at the hope they now feel.

Ryan gets excited at the memory of his own favorite part in the downfall of the Council. He says with great enthusiasm, "You mean, we've got Chrysalene butterfly *MOLES* infiltrating the bad guys?! *COOWAL!*"

Everyone chuckles, and Angie and Liling get one more message from the Monarch in their hands.

Liling says, "Eve Elli has already sent out word to the Monarch Angel, who is alerting Monarch Butterflies around the world to go to the Yucatan."

Angie says, "And she is also alerting the pigeons! Oh, and we are all to go the to the Pyramid of Chiconahui at once!"

Angie and Liling both laugh as they speak the final command of the little being of Light and Love in their hands. *"HOP TO IT, HUMAN CREATURES!"*

* * *

ES and SPA are still stinging with the realization that their appearance has not transformed at all and that they will be completely exposed to anyone who might find them.

The two techies, however, look at each other in amazement. Each one is thinking, *Hm . . . if she looks that good, I wonder what I must look like.*

"What is your name?' one of them says to the other.

"My name is Ruth. How about you?"

"Hi, Ruth, my name is Nita," she says, extending her hand. The newly transformed techies shake hands.

ES hands the Metatron device to Nita and says, "This is the box that we were supposed to retrieve and the two of you are supposed to decipher."

Ruth and Nita are curious as they open Metatron and start to go through Kookie's programs.

"This is really flawless," says Ruth.

She is looking at the 369-program that changed a bioweapon into a creator of an evolved human being, which unintentionally gave rise to the Chrysalenes. Shaking her head she remarks to Nita, "I mean all this guy was trying to do was stop the UC from killing people. And he ended up creating these super-humans instead."

Before they can say anything else an apparition materializes before them. ES and SPA are apprehensive about whatever Bella's next instructions might be. She approaches the four of them and speaks to the techies first. "Well, well, that is quite an improvement my dears, wouldn't you say?"

Ruth and Nita look at each other and then at Bella. They too were escapees from the Isle of Bella just before it was destroyed. Suddenly, they are frightened when they remember Bella's ruthless spirit in life. The queen of the underworld senses their fear, as well as the trembling of ES and SPA standing nearby.

She addresses the four of them. "Now, now, you four. No need to fear. So far you have all done a *wonderful job!* I must say that Lucifer is well pleased with the lot of you!"

Somehow, they do not really believe that Bella is speaking the truth, which is making them even more anxious and fearful.

"Well then," Bella continues, "Let us move to the next phase of your assignment, shall we?"

She is met with gaping stares and silence.

"Fine!" Bella quips. "First, you are to give me the Metatron device."

Nita gingerly hands it to her. Bella turns it over in her hands as if she is inspecting the thing and says, "My, my, is that all there is to it? Our whole world was brought down by something as small as this?"

She looks up for a moment at the others expecting an answer. She gets more frozen silence.

"Yes, I quite agree," Bella smiles. "We are now about to turn the tables on them with this device of their own making."

Turning to the techies, she hands the Metatron device back to Nita and says, "It is now up to you ladies to finish them off, so to speak."

Nita speaks cautiously to Bella as she asks her, "What would you have us do with the device, ma'am?"

"You are to figure out how to use Lord Kenneth's 777-program on this device, sneak in undetected to the pyramid at Chiconahui, and set in reverse whatever it is that they recently did. In other words, ladies, you are to take away all this blissed-out, lovey-dovey junk that they are feeling, this connection to each other and to their Creator, and send the divine energy of absolute power to where it belongs: *TO LUCIFER!* It will instantly send all the people of the world into a state of terror and paranoia, where it will be easy pickings for the beast. Yes indeed! My husband will have his way with them after that!

"AND SO SHALL I!" Bella screams followed by maniacal laughter, waving her serpentine staff in the air.

"CHRYSALENE! THIS HOUR IS YOUR LAST!"

Suddenly, Bella turns around and spots the little mesh cage with the baby Monarch Butterfly trapped on the inside and her mama sitting on top. Chrysalene Monarch Eve Elli is fully focused on the approaching wrath of hell. Bella starts screaming and racing towards Eve Elli, holding Andre high over her head. His fangs protrude and his mouth salivates, anticipating the sweet taste of butterflies.

DIE, CHRYSALENE! DIE! Bella screams, only a few feet away from Eve Elli and Eve Bi. The Monarch Chrysalenes both start glowing and they hear a voice from above calling to them, *"I will never leave you nor forsake you."*[12]

Suddenly, a Bright White Light pours down from Heaven into the bodies of the Chrysalene Monarchs. Their Light is amplified so much that they are as bright as the sun, and Bella is blinded by its intensity. She stops dead in her tracks and screams out in pain from the fierce burning in her eyes.

"NO! NO! NO!" she cries out in horror, dropping Andre to cover her scorched eyes.

"YOU WILL NOT HONOR MY SISTER! YOU WILL HONOR ME! . . . ME! ME! ME! . . . OR YOU WILL DIE!"

Bella drops to the ground in the agonizing pain of her tortured spirit, crying out to the heavens above, "Why did you love my sister and not me?" Holding her hands up to the Light above she continues to wail, "Why? Why? *WHY?!"*

And another voice is heard from Heaven, piercing through the fury of a broken soul. It is the voice of Bella's sister Bi. She is whispering, once again, the last words she spoke to Bella on earth,

---

[12] *Hebrews 13:5, ESV*

at the very moment that her tortured body lay there dying: *"But **I** love you, my sister."*

Bella puts her hands over her ears and lets out the most sorrowful cry, *"NOOOOOO!"* as she collapses in a heap.

The Bright White Light fades and so does Bella, returning to the underworld where her master awaits.

Eve Elli looks at her little one and sighs. Then she looks up to the heavenly realm and says with love and compassion, "Lord, have mercy on the tortured spirit of our sister Bella."

And the voice of Bella's sister Bi, from the heavens above says, "Thank you, Eve Elli, and bless you. It is already done" . . . Amen.

* * *

While Bella was screaming and carrying on, ES, SPA, Ruth, and Nita were hiding inside their huts. They did not dare come out and see what was happening. And when the Bright White Light came, they quickly covered their eyes until the Light was gone. Now that all has gone quiet, they cautiously peep out of their huts. All seems peaceful and still and they are quite relieved to see that Bella is gone. Ruth and Nita return to their work with the 777-program on Metatron, and ES and SPA go back to hiding inside their hut.

ES looks outside for a moment and notices something out of the ordinary which he mentions to SPA.

"Brother, have you noticed that there seems to be several butterflies hanging around that mesh cage over yonder? I mean, initially there was only one sitting on top of it. And now there are at least seven, or so."

"No brother, I haven't noticed," says SPA, who wonders what the women are getting up to in the other hut and when they will be ready with the 777-program.

"And then there are those infernal pigeons!" ES exclaims. They just keep wandering around out there making the most dreadful noise!"

"I believe that is called *cooing,*" SPA says. "Perhaps those infernal pigeons are hungry. Have you tried feeding them?"

ES just snickers at SPA and shakes his head. Then he replies. "I know this is going to sound strange, but it is almost as if they are restless or something. Now what the blazes could a nasty little beast such as a pigeon be restless about, brother?"

SPA is in no mood for trivialities, and he brushes ES off. "Well why don't you just go on out there and *ask* one of the nasty little beasts?!"

"Fine!" says ES as he huffs off to get a closer look at the noisy birds. And when he does so, he is almost knocked to the ground.

Suddenly, he sees the entire Garden of Josef filled with thousands of Monarch Butterflies. His heart begins to pound as he cries out to SPA, "BROTHER! COME QUICKLY!"

The last thing SPA wants is to draw attention to themselves, so with much irritation he goes outside to hush up his brother. But when he sees what is going on, his heart begins pounding too. And as the brothers look up to the sky, they see more butterflies arriving. They have completely surrounded and covered the mesh house with Eve Bi on the inside and Eve Elli on the outside.

"Where is the mesh cage?" yells ES.

"I don't know, brother! I do believe it is over there somewhere!" SPA says, without really having any idea where the cage is anymore.

At that moment, ES and SPA hear another cry coming from Ruth and Nita's hut. The two women come running out of the hut saying, "We've got it! We have unlocked the key to the 777-program!"

And then they see all the butterflies and their hearts start pounding too.

"Good heavens!" Ruth cries out. "What the blazes is that?"

"I don't know," says SPA, "But I think we had better just get ourselves over to the Pyramid of Chiconahui. There is an autovan waiting for us over there in the clearing. Bella said it would be preprogrammed to take us to our destination and that it would not take us long at all to get there."

"Yes, but what about the baby Chrysalene?" ES says rather frantically. "You know that is part of the deal!"

"Do *YOU* want to try and comb your way through all those winged little beasts and probably miss our opportunity of getting to the pyramid before our enemies? We can always come back for the Chrysalene. I do not think she will be going anywhere!"

Chapter 17 – 777

THREE CLOUDTRANSPORTERS are on-route to the Yucatan. Kookie, Yakov, and Rudolpho, the top technical and strategical geniuses are huddled together. They are analyzing the possible plans of ES and SPA, and what damage they could inflict with the Metatron device in their possession. Angie, Liling, and Emeka have organized a team to comb through the rainforest with Eve Elli's butterfly as their guide. They will be searching at a low altitude in one of the Cloudtransporters. Sergio, the Major, Ryan, and the rest have organized themselves into small groups to guard both the pyramid and the village of Chiconahui. They are to watch out for anything or anyone who looks at all suspicious.

ES, SPA, Ruth, and Nita are almost at the village of Chiconahui. The brothers know the geniuses that they are up against and are fairly certain that Kookie and company are close behind, if not already there.

* * *

Kenny and his young recruits leave Judy's Garden, heading for Bear River. Once they arrive everyone goes straight to the pigeon coop. Kenny shows the youngsters how to prepare the messages for the pigeons and attach them to their leg bands, and in no time at all 144 pigeons are ready.

"Okay, guys," Kenny says. "Let's send these birds out to garden communities throughout the Yucatan."

Ivan and Boris are especially excited to be a part of this venture with their new little winged friends.

"These guys are so cute!" Boris says, fawning over the little critter nuzzled against his neck. "Is this really going to help find Eve Elli and Eve Bi?"

"Absolutely," replies Kenny. "When people throughout the Yucatan join together in sending out positive energy, the natural world as well as the heavenly realm will hear it."

Meiling smiles, adding, "And as Angie is always reminding us, "With love all things are possible."

On that note Kenny and his recruits release their pigeons into the air.

"Okay," Kenny says to the youngsters. "Now let's track those little guys and see where they are going to."

Ivan and Boris are new to all of this and are very confused. Ivan says, "How are we supposed to do that, Kenny?"

"Oh, it's all quite simple," Kenny explains. "We close our eyes, put our hands on our chests, and connect our hearts to the hearts of the doves. They will communicate with us and let us know where they are going."

"Wow," Ivan and Boris both exclaim.

Beth and Meiling look at each other and chuckle, and Meiling says to the brothers, "It's okay you guys. You'll get used to it."

The young folks, together with Kenny and Lisa put their heads together, close their eyes and ask the spirit within to connect with the hearts of the doves.

And that is how they discover that the birds are enroute to a garden plot somewhere in the Yucatan, not far from Chiconahui. The doves say that they are on their way to a garden plot with 16 bewildered fledgling pigeons, 3000 Monarch Butterflies, and the guardianship of Eve Elli and Eve Bi.

"WHOA!" Everyone cries out all at once.

And Kenny howls, *"LET'S GO!"*

Kenny, Lisa, and their group board the Cloudtranporter that Kookie left behind for them and head to Chiconahui.

* * *

In the middle of the Yucatan rainforest, on a brand new garden community spot, Kenny's 144 pigeons have just arrived. They discover 16 new pigeon buddies who are rather dazed and a bit confused at their sudden change of "circumstances." However, the more seasoned pigeons are quite happy to indoctrinate the newbies into pigeon-hood, including the new lifestyle that goes along with their recently acquired form.

The myriad of Monarchs is happy to meet the legendary Eve Elli; best buddy of the Monarch Angel, and her baby daughter, who have come to join them as one of their own. They are honored to be protecting and hiding them from the unfriendly human creatures.

* * *

In the village of Chiconahui, Kookie, Yakov, and Rudolpho have come up with a strategy which they are ready to put forward to the group.

"Okay friends! Listen up!" Kookie exclaims. "There is not much time. Yakov, Rudolpho, and I think that we've analyzed their plan, and if we are correct, ES and SPA should be here momentarily, if they are not here already. We also think that they are not alone. Those guys just aren't smart enough to figure out what to do with Metatron, so they are undoubtedly being helped."

Kookie turns to the patrol group and says, "For Sergio, Ryan, and the Major, and the rest of you who have decided to stay close by and help protect us, be on the lookout for two old guys and a few helpers. I think they will be easy to spot once they get here.

"Angie, Liling, and Mimi's team, go ahead and take your Cloutransporter across the rainforest."

Turning to Angie he says, "Please, honey, as soon as you think you have found something, message me immediately! Yakov, Rudolpho, and I will be staying in our Cloudtransporter watching everything with some of the old surveillance equipment I've got in there. Once we hook the surveillance equipment up to Metatron it should be reasonably effective. Also, if we work out of the aircraft we will be ready at a moment's notice to join either of your teams, whoever spots ES, SPA, Eve Elli, or Eve Bi first."

They all look at each other and nod with confidence.

"Is everybody ready, then?!" Kookie shouts.

"Yes! You betcha! We got this!" They shout back as each one heads off to his or her assignment.

Not one of them notices four people standing behind some nearby trees or the well-concealed autovan in the woods. ES, SPA, Ruth, and Nita were about to reach the pyramid when they saw the Cloudtransporters landing. It was too close for comfort with not enough time for them to reach the top of the pyramid undetected. So they had to pull back.

Ruth and Nita explained to ES and SPA that the 777-program will have to be activated from the apex of the pyramid. And they know that they will only have one shot at it without getting caught.

The four of them were listening to Kookie's plan and decided to head back to their autovan. They must now reorganize and re-strategize according to what they just heard.

* * *

In Cavern Village, Wyoming, Leo, Viktor, Marie, and Pasha are camped outside the mouth of the cavern. They are all hooked up to Kookie's Metatron, waiting for the word from him to go into the Hidden Cavern of the Great Quartz Crystal. Speaking to each other in Russian, they commiserate over the dark times behind them.

But Marie reminds them of the lives they now have lying ahead. She says to the men: "We have been through much suffering these past 18 years, but I *do* believe in this *'Kind One'* I hear these people talking about."

She takes her husband Viktor by the hand and says, "It is just the way I felt that time when a group of us were kidnapped by Bella's minions and held prisoner on that deserted beach."

She turns to Leo and Pasha and continues, "I was pregnant with Boris and had little Ivan in captivity with me."

Then Marie looks deep into her husband's eyes and says, "But I never gave up hope that we would see you again." Tears are now forming in her eyes, "And I always felt that someone or something was guiding us to a better life where someday, we would all be happy and free."

With tears flowing down her cheeks Marie proclaims to all of them, "And I believe that time has finally arrived!"

Viktor embraces his wife and the other two close their eyes and smile. For they are all feeling the truth of what Marie has just expressed that, "With love all things are possible."

* * *

Sergio, the Major, and Ryan are organizing the security team at Chiconahui. Gathering the villagers and Chrysalenes together Sergio says to everyone, "Okay, folks. I want all the Chrysalenes to go to the pyramid. They need to surround the place with their high vibrations. Elena, why don't you help me round them up."

Ryan interjects, "I would like very much to climb to the top of the pyramid and act as a lookout. If anything happens, I'll give you all a holler on Metatron!"

The Major says, "And I will go back and forth from the village to the pyramid, keeping an eye on anyone who might show up in either place. If there is a con artist anywhere around I'll be sure to know it. After all, as the saying goes, it takes one to know one! Any other tricksters in the group wanna join me?"

Everyone has a chuckle and Vi says, "Sure, my henchman husband! I got your back!"

They form two groups and disburse. All except Ryan that is, who is headed for the pyramid.

Alone.

As Ryan reaches the pyramid, he is not aware of four people who have also just showed up and are hiding in the thicket close by.

Off in the nearby field, a Cloudtranporter has just landed. Kookie has been watching the aircraft arrive and he recognizes it as the one he left Kenny and Lisa.

"Something has happened over there!" Kookie exclaims to Yakov and Rudolpho. I'll go meet them. You guys stay here and I'll be right back."

"Okay, bratan," they say.

* * *

Angie and Liling's group are flying low over the trees and vegetation in search of Lord Josef's estate.

Liling says to Paul, "Does any of this look familiar?"

Paul is embarrassed as he sighs. "I'm sorry, but I never really paid attention to anything while flying in the Cloudtransporter. It all looks the same down there anyway."

He sighs again and says, "How about the butterfly? Getting any messages from her?"

Angie and Liling look at each other and then they look at Paul.

I don't know," says Angie, "I mean it's weird. All I keep hearing and seeing over and over is *Wings!* Wings, wings, wings, wings, *WINGS!*"

Liling looks at her. "Did you say you are *seeing* wings? 'Cause all I'm getting is a voice, not a vision."

Suddenly, Mimi is having a vision. She remembers the rescue of Eve Elli when she was three years old and about to be executed along with her mom and dad and the other Chrysalenes in their group. Mimi sees it all happen again. How she screamed when she saw the commandos aim their guns at her granddaughter, and suddenly a swarm of thousands of butterflies filled the night sky.

All at once, Mimi screams out with passion and hope, *"WINGS! YES! IT'S THE MONARCHS!"*

Emeka and the others jump as they look at her, *"What?! What Monarchs?! What are you saying?!"* Emeka wails.

Mimi laughs and cries at the same time. "We are to look for the Monarchs!" she proclaims. "Thousands of Monarch Butterflies! *Not* Lord Josef's Estate!"

Angie and Liling give a sudden start and they too begin to laugh.

Angie says, "This little one in our hands is suddenly fluttering away like crazy."

Liling says to the little Being of Light, "Can you take us to the butterflies?"

* * *

David is the first one of Kenny and Lisa's group to come racing down the ramp of the Cloudtransporter. He runs to his father with Kenny, Lisa, and the other young folks right behind him.

"DAD!" David cries out when he sees Kookie coming quickly towards them. "It's the pigeons!"

"What?!" gasps Kookie. He is all out of breath as he reaches his son.

"The doves!" Kenny cries, as he too is out of breath with excitement when the rest of them reach Kookie. "We directed the pigeons to 144 different garden communities in the Yucatan, but when we connected with their hearts we discovered that they were all heading this way."

"Really?!" Kookie's eyes go wide with amazement.

"That is their dove nature, dad!"

"Their *what?!*"

Lisa and the youngsters chuckle since they all got the full explanation on the way over.

"Okay, brother. Why don't you explain it to *me* while we walk back to my Cloudtransporter. Yakov and Rudolpho are waiting. Looks like we're gonna have to track those pigeons!"

Ryan has climbed to the top of the pyramid. Remembering how he made little Bi giggle at the pyramid near Johannesburg when he beat his chest from up there, he has a sudden moment of sadness. He looks up to the clouds and says aloud, "If you can hear me, Angel, please let me beat my chest again for little Bi. Why, I'll even beat my head and knock my brains out if you will let me hear her giggle again."

"That can be arranged," a voice answers. But it is not from above nor speaking to his heart.

Ryan turns around and looks down to see who the voice belongs to.

There is a man smiling at him, climbing up the pyramid. He is holding a large staff with the head of a serpent on the end of it.

* * *

Kookie, Kenny, Lisa, and all the kids pile into Kookie's Cloudtransporter. David jumps on his dad's equipment and exclaims to Kookie, Yakov, and Rudolpho, "The pigeons! The pigeons! We've got to track the pigeons!"

"What?" Yakov and Rudolpho look at David, confused.

As Kenny explains what is happening, David and Kookie are already in front of their screens. Everyone has gathered around them and are looking on with utter fascination. Father and son work quickly, touching the screens and zeroing in until they get a lock on the exact location of the pigeons.

"*There they are!*" David exclaims.

And everyone excitedly cries out at once, "*HUZZAH!*"

"*LET'S GO!*" shouts David.

But suddenly Kookie's expression changes as he looks at the screen again.

David notices the worried look on Kookie's face and says, "What is it, dad?

Yakov and Rudolpho stare at their screens as Kookie looks up and they all lock eyes with each other. Yakov says to both of them, "I'm on it! Notify the Major and have their whole team meet me there immediately!"

He dashes out of the Cloudtransporter and Kookie nods to Rudolpho, who messages the Major.

Meanwhile, the whole group stares at Kookie wondering what just happened. And then David sees it; his father's penchant for flashing red lights. All at once it starts flashing red at the pyramid.

David and Rudolpho look at each other and the thought occurs to them at the same time. David cries out, "The Great Quartz Crystal!"

"Yes!" Rudolpho agrees. "I will message Leo at once! Time to get the positive energy from that badass crystal, laser focused on our pyramid!"

* * *

"Emeka!" Angie cries out, "Get in front of the programming panel! We need to set the coordinates!"

"Already there!" Emeka exclaims.

Angie motions to Mimi to join her and Liling. As Mimi cups her hands over Angie and Liling's hands with the butterfly inside, they all move to the programming panel. Angie puts one of her hands on the panel sensors and Emeka watches as the numbers appear on the screen.

Paul looks on, stupefied. He is dying to ask questions about what is happening but knows to just keep quiet for the moment. He has never seen intuition, the natural world, and technology all work together.

In no time at all, the butterfly in the women's hands has the location pinpointed and Emeka locks in the coordinates. He hits the velocity link and they are off.

* * *

ES reaches the top of the pyramid. Without warning (and still smiling at Ryan), he swiftly thwacks Ryan over the head with the staff. Ryan tumbles to the ground and lies still.

SPA and the women are perplexed.

"Why didn't you use the serpent's fangs to tear into him, My Lord?" asks Nita.

ES replies, "I heard the master's voice in my head saying, *Beware! There must NOT be the blood of a righteous man spilled on these stones!*"

Ryan is motionless with blood from his head spilling on the ground within inches of the bottom of the pyramid.

* * *

Everything goes dark for a moment, until Ryan is aware of a Bright White Light at the end of a Kaleidoscopic tunnel of beautiful colors. There is a warm Presence radiating around him, the likes of which he has never felt. It is so peaceful that Ryan is compelled to move forward through the tunnel toward the loving Presence of the Light at the end of it. And the Monarch Angel appears before him.

"You may come home now if you wish, Ryan creature. The choice is yours. However, should you choose to remain here on earth for now, this is what lies ahead for you."

Ryan sees the Cloudtransporter with Mimi in it racing toward the butterflies. Then he sees the garden with 3000 butterflies, 160 pigeons, and the two they are guarding. He hears the voice of Eve Bi giggling as she joyfully plays with the Monarchs in her charge.

Then he sees Eve Elli in the form of a butterfly, looking directly at him . . .

"You may go home now if you wish, grampa. I will let Eve Bi know all about her courageous great-grampa and how he loved her so."

Then she smiles at Ryan with all the love and compassion of a Chrysalene, and Eve Elli says, "It's okay. You can go home now and be with the Lord. It's okay. I love you, grampa. You can go."

* * *

"I hear voices! Hurry!" ES yells at Ruth and Nita, as they quickly set up the Metatron device.

SPA suddenly hears another sound. It is the sound of giggling from a little angel who is planting baby angel kisses all over his face.

Then SPA hears a voice speaking to his heart saying, *Come, Follow Me, human creature! The choice is yours! There is still time! Follow me!*

With tears in his heart, SPA answers the voice out loud saying, "Yes! I will follow you! What would you have me do?"

ES hears his brother's words, looks at him and fears the worst, but he knows there is no time to stop him as the Major and Yakov now appear in the distance. They are running toward the pyramid with a flock of people and Chrysalenes right behind them.

SPA climbs down the pyramid and goes to Ryan while ES yells at Ruth and Nita. Only it is not the voice of ES. It is the voice of Lucifer who has been watching everything from the depths of hell. He screams up from hell through the mouth of ES with all his might:

"DO IT! DO IT! DO IT NOW!"

SPA reaches Ryan.

Leo reaches the Great Quartz Crystal and turns on Metatron.

The Major and Yakov are only a few feet away from SPA and Ryan.

SPA scoops up some of Ryan's blood and wipes it on the stone just as the women press the button on top of the pyramid and trigger 777.

Suddenly the ground begins to shake and the pyramid starts to rock with a thunderous rumbling from within. At that moment, the Major and Yakov reach Ryan and SPA falling on the ground in front of them. They instinctively grab Ryan's lifeless body and drag him across the shaking ground away from the pyramid. The others all catch up and the Chrysalenes surround the Major, Yakov, and Ryan.

In a flash, the pyramid erupts like a volcano, throwing a tower of flames high into the sky. ES, Ruth, and Nita are thrown off the apex with the force of the blast and crash onto the stones below. Everything goes black for them, and ES continues to fall downward into the dark underworld where Lucifer is awaiting his arrival with great anticipation.

As the pyramid continues to shake violently, one of the large stones loosens and comes crashing down on SPA.

The earth is still shaking but starts to steady, and the Chrysalenes form a tight circle around Ryan's lifeless body. The shaking beneath them gradually stops, the pyramid settles, and the bellowing fire subsides.

All the people surrounding Ryan and the Chrysalenes close their eyes and bow their heads as the Chrysalenes put their hands on Ryan's body and sing the healing song of the angels.

Chapter 18 – I AM

"WE'RE ALMOST THERE!" Emeka cries out.

Mimi anxiously scans the treetops and clearings below. Her heart is racing and she can hardly breathe.

Paul comes over to comfort her. "It's okay," he says. "I'm sure Eve Elli and Eve Bi are just fine."

"I'm sure they're okay, too," says Liling.

"We are all feeling the same thing Mimi," Angie chimes in. "It won't be long now!"

* * *

Eve Elli sits on top of the mesh house along with her new friends. They watch as Eve Bi eats a piece of apple that appeared in her cage.

Speaking to their hearts Eve Elli says, *Sweet friends, I am so honored to be a part of your world.*

The Monarchs all twitter and giggle. *And we are so happy to have you and the little one among us, dear sister. It is our greatest honor to protect you!*

Thank you! Eve Elli replies graciously. *It was quite by chance that little Eve Bi and I became one of you.*

Really? Gracious! How is that?

Well, when I stepped outside the aircraft, the first thing I saw was all of you Monarch Butterflies fluttering around by the flowers, sipping nectar, and looking so happy.

More giggles. *Ah yes! That is true. We do love sipping nectar!*

The Chrysalene Monarch begins to glow with joy. *And my very next thought was to go inside the craft and join my little one. As I was thinking about those two things, suddenly the surroundings changed. And, well, it seems that my thoughts became reality for both me AND my child!*

The Monarchs are stunned. *Wow! Amazing! Thoughts becoming reality!*

Yes! Eve Elli says. *I Am my thoughts, manifest!*

More giggling, and then a loud signal is emitted by those who are keeping watch.

The human creatures! They are here! Up we go! Goodbye, Eve Elli, and Eve Bi! Always remember we love you, and love manifests all.

Off in the distance everyone in the Cloudtransporter suddenly witnesses an amazing spectacle. Three thousand Monarch Butterflies swarm up into the air, together with 144 pigeons.

"That's it! That's it!" all the human creatures in the Cloudtransporter yell at once. "The Monarchs Rising!"

Emeka brings the craft down underneath the Monarchs and doves, slowly circling around an empty garden plot. All they can see is four huts, a few trees and shrubs, and a large clearing.

Then Angie sees it. "What's that?" she asks, looking at something small on the ground.

"I'm taking her down!" Emeka cries, landing near the object.

He bolts out of the Cloudtransporter with Mimi and Angie right behind. They come upon the mesh butterfly cage and in an instant, the butterfly sitting on top flutters over to Emeka and nestles in his hair. Mimi picks up the cage and sees the little one fluttering about inside.

Eve Elli speaks to their hearts, *It is I, Eve Elli and the little one is Eve Bi!* she proclaims as the two Chrysalene butterflies begin to glow.

"Eve Elli! Eve Bi!" Emeka, Mimi, and Angie cry out. "What?! How?! What can we do?!"

Don't worry, Eve Elli says with compassion, *everything is gonna be okay. Just get us back to Kookie. He will know what to do.*

Emeka and Mimi are in tears as they hold their precious loved ones close to their hearts.

Angie exclaims, "Come on, you guys. Let's get back to Chiconahui!"

As they all get into the Cloudtransporter Liling looks at them in sorrow. Kookie just messaged her and she does not have the heart to give Mimi the news about Ryan.

* * *

Ryan's spirit is in the tunnel of light, holding onto Angel. She guides him to the Gates of Heaven and he is almost home.

As he gazes upon the warm, Bright White Light he sees a familiar face. It is his sister waving to him, the one he wanted to introduce Mimi to on Amber Beach many years ago. His sister was killed by the Ebola bioweapon shortly thereafter, and the two women never did get to meet. The memory saddens him, but he is happy to see her now.

All at once, Ryan is aware of another presence coming up behind him. He stops for a moment and turns around. To his amazement there is SPA with two angels on either side guiding him to the Light.

SPA is most happy to see Ryan. He catches up to him and explains, "It was your blood that saved me."

"How so?!" asks Ryan, perplexed.

"The blood of a righteous man was needed to block the effects of the reversed 777-program. The voice of Love called to me one more time and I saw my little great-granddaughter, your granddaughter, Eve Bi, and my heart knew what path to choose. I could not let Lucifer destroy little Bi's world. So the voice of Love told me to wipe your blood on the stone and all would be saved.

"Thank you and bless you, Ryan, for being the chosen righteous one. As Heaven welcomes you home surely the world will miss you."

And with that, SPA goes before Ryan and enters the Gates of Heaven.

Ryan looks at Angel who says to him, "There is one more thing I think you should see, Righteous Creature, before we go any further."

He looks back through the tunnel as Angel gives him one last vision of what is happening on earth below. "The choice is yours," Angel says with much love and compassion.

* * *

Emeka, Mimi, the Chrysalene butterflies, and the others have just landed at Chiconahui. Emeka has both butterflies nestled in his hair as he dashes down the portal of the Cloudtransporter headed for Kookie.

The others are getting ready to follow him, especially Mimi. But as she rushes to the portal Liling stops her. "Mimi!" Liling says with urgency. "I must tell you something first."

The others all look at Liling wondering what is going on.

"While you were outside getting Eve Elli and Eve Bi, a message came in. I did not have the heart to tell you right away. But now you must know what happened."

"What! What happened?!" Mimi yells. She is instantly filled with anxiety.

The others are also visibly upset at whatever this news could be.

Up above in the tunnel of Light, the spirit of a righteous man witnesses his loved one below as she hears the news of his passing.

Mimi is stricken with agonizing despair and lets out a gut-wrenching scream, ***"NOOO! NOOO! NOOO! OH GOD! NOOO! RYAN! MY SWEET RYAN! NOOOOOOOOO!"***

She runs down the portal ramp and almost collapses as the others come quickly to her aid. They hold her up as Mimi cries and screams all the way to the pyramid, where Ryan's body lays. The Chrysalenes are still singing angel songs of healing to him and the villagers of Chiconahui have adorned his body with many flowers.

As Mimi reaches Ryan she falls to the ground in front of him. Inconsolable, she takes her beloved in her arms. Rocking him back and forth Mimi says, "I love you, my angel. I love you so much. I'm so sorry I wasn't here. I could have gone with you."

Looking up to the heavens Mimi cries out, "Please don't leave me here without my angel. Please dear Lord, please take me home too."

Mimi bows her head over her husband and kisses him, washing his face in her tears.

The Chrysalenes continue singing with the group seated around them. All eyes are closed and heads are bowed. Mimi rocks the body of her husband and weeps in great agony.

Suddenly, Ryan's body jolts causing Mimi to jump. The Chrysalenes stop singing and everyone else looks up.

Ryan's face starts to twitch and low and behold, his eyes slowly open.

Way up high a voice speaks to his heart saying, *Good choice, Righteous Creature!*

Mimi's tears turn to tears of joy and gratitude holding her angel tight. Kissing him softly she says to her Ryan, "Thank you, my darling. Thank you for coming back to me."

Ryan smiles at her and whispers, "I love you, Mimi." And he closes his eyes for a good healing rest.

* * *

Emeka is frantically watching Kookie, Yakov, and Rudolpho as they open the programs on Metatron and get to work.

After a preliminary scan, Kookie sighs and sadly says to Emeka, "I'm sorry bro. This one is not going to be that simple. It's going to take a bit of time for us to figure out a way of returning Eve Elli and Eve Bi to their human form. But don't give up hope. We have a good team here. You know we'll do all we can."

Emeka looks down as his heart sinks. "I was afraid you might say something like that." Yakov puts his hand on Emeka's shoulder. Emeka says, "She is my very best friend, my angel, my soulmate. I knew that from the moment I first heard her voice in my head."

Still looking down and with tears in his eyes he says, "I was only five years old and Eve Elli was only three. But we knew even then that we were the bestest of best buddies, ever."

Yakov and Kookie look at each other. They each have a story of their own of how the three-year-old Eve Elli gave them hope when they had none. Her love and compassion have been a gift and a blessing to so many throughout her short life. Kookie and Yakov know that they will never give up on her.

Back at the pyramid, the Major, Sergio, and some of the other men have created a blanket carrier and taken Ryan to one of the huts. Adam Mateo and Eve Sophia are singing him back to health, while Doc and Vi pick healing plants for herbal preparations. Ryan was gone for some time, and they are all hoping that when he has fully recovered he will remember enough of what happened to share his story.

Paul stands over SPA's body. He is just hearing from the Chrysalenes about SPA's part in saving everyone and wonders where his brother's soul is now.

Eve Maria says, "I am certain that Brother SPA has found peace and is now in the House of the Lord. Look, Brother Paul and behold SPA's face. Is he not shining with the light of the Holy One in his eyes?"

Paul looks at his brother's eyes and knows in his heart that Eve Maria is speaking the truth. "Indeed, it is so, Eve Maria. Indeed, it is so," Paul says.

Not far away are the bodies of ES, Ruth, and Nita. Paul says to Eve Maria, "What do you suppose happened to them?"

Eve Maria gives it some thought before answering. "There are many concepts about eternity, brother. Many ideas and many things that can happen. One thing we do know for sure though, is that with love all things are possible. And that love is the greatest power of all."

Paul begins to feel a ray of hope. "You mean whatever happens to us can always be changed?"

Eve Maria smiles at him with much compassion. "Yes. That is exactly so."

Some of the villagers have prepared a burial place for the fallen. They do not distinguish between those who aligned themselves with Love or with fear. The bodies of ES, SPA, Ruth, and Nita are taken to the burial ground which the Chrysalene's have consecrated. They say a blessing over the four, finishing with, "And they shall dwell in the House of the Lord forever."

* * *

Deep in the bowels of hell an angry Lucifer responds, *I don't think so! Oh no! I do NOT think so! At least one of those characters is now dwelling in MY house! And if I have any say in the matter IT WILL INDEED BE FOREVER!"*

BELLAAA!

The angry beast shouts for his queen. "You have failed me, woman!"

Bella looks at him with narrowed eyes. "I? I have failed YOU?"

"YES, MY QUEEN! YOU – HAVE – FAILED - ***MEEE!*** *And now I must consider a suitable punishment for you!"*

It seems that the beast has not quite learned his lesson yet. Nor is he familiar with the quote, "Heav'n has no rage, like love to hatred turn'd, Nor hell a fury, like a woman scorn'd." In its day it was simply known as, "Hell hath no fury like a woman scorned."[13]

If he ever does learn that lesson he will know never to scorn his woman.

----

[13] *"The Mourning Bride"; William Congreve, 1697*

Bella struts over to him and says sarcastically, "I'm not quite sure I heard you correctly." Bending her ear towards him she says, "Did you say I failed you? Did you say PUNISH? MOI?! **REALLY?!"**

In one swift motion Bella raises her arms high over her head and screams, "ANDREEE!"

Her serpent buddy appears in her hands with gaping fangs and a great big smile. Andre, at least, knows the drill already.

As she comes down upon her seemingly unsuspecting mate, this time Bella slashes him to more than a hundred pieces and it takes him more than just a few minutes to pull himself back together again.

He then crawls over to his queen, his throbbing lust for her overflowing, and says, "Ah, my woman, you are forgiven."

Just then a voice is heard from above and says to Lucifer, "Ah, beastie creature, but you are NOT forgiven so quickly. It has been decided that there will have to be some limitations placed on your trickery and shenanigans with the human creatures for the time being."

"Yes indeed!" Angel continues, "In fact, that woman of yours and her serpent are also being temporarily diminished. The Garden is back! And this time NO SCALY CREATURE will be telling a woman what to do! Of this I AM CERTAIN!"

Lucifer and Bella are left speechless. But Andre whimpers.

The scaly creature was truly beginning to enjoy himself.

Epilogue – Eden

OVER THE NEXT SEVERAL DAYS, Kookie checks in with various garden communities all over the world. And he is happy to discover that no one seems to have sustained any damage. On the contrary, there is an absence of fear and increase of love everywhere. There are also reports of people remembering who they and their people are, and their purpose here on earth. It is this very thing that Kookie, Yakov, Liling, and the others are most excited about.

That evening Kookie calls for a gathering at the village of Chiconahui where he will share with everyone his ideas for a big event. Ever since their summit conference many years ago when the plans for a free world were first discussed, Kookie has been fascinated with something he read in a history book. He shared it with his friends at the time and they all got excited about it too.

Now it is time to recreate and manifest this thrilling historic event.

Everyone gathers around the campfire bringing food and a joyous spirit. Ryan has been recovering steadily day by day and he is about to share his story with his friends and all the villagers.

Kookie says that he, Yakov, and Rudolpho are close to figuring out the mechanics of the shape-shifter program that turned Eve Elli and Eve Bi into Monarch Butterflies. Although they are all frustrated by the fact that they haven't figured it out already, Eve Elli has been most encouraging.

Everyone is seated and Angie stands up to speak, "Thank you all for gathering together this evening. We are anxious to share with you our plans for an exciting upcoming event!"

The villagers and friends look at each other with great anticipation as Angie continues, "A long time ago my husband found something in a history book that captured his imagination. Before the Council took control of our minds and our lives people were free to do all kinds of things including expressing their love, joy, and creativity together."

There are nods of understanding and sighs of regret from one and all.

"Since we won our freedom and have become a new free world of garden communities, we have been focusing a lot of energy on reuniting the people, networking, and coming together in regular summit conferences. I believe that we have all benefited from regular local gatherings, as well as greater global summits. It has helped us to share our knowledge and become united in our efforts."

Everyone agrees, with many index fingers pointing in the air.

"It has been necessary for us to rebuild our lives from the broken place we came from, to the thriving garden villages and communities of today. And now, my wonderful friends, we are ready to take the next step forward!"

"Oh my! What could that be!" the crowd murmurs.

"I will turn it over to Kookie and let him share with you what he discovered in the history books of long ago."

Everyone applauds as Kookie rises and takes the floor. Closing his eyes and breathing deep, he smiles, taps the tips of his fingers together, and begins, "Those of you who remember our very first summit conference might recall the fun we had sharing our new ideas of what it would be like to have a life of freedom."

Everyone smiles as they recall the loving, positive, hopeful energy they were filled with at the summit.

"Well," Kookie continues, "At the time I mentioned to a few of you that the summit reminded me of something I had read about in our past."

Looking out at all the eyes focused on him, Kookie says, "It was an event called a Music Festival!"

"Ha ha! Yes!" Liling, Vi, and Doc jump up and yell.

Vi howls, "Oh my, how I *do* remember you saying that Kookie! Are you saying that we should have a Music Festival?!"

"Actually," exclaims Kookie, "what I am suggesting is that we have a *worldwide* music festival all over One Garden. The larger garden communities can connect with each other through the 36 Metatron devices out there.

"I propose doing this for three days, just the way they described it in the history book. They called it Three Days of Peace and Music, which is what they were manifesting. But I propose that we call it Three Days of Love and Music, as we all move forward together, all people everywhere around the world, ushering in a higher level of divine love!"

"Whoa, brother! Huzzah! Awesome! Let's do it! Yes!" the crowd shouts around the campfire, with much laughter, backslapping and hugs all around.

When the excitement quiets down, Kookie remarks, "I guess that means you all like the idea, then!"

"Hahaha!" more laughter erupts, with a resounding, "Amen!"

"There is one more announcement that we need to make but first, I would like to invite our brother Ryan to share with you what happened to him recently at the pyramid."

Everyone applauds as Ryan stands and begins to tell his story. "Thank you, everybody. Thank you for being there when I had the fall and for your kindness in helping me through my recovery. I would like very much to share with you what happened. It was quite a journey which has changed me forever."

Ryan tells the crowd how he was attacked by ES at the top of the pyramid and fell into a pool of darkness. Then he found himself in a beautiful tunnel of Light and was filled with the warmth and love of the Creator.

Ryan shares how he wanted very much to cross over and become one with the Light, especially when he saw his sister waiting for him. But then something happened. Angel was with him and she said he could choose whether or not to go home at this time.

"As I looked behind me, I saw SPA coming up from below, being escorted by two angels. SPA was so happy to see me. He told me how I helped him and thanked me as he crossed over into the Light."

Paul listens intently as Ryan describes SPA's journey home to the Creator. He has a tearful breakdown, and through heavy sobs says, "Thank you, Ryan, my brother. Thank you and bless you."

Liling and Dumaka sit on either side of Paul and they wrap their arms around him. Dumaka says, "It is truly a miracle. We are all so happy for SPA and for you too, Brother Paul."

Ryan looks at his wife and continues his story. "It was then that I saw my beloved Mimi receive the news about me. I could hear her screams, but more than that, I could feel what she was feeling. I watched as she was escorted to the pyramid where my body lay, covered in flowers and being sung to by the heavenly choir of Chrysalenes.

"I looked at Angel, who knew exactly what I was feeling. She smiled and said, *It's okay, Righteous Ryan Creature. We shall still be here when you are ready to come back.*

"Angel then brought me back down through the tunnel until I saw myself hovering over Mimi. I watched and felt her heart as she was tearfully holding and rocking me. Then Angel sort of pushed me and I felt myself jump back into my body. As I opened my eyes I saw the beautiful face of my beloved and knew in my heart that I would never leave her like that again."

With those words Ryan sits down and takes Mimi in his arms. And everyone knows that he truly will never leave his beloved again.

Angie stands up one more time to give the final announcement. "I know that we have all been waiting for the return of Eve Elli and Eve Bi to their human forms, and that Kookie, Yakov, and Rudolpho, with the help of David and a few others, have been working day and night to figure out how to do that. I'm also sure that sooner or later, they will come up with the solution. But in the meantime, Liling, Vi, Doc, myself, and a few others have been talking to Eve Elli through our hearts every day. I have asked her if she would speak through me to all of you here this evening. And of course, she said that it would be an honor for her to serve you."

Everyone smiles as their hearts are warmed, looking forward to what Eve Elli has to say to them.

Angie goes over to Emeka who has his wife and baby daughter nestled comfortably in his hair. The Chrysalene Monarch flutters from Emeka to Angie and nestles in *her* hair.

Angie closes her eyes, puts her hands over her heart and speaks the words she hears from Eve Elli:

I am so happy to be a Monarch Butterfly! It has truly been a blessing to experience the exquisite passion and love that these beautiful creatures feel! Their love for life is so great that it is easy to see how they can manifest anything with the love in their collective soul.

My dearest friends, I believe with all my heart that we human creatures can do the same.

* * *

The next day, everyone is excited heading to their Cloudtransporters. Kenny and Lisa are returning to Bear River Garden, dropping off Ivan and Boris in Wyoming, along the way. The Major, Vi, their boys and Henrietta are returning to Howard Pharmaceuticals. Doc is staying in Chiconahui for a while, along with Suzie of the Seashells, Rudolpho, Sergio, Elena, and the children. And everyone else is going to Emeka and Eve Elli's estate in Johannesburg.

Kenny and Lisa arrive home with quite a surprise waiting for them.

Kenny goes to the back garden to check on his pigeons and, lo and behold, he finds his 144 birds in various locations around the garden attending to 16 new little critters, who look lost and out of place!

"Huh?!" Kenny says, scratching his head. "Now where in the blazes did *you* guys come from?"

He yells out to his wife in the cottage, "Hey Lisa! Come on out here, honey!"

Lisa comes to the back garden, sees what her husband is looking at and places her hands on her hips.

"Huh?!" Lisa says, "Now where, in all of One Garden, did *you* guys come from?"

She looks at Kenny and says, "Well, my goodness! *That* certainly is a mystery!"

Kenny has a thought, "I guess our little guys must have picked up a few strays along the way!" He and Lisa chuckle and he says, "I guess I had better make a few more coops to house 16 new pigeons!"

The Chrysalenes from Bear River Garden join Lisa and Kenny.

Adam Nelson says, "The doves returned a few days ago with the new ones in their fold. We have been feeding them since their return and connecting to their hearts. Their messages have expressed much confusion and uncertainty as to their very identity! So this morning we decided to start singing the angel songs of healing to them."

"Well," says Lisa, "It will be quite interesting to see what comes of that!"

The men nod in agreement.

"Meanwhile," says Kenny to Lisa, "We've got a job to do. Let's get those announcements about the Worldwide Music Festival written and sent out to 144 garden communities. Who knows, maybe in a few days we will have 16 more carriers ready to go to 16 more gardens!"

They all have a chuckle and Adam Nelson says, "I guess that means we Chrysalenes have a job to do, too!"

* * *

In Cavern Village, Wyoming, Leo, Pasha, Viktor, and Marie, decided to remain for several days at the Cavern of the great Quartz Crystal. With Viktor's technological expertise and the Metatron device that was left with Leo, he has been working on programs to harness the energy of the crystal for other possible uses throughout One Garden.

They are all intrigued about what Viktor has been working on, and are looking forward to sharing it with Kookie, Yakov, and Rudolpho.

They have finished their work at the Hidden Cavern and are just arriving at the Garden of Tom in Cavern Village. When they learn what has happened during the time that they were gone, and the pyramids were activated, they are completely amazed. Families all over the area have been reporting a huge, miraculous upsurge in pregnancies. It is the talk of every coffeehouse for many miles around along with the boom in crop production.

Life is suddenly proliferating in a way it has not done for several generations. The old Council destroyed so much of the presence of love, and instead created a physical and emotional toxicity from too many years of greed. And with that, the will to live seemed to just give up in much of life on earth. But in the time that Leo has been gone, the green landscape is now blossoming and blooming everywhere, the likes of which they have never seen. Even the corn stalks appear to be twice their size.

Master Sam and several of the villagers see Leo with the five newcomers and come over to welcome them. "Hey there, folks!"

Master Sam exclaims, "Welcome back Leo! And Welcome to the newcomers! My, it's good to see you all! And who might these new folks be?"

Leo introduces them to everyone and says, "My dearest friends, these good people are Slavs who have been displaced and are in need of a home. They are, Viktor and his wife Marie, their two sons Ivan and Boris, and a friend Pasha. I was hoping that you all would welcome them into our community."

Master Sam holds out his arms to Viktor, Marie, Ivan, Boris, and Pasha. "Good people, it is my honor to welcome you into our garden community. May we invite you to make your home here with us."

Viktor and his family and Pasha are touched and deeply grateful for the loving welcome they receive. They bow their heads with great humility and say, "Spasiba and thank you," to their new community.

There are warm hugs and laughter all around.

One of the men, Frank, is there with his daughter, 18-year-old Annamarie. He comes over to welcome Pasha and the two men look at each other for a moment.

"Don't I know you from somewhere?" Frank says rather puzzled.

Pasha already knows who Frank is and he tells him, shyly, "Yes, Commando Vladimir, it is I, your old comrade Pasha."

Frank's eyes widen as he explodes with laughter. "BWAHAHA! Well, my goodness! Commando Pasha! Will wonders never cease!"

The two old friends laugh and embrace each other warmly.

Meanwhile, Annamarie has been staring at this very handsome man called Pasha, drawn to his sparkling eyes. And suddenly, old sparkling eyes notices Annamarie.

He sparkles.

She twinkles.

And with a sweet smile they both sigh.

Leo gets down on his knees, and his wife and daughters, along with Viktor, Marie, Ivan, Boris, Master Sam, Frank, Pasha, and Annamarie, join him. With an overwhelming feeling of gratitude Leo says, "Thank you, thank you, Kind One! Thank you for the abundance you have given us; the abundance of life."

Looking at his family and friends he adds, "And thank you for the abundance of love. Bless us, and our new friends."

Then Master Sam gives everyone the news he just received from Kookie about the Music Festival.

"*YAY!*" Leo's daughters howl and the rest all laugh and cheer.

With one final thought, Leo holds his hands up to the heavens above and proclaims, "May this Music Festival truly be in Your honor, Kind One!"

And Pasha gazes at Annamarie as he says, "Amen!"

* * *

The Major, Vi, Henrietta, and the boys walk into Howard Pharmaceuticals and are instantly struck by something different about the plant. They look at each other and the Major says, "Wow! Is it my imagination or has it suddenly gotten a whole lot brighter in here?"

The others nod in total agreement.

Jayson says, "Gee dad, it looks like someone added a whole lotta light bulbs to the place!"

As they look at each other in bewilderment, they are greeted by the senior shop manager, Reggie. The Major and his family gape at this man who looks as bright as the light bulbs.

"Hello, hello, everyone! My goodness, how wonderful it is to see you all again! We have missed you all so *very* much! Why, Henrietta darling, you look absolutely *ravishing,* my dear!"

She giggles.

Reggie continues, "And don't you handsome young men look just as wise as your wonderful old man!"

The handsome, wise young men chuckle.

Finally, Reggie turns to the Major and says, "And don't you and the Mrs. look like the picture of health, beauty, and sweet, coo-coo, love birds!"

With that everyone laughs out loud, and the Major says to him, "My man! Whatever it is that you've been eating, drinking, or smoking, bring it into my office at once! And *DO* share it with your boss!"

* * *

The last Cloudtransporter has just landed in Johannesburg.

Emeka, Kookie, Liling, Yakov, and company arrive to find the Trader's Market underway in the back field of the estate.

Emeka remarks, "How excellent is that? With so many people here today, we can announce the upcoming Music Festival!"

The others enthusiastically agree, and Neely says, "I should like very much to go to the Village of the Holy Ones right away and share all the news with them. I don't know why, I just have a need to connect with Mama Eve Zula, Papa Adam Makena, and Eve Gerda right now."

Turning to Yakov she says, "Would you come with me, my darling?"

He gives her a smile, a great big kiss, and says, "Let's go."

Turning to the others he tells them, "We'll catch up with you guys later at the Big House."

"Will do," says Kookie.

Meanwhile a crowd of people have noticed the return of Emeka and are coming over to greet him.

"Hello, Lord Emeka! How wonderful to see you again! The market has been doing exceptionally well since you were last here! Where is Eve Elli and the little one?"

Emeka swallows hard and says, "They will be along shortly," with the two of them nestled in his hair.

He is becoming more proficient at hearing his wife speak to his heart as she says to him, *"I am so proud of you my darling, you are so very brave. And I know that you have spoken the truth, for I do believe that Eve Bi and I SHALL be along, shortly."*

* * *

The next day, 160 copies of the same message are delivered through the Pigeon Communication Network. It reads:

***THREE-DAY WORLDWIDE MUSIC FESTIVAL,
BEGINNING IN 9 DAYS!***

***ALL GARDEN COMMUNITIES, VILLAGES, AND
CENTERS INVITED TO PARTICIPATE!***

***WE WILL CELEBRATE THE JOY THAT HAS BEEN
GIFTED TO US ALL, AND USHER IN A HIGHER
LOVE, WITH MUSIC, FOOD, AND EACH OTHER!***

The message spreads rapidly from one garden community, one village, one center, and one coffeehouse, to another, reaching every corner of the globe. Kookie and Yakov also put the message out to the owners of the 36 other Metatron devices, all of whom have extensive communication networks of their own. Anyone with any kind of instrument is thrilled to participate in the upcoming festival, as well as singers and dancers of all descriptions.

Master chefs such as Yakov and Neely, Lisa, Judy, Henrietta, and Vi are most delighted to share their culinary talents with others. And of course, the simple fare of fruits, vegetables, and bread of every description will be shared by everyone, all throughout the world of One Garden.

One thing all the participants have in common is that their gifts are all created, prepared, performed, or shared with lots and lots of love.

* * *

The big day of the Music Festival is now upon them. Wherever people are all around One Garden, they are gathering at the heart of their community, be it a fire pit, center coffeehouse, or back field of a lord's estate. People arrive with instruments of all kinds mostly homemade and food of every description, *all* of it homegrown and homemade.

The Chrysalenes are prepared to sing their angel songs of healing and lead the festival in blessings and prayers.

With the energy of higher love all around, another special event is going to happen over the next three days. Many couples will be getting married at the Music Festival!

Kookie, Angie, and David are setting up their little booth where Kookie will play his tuba. They will be joined by Eve Gerda and a few other Chrysalenes from the Village of the Holy Ones, singing angel songs of peace and love.

Angie is setting out the offerings of their booth with a little sign that reads, "Kookie's Cookies."

* * *

The Chrysalenes and the other participants have arrived and are ready to begin.

Liling gets on the podium and addresses the crowds. "Welcome, everyone! Welcome to the first Worldwide Music Festival of One Garden!"

Huge cheers go up along with thunderous applause.

Liling continues, "Welcome to three exciting days of Music, Food, and Love!"

More cheers and applause.

"Our purpose for organizing this festival is to usher in a Higher Divine Love to our planet, which began with the activation of the pyramids. Now the rest is up to us as we reach an even greater level of healing, love, and compassion. May we all become the true stewards of life on earth that we were born to be."

More applause, as Liling holds her hands up and says, "Throughout this event we will be asking the Chrysalenes to offer their blessings. At this time I would like to ask Mama Eve Zula to come up here and bless the opening of our Music Festival."

Mama Eve Zula comes up to the podium smiling at everyone. She holds her hands up to the heavens, closes her eyes and says, "Heavenly Father, our friend Dumaka once called You the Kind One. Indeed you are most kind, most loving, and most forgiving, to bring us all out of the darkness and bless us with a wonderful life of abundance and love.

"As we move forward over the next three days, may we learn to give back to each other and to all life on Earth that which You have so freely and lovingly given to us. Thank You and bless this wonderful music festival. And now, let us 'Make a joyful noise unto the Lord'[14] and eat, very, very much! Amen!"

And the people all say, ***"YEEEHAAA!"***

* * *

Music, gaiety, and laughter resound all around the world. The hearts of everyone swell to the ecstasy of joyous dancing, music, and singing, and the best cuisine anyone has ever known.

---

[14] *Psalm 100, KJV*

Kookie is in tuba heaven playing his deep haunting tones, as Eve Gerda, Mama Eve Zula, and Papa Adam Makena sing the song of the angels with him.

Ryan is teaching Paul how to play the drums in their drumming circle, and Paul is sure that he is in heaven itself.

In California at Judy's Garden, Kenny and Lisa have joined the crowd along with the Major, his family, Reggie, and his wife Helen. Henrietta, Lisa, and Judy keep the crowd well fed with the most exquisite pies and pastries anyone has ever tasted. One hundred and sixty pigeons have also joined the party, and they are all attached to the shoulders of anyone who is dancing or bopping to the music.

Reggie is the delight of the party. He is dancing from one drumming circle to another, getting in the center of the circle and letting himself go.

And the Major keeps shaking his head and asking him to "share."

"Come on, my good man!" the Major keeps nagging him, "Whatever it is, just pass it around!"

In Chiconahui, Daniela and Tomas lead the other children in a percussion band, with instruments made from all sorts of tree branches, twigs, and shrubs. Doc is delighted to dance to the children's music. Rudolpho joyously plays his homemade drum and Suzie of the Seashells jingles away on her seashell necklace, while dancing with her mama, Doc.

Couples are getting married everywhere and their higher love radiates outward to everyone. Among the Music Festival newlyweds are:

Judy and Adam Tate, Rudolpho and Suzie of the Seashells, and the newest lovebirds, Pasha and Annamarie!

Toward the end of the third day of celebration, the Chrysalenes and people everywhere feel the need to begin to quiet down. There is a calling in everyone's heart to turn their attentions to the heavens.

And then it happens.

Everywhere, at the same time all over One World, a Light appears in the sky. Everyone stops and looks up as the Monarch Angel appears.

Speaking to their hearts, Angel says:

"Human Creatures everywhere, with you, ALL of heaven is well pleased! You are now ready to open your hearts further and live in Divine Love and Compassion. Hear the words of the Heavenly Father that you may live with Him always, blessed, sacred Human Creatures:

I AM THE PRESENCE WITHIN YOUR HEART,
STRONG AND ENDURING,
TRUSTING AND TRUE.
I AM THE KINDNESS WITHIN YOUR SOUL,
LOVING AND TENDER,
MERCIFUL, TOO.
I AM THE LIGHT FROM HEAVEN ABOVE
SHINING UPON YOU
WITH ALL OF MY LOVE.
AND WHEN YOU ARE LOST, OR STUMBLE AND FALL
I AM THE PRESENCE
ON WHICH YOU CAN CALL.

NOW AND FOREVER, ETERNALY YOURS,
I AM.

The Angel of the Lord goes back up into the clouds and all are at peace.

All, that is, except for 16 pigeons and two Monarch Butterflies.

At the Garden of Judy, 16 pigeons suddenly fall off the shoulders of the people they have attached themselves to and everyone witnesses a miracle. The pigeons transform into men, kneeling on the ground. The people gasp and gaze in bewilderment, but Kenny and Lisa are beginning to understand.

Kenny approaches one of the men and says to him, "May I ask you brother, who you all are?"

The 16 men look at each other and smile as they rise from their knees. The one speaks to Kenny and says, "We were once fallen men, Master Commandants of the Council. But now, though we are most undeserving, the Kind One has given us another chance."

The man bows his head, and the others all do the same as he says, "May we be of service to you?"

Adam Tate comes over, embraces the man and says with a warm smile to all of them, "Welcome to our fold, brothers. May we all serve each other."

* * *

Lord Emeka, Mimi, and Ryan were also listening to the beautiful words spoken to their hearts by the Monarch Angel. It has given them hope and they are greatly uplifted by the loving message, amid their sorrow over Eve Elli and Eve Bi. They gaze at each other, sigh, and start to walk back to the Big House.

Suddenly, Emeka feels a weight upon his head. The unexpected weight causes him to lean forward, and the two beings perched in his hair fall to the ground. And behold! All the people and Chrysalenes nearby witness the miracle.

Eve Elli and Eve Bi are on their knees back in their human form!

Emeka lets out a shriek and drops to the ground, throwing his arms around his wife and daughter. He rocks them back and forth with tears of joy and laughter.

Mimi is thrown into a state of euphoria. She wants desperately to join Emeka, Eve Elli and Eve Bi on the ground in a massive hug-fest. But Mimi knows that this is a private moment for her three loved ones, and she will have plenty of time for great-gramma hugs later.

Emeka finally stands up with Eve Elli who is holding their little one, and with a great big smile he says, "Can we go inside now?"

Then, as an afterthought he turns to Kookie, points his index finger in the air and says, "Ah! Kookie! Just one more thing. I believe that my wife and daughter here would love some chocolate chips cookies. Got any left?"

Everyone laughs and Kookie says, "I will go straight to the kitchen, bro, and make a fresh batch!"

As they all walk back to the Big House together, Kookie ponders the big lesson he has just learned. He looks at Angie and says, "My love, I understand now why I was not able to figure out how to reverse the shape-shifter program."

"Why is that, my husband?" Angie says with a loving sparkle.

"Because, while most of the time brains and technology are a good thing, we are never to forget what is better, greater, and even more powerful than any of that."

"And what is that, sweetie?"

"It is the Highest Power of all. The Absolute Power. The Power of Love."

AMEN!

About the Author

SYLVANA C. CANDELA is a licensed acupuncturist, author, and book publisher, who resides in Sherwood, Oregon. She has supervised in community acupuncture clinics in Los Angeles, California, including Samra University, and Yo San University of Traditional Chinese Medicine.

She received her Bachelor of Arts degree in special education from Queens College of the City University of New York, and taught children on the autistic spectrum at the Sybil Elgar School in London, England.

Sylvana started her own publishing company in August 2020, called Peaceful World Publishing. The books promote healing, love, compassion, and understanding of people all over the world.

She has five children and six grandchildren. In her "spare time" she enjoys doing jigsaw puzzles, Sudoku, word games, visiting with family and friends, and relaxing at Starbucks.

Sylvana is currently working on her first screenplay, an adaptation of her novel *AWAKEN – Book 1 of the Monarch Rising* series.

For more information please visit:
www.sylvanacandela.com
www.peacefulworldpublishing.com

Other Books by the Author

GENTLY HEAL THYSELF: Healing the Soul with Energy Medicine

The Monarch Rising Series:

Book 1 – AWAKEN: Greed is the Root of All Evil
Book 2 – GATHER: A House Divided Against Itself Cannot Stand
Book 3 – ARISE: From the Darkest Night Comes Courageous Love

Acknowledgements

Many, many, heartfelt thanks to all the people who have inspired me throughout my life, to bringing my visions to the **Monarch Rising** series. We never truly know how we touch the lives of others, in ways that are both great and small. So many of you have touched my life very deeply over the years, and will remain forever a blessing in my heart.

Thank you, Wendy C. Garfinkle, and Leanne Sype, for your incredible talent and editing skills. You have each contributed wisdom and insights that have truly helped me to bring forth my visions in REMEMBER. And of course, I greatly appreciate your dedication, time, and energy, as well as your sharp eyes for details.

Thank you, Glenda Nowakowski, Elise Cadwell, Perry Beliz, and Leanne Sype for reading the first draft of REMEMBER, and coming up with wonderful suggestions. And thank you all for listening, and responding to the questions I threw at you.

Thank you Evenia Olivares, and Louie Olivares for your Latin American historical contributions, including your heartfelt candor in sharing your personal stories with me. And most of all, thank you both for your beautiful Spanish words of a mother's broken heart to her deceased child, on page 150 of this book. You have given me much to think about regarding the deeper, universal meaning of love that words carry, crossing all cultural and human boundaries.

Finally, thanks to the truly fabulous baristas at the Safeway Starbucks in Sherwood, Oregon. You have watched me grind out this novel, keeping me well fed and coffee-d. But most of all, you are among the kindest, most loving people I have ever known. I appreciate you all, so very much.